PRAISE FOR *NUNZIO'S WAY* AND NICK CHIARKAS

"Writers are always told, *Write what you know*. Nick Chiarkas knows New York, organized crime, and how to write an engaging story. *Nunzio's Way* is gritty and thoroughly gripping."

~ John DeDakis, award-winning novelist, writing coach, manuscript editor, and former senior copy editor for CNN's "The Situation Room with Wolf Blitzer." www.johndedakis.com

"Nick Chiarkas brings a great deal to the table for a novel like *Nunzio's Way*: a childhood in New York City's hardscrabble public housing that led to a career in law enforcement, which in turn gave him a unique familiarity with the ways of the street and the Mafia. In a tale that evokes in its own special way *On the Waterfront* and *The Godfather, Nunzio's Way* is a fast paced and engrossing story based in New York City during the early 1960s, a time when street gangs and organized crime had power that extended from the gutter to government.

Chiarkas knows his stuff and it shows in this wild story of international intrigue and vengeance. There is a body count in *Nunzio's Way* that a reader needs a scorecard to keep track of in this driving narrative that never fails to entertain."

~ Tony M. DeStefano, award-winning author of *King of the Godfathers, The Deadly Don: Vito Genovese, Gotti's Boys, The Big Heist*, and *Gangland New York*. https://www.tonydestefano.com/home

"Nick Chiarkas's eagerly awaited return to the mean streets of Lower Manhattan is even better than his award-winning *Weepers*. There is much to like and admire about *Nunzio's Way*, including the first appearance of Heather Potter, which will endure as one of the great entrances in crime fiction. What a character! Revenge may be a dish best served cold, but *Nunzio's Way* sizzles, and readers wouldn't want it any other way."

~ Review by Doug Moe, journalist, and author of *The Right Thing to Do: Kit Saunders Nordeen and the Rise of Women's Intercollegiate Athletics at the University of Wisconsin and Beyond*. https://www.dougmoe.org/

D1117816

"From the first page of *Nunzio's Way* by Nick Chiarkas, I knew I was in the hands of a master storyteller. The reader will experience New York's Little Italy in 1960 as Chiarkas brings it to life with vivid descriptions of the sights, sounds, and smells of the ethnic neighborhood. This high-octane thriller moves fast with a captivating mix of violence and compassion as rival street gangs fight for control. The beautifully flawed main characters are well-drawn through Chiarkas' use of authentic dialogue and action scenes that jump off the page. Gripping tension escalates throughout this skillfully plotted story, ending with a well-earned riveting climax."

~ Gregory Lee Renz, multi-award-winning author of
Beneath the Flames. glrenz@hotmail.com

"Fabulous! *Weeper*'s Nunzio Sabino returns triumphantly in the all-consuming crime-thriller, *Nunzio's Way*. He is all-powerful on the streets of NYC, but can anything make up for what Nunzio lost all those years ago? Author Nick Chiarkas superbly shares the lives of five teenage friends (*Weepers*), now older, in this consummate sequel. Surely another award-winning best-seller by Nick Chiarkas!"

~ Luca DiMatteo, award-winning author of *Green Haven*.
https://www.luca-dimatteo.com/

"*Nunzio's Way* was worth the wait. Chiarkas' follow-up to *Weepers* deftly spins a tale that you can see, hear and feel, from the donkey stable to the trattoria, from the rough streets to the church pew. To read *Nunzio's Way* is to live in these moments and places, brimming with guile, tough lessons, and most of all, humanity and wisdom. As always, Chiarkas writes a gripping story with a hardboiled heart of gold."

~ Matt Geiger, award-winning author of *The Geiger Counter: Raised by Wolves and Other Stories; Astonishing Tales*. Middleton and Cross Plains newspaper editor. mgeiger@newspubinc.com

"If you're a fan of Mario Puzo's *The Godfather, The Sicilian* and *The Last Don* you will want to read Nunzio's Way. Nick Chiarkas reveals the gang world of 1960's New York City in this fast-paced novel. Nunzio Sabino is intuitive, cunning, secretive, and loyal to his gang, the Weepers. Learn how Nunzio becomes and remains the "boss of bosses" by following his own way—'Nunzio's way'."

~ Rex Owens, author of *The Life and Times of Rowan Daly*
and host of the award-winning radio talk show "My World and Welcome to It,"
on 103.5 FM KSUN. https://rexowens.us/about.html

"Chiarkas is a master at bringing to life an era ruled by the Mafia and gangs of 1960's New York, complete with their code of honor, family ties, connections abroad, and a memory longer than all the streets of New York. And yet, the story takes an unexpected turn when an outsider proves to be the most ruthless of all. The writing is smooth with dialogue so authentic and visual that you hardly realize you're reading a novel and not watching it on the big screen."

~ Margaret Goss, author of *The Uncommitted*,
award-winning paranormal suspense novel.
http://www.margaretmgoss.com/

"Chiarkas takes readers back to Nunzio's world: a world of hierarchies and revenge, loyalty and betrayal, a world where "The Code" is clear and en-forced—sometimes brutally. Like an action movie playing out across the page, this fast-paced novel leaves the reader breathless. Its gritty characters and surprising twists grab our attention and don't let go. If you enjoyed *Weepers*, you will love *Nunzio's Way*.

~ Kim Suhr, award-winning author of *Nothing to Lose*
and director of Red Oak Writing. kim@redoakwriting.com

"In *Weepers*, the novel where Nunzio Sabino made his first appearance, Nick Chiarkas showed himself to be the rare author who can create a vividly drawn world that both immerses and addicts the reader. *Nunzio's Way* fulfills the promise of that earlier tour de force. Begun, it is hard to put down. Entered, the experience is not of language on a page, but directly of another time and place with other rules. Finished, it is set aside with satisfaction, tempered with sadness only that its story is, for now at least, over."

~ Jeff Scott Olson, Madison attorney https://www.scofflaw.com/

"*Nunzio's Way* is a story of the wounded heart's cry for vengeance and its hunger for home. In this suspense novel, Nick Chiarkas does more than tell a story—he invokes the past of a tribe of boys wanting to be loved, wanting to be feared, all grown up—real tough guys from New York's Canon Street tene-ments. Chiarkas draws out their characters—kids and men with the shadows of lions—and their fight to claim a piece of their Lower East Side streets, where prosaic rituals in diners are as holy as those in a church. Pleasurable, evocative details sizzle on every page. You can hear the jazzy music and smell the smoke of the silenced .32 Barretta. You can sense the cold desperation in these crime bosses—their drive to build an empire of power. And you can feel the agony in their longing for the warmth of home."

~ Tricia D. Wagner, creator of *Swift and the Star of Atlantis*
YA literary fiction series. https://www.triciawagner.com

"If you liked *Weepers*, you're going to like Nunzio's Way. It's got some of the same great characters and a new really nasty villain. It plops you into Manhattan's Lower East Side with details that tell you Nick knows of what he writes, whether it was from growing up there or from his time on the NYC police department."

~ Christine Keleny, CKBooks Publishing.
https://ckbookspublishing.com/

/

"It was at page 30 that the hook sank in deep. When I was a little kid, my bedroom faced the street. I could hear the folks in the apartment building across the way as they stood out front and carried on. But what I loved was the sound of taps on the sidewalk. It wasn't a neighborhood of prosperous people and putting taps on shoes meant you didn't have to replace soles and heels as often. As older boys walked down the street, the double click of each step would fill your ears. Often, if two or three abreast, they'd fall into a rhythm; more gloriously, but rarely, a tune.

Alas, taps have lost their ubiquity and I'd forgotten about them. Until page 30. The year is 1960, but it's not referenced by events that kids learn about in history class. Instead, Nick Chiarkas takes us back in time in subtly effective ways: the tunes playing in the background, a scooter made of wood, and taps on shoes. Thus, that which marks time becomes timeless. As is the story. It's about the bonds of family; bonds that are universal, here finding expression in a family tethered on one end by a man on the wrong side of the law and on the other, by a boy trying to figure out which side he's going to grow into.

Uncle Nunzio is no stereotype. More layered than a *mille feuille,* he is patriarch and foe, caring and vengeful, mentor and murderer. Though he could afford it, he doesn't give his family monetary wealth, but lavishes guidance and protection. He grieves deeply at the loss of a loved one and soothes himself by ordering the death of others' loved ones. A lion and a fox who nuzzles his brood and eats the rest. Always the smartest one in the room, he explains his *raison d'être* and you see the sense of it. It's not enough to know about Nunzio. You want to meet him, talk to him. But only if you're introduced by family. You want to make friends with a guy who won't let anyone outside the bloodline close; except one, and maybe not even him. By word and example, he teaches his nephew while not pushing his nephew to succeed him.

Drawn to this man, you root for him. It's not rational if you think about it. But neither is a roller coaster. Nunzio and the Coney Island Comet, though, are fabulous rides."

~ Steve Hurley, whose scriptwriting won an Oscar for the movie *Primal Fear* starring Richard Gere and Edward Norton. Steve is a Madison attorney. https://hurleyburish.com/

"Picking up where Weepers left off, Nunzio's Way transports readers to the beginning of the Kennedy era in a hostile corner of New York City where organized crime reigns supreme. As the bodies pile up, tensions rise—culminating in a finale that's as gratifying as it is grim. This is a brisk read about the bulletproof bonds of family and friendship, written by a former New York City cop skilled in delivering an uneasy fusion of violence and wit."

~ Michael Popke, Wisconsin-based writer and critic.
https://www.linkedin.com/in/michaeljpopke/

NUNZIO'S WAY

(A NOVEL)

Other books by Nicholas Chiarkas:

Weepers

Forthcoming novels:

A Lion and a Fox

Blue Bounty

Black Tiger Tea

Stories from a Radio Car (a collection of short stories)

NUNZIO'S WAY

(A NOVEL)

NICK CHIARKAS

Three
Towers
Press
MILWAUKEE, WISCONSIN

Published by
Three Towers Press
An imprint of HenschelHAUS Publishing, Inc.
www.henschelHAUSbooks.com

Paperback ISBN: 978159595-908-6
Hardcover ISBN: 978159598-909-3
E-Book ISBN: 978159598-910-9
Audio book ISBN: 978159598-911-6

LCCN: 2022938528

Author photo by Judy Olingy

Cover design by Mark Schmitz, https://www.zebradog.com

Printed in the United States of America.

Dedicated to my brilliant and beautiful children:
Erica L. Chiarkas, Nicholas L. Chiarkas III,
Christopher J. Chiarkas, Adrienne M. Marchioni, and
Gerard (Josh) A. Chiarkas

And to Attorney and Law School
Clinical Professor, Emerita,
Judith E. Olingy—
My amazing wife, best friend,
and initial and final editor reader

And a big thank you to the gang—
Angelo, Anthony, Barbara, Beverly, Billy, Bobby,
Bruce, Carl, Carol, Cathy, Chico, Denise, Dennis,
Diane, Eddie, Georgia, Harriet, Harry, Howie, Jack,
Jimmy, Joey, John, Johnnie-girl, Johnny, Kenney,
Larry, Lydia, Marie, Mary, Mike, Natalie, Rennie,
Richie, Robert, Ron, Salma,
Steve, and Tommy
—for always being there with me,
on those streets, so long ago.

Until the lion learns to write,
every story will glorify the hunter.
— African Proverb

The Devil hath power to assume a pleasing shape.
— William Shakespeare

One must be a fox to recognize traps
and a lion to frighten wolves.
— Niccolo Machiavelli

CAST OF CHARACTERS
IN *WEEPERS* AND *NUNZIO'S WAY*

Names that are bold indicate a main character, standard type indicates a secondary character.

	Age in 1960
Nunzio Sabino (the Boss)	54
Pepe (Nunzio's right hand)	
Natale Ventosa (owner of Caffe Fiora and Nunzio's adopted daughter)	42
Fiora Ventosa (Natale's mother, died on Jan. 3, 1920, in what is now Caffe Fiora)	
Father Joe (Father Joseph Bonifacia)	55
Father Cas (Father Robert Casimiro)	31
Declan Ardan (Nuzio's lawyer, running for mayor of NYC)	54
Heather Potter / Angie Zara	22
Ignazio ("Iggy") Zara (killed in 1948 by Mac Pastamadeo, Angelo's father)	
Remo Zara (killed in 1948 by Mac Pastamadeo)	
Fabia Zara (Angie's mother, killed in 1957 by Camorra in Italy, ordered by Nunzio)	
Aldo Emetico (Angie's stepfather, killed in 1957 by Camorra in Italy, ordered by Nunzio)	
NYPD Detective Clarence Hartz	35
Anna (Terenzio) Pastamadeo (married to Mac, Angelo's mother, Nunzio's goddaughter)	34
Frank Terenzio (Anna's older brother, owns Lilly's Liquor Store)	36
Danny Terenzio (Anna's younger brother, US Army, NYPD)	22
Pompeo Terenzio (Frank, Anna, Danny's father, works at the meat market, also goes by "Pomp," "Pompa")	54
Nonna Terenzio (Anna's mother)	52

WEEPERS (gang, 24 members by 1960)

Angelo Pastamadeo (leader of the Weepers)	16
Audrey (Angelo's girlfriend)	16
Tate Kramer (Angelo's best friend)	17
Bobby	16
Howard ("Howie")	16
Carl	16

SATAN'S KNIGHTS (gang with more than 100 members by 1960)

Rico Cruz (leader of Satan's Knights and Heather's main contact in NYC)	26
Andrew ("Andy") Noonan	19
Derick Blassano	18
Dominick ("Dom") Blassano	22
Domingo Rio	19
Mike	23
Mac Pastamadeo (Angelo's father, Anna's husband)	35
Johnny Pastamadeo (Mac's brother, works with a security agency)	31
Adam Pastamadeo (Anna and Mac's son, Angelo's brother)	8
Rosemarie (Gostopolas) Moran (Anna's best friend)	34

ROOSEVELT STREET BOYS

Daddy Bruce (leader of the Roosevelt St. Boys)	28
Nicky Two-Bridges	26

HELL'S KITCHEN (10th Ave.) Boys

Tommy Sullivan (leader of this gang)

South Street Boys ("Popeyes")

PROLOGUE

For those who have read *Weepers* a while ago, and for those who have not read *Weepers,* here is a brief description of Nunzio Sabino, as told by Father Joe to Father Casimiro (Father Cas) in *Weepers.*

* * *

"In 1920... Caffè Fiora was the Baling Hook, a tough bar owned by an ex-longshoreman, Stanley Marco, and his wife Sylvia—who was every bit as tough as Stan. The place was decorated with nets, anchors, and baling hooks hanging all over the walls. It had a long bar and small tables."

"Sounds charming," Father Casimiro said sarcastically.

"In a strange way, it was. The booze was good. The food was tolerable. And the dancers were okay—that is, except for one. Fiora Ventosa was a delicate breeze in a cigar-filled room. And when she danced, the room dropped silent. She was sensational."

"A stripper?"

"Not completely, more burlesque. The dancers would take off this or that but never stripped completely. Each night of the week featured a different dancer. Fiora danced on Tuesday nights. And Nunzio fell in love with her."

"How old was he?"

"Thirteen. We were all kids about the same age. There were five of us—me, Nunzio, Pompeo—Anna's father—

George, and Nick. We would sneak in every Tuesday night. Sylvia knew, but let it slide."

"Did Fiora know how Nunzio—"

"Probably. She would sometimes sit with us after her show. Thinking back, she probably thought it was cute, and compared to the rest of the clientele, we were safe, adoring fans. We would sit there and Nunzio would be transfixed. She was seventeen and Nunzio figured a four-year difference wasn't that much. So, after watching her dance every Tuesday for seven or eight months, on the third Tuesday in January 1920, Nunzio decided to tell Fiora he wanted to marry her. Seems silly now, but back then...what did we know? Anyway, Nunzio had to work late, so we waited for him and then we beat it over to the Hook."

Father Casimiro loved these stories. They gave him a history, like he belonged to the neighborhood. "Did he tell her?"

"When we got to the Hook, Stan was shoving everyone out of the place, telling them to go home. Somebody, I don't know who, said, 'You kids better not go in there tonight.' We pushed our way in against everybody leaving. There were several overturned tables and a couple of people standing around looking down."

"Looking down?" Father Casimiro dodged several kids running along the sidewalk.

"Sylvia was sitting on the floor crying. Fiora was lying on the floor, covered by a large flannel shirt. Her head in Sylvia's lap. Stan was arguing with a big guy they called the Bear. He was six- foot-six and must have weighed in at over three hundred pounds. He was a foreman on the docks and a neighborhood bully. The Bear stood there in a T-shirt and said to Stan, 'Don't you say nothing, you hear me? Nothing.' Sylvia shouted up at the Bear, 'You sonofabitch, you killed this little girl.'"

"What? She was dead? He killed her? Why?"

"The drunken Bear wanted to see more skin. He yanked her off the dance floor. She fought and he broke her neck." Father Joe lit a cigarette and handed the pack to Father Casimiro.

Father Casimiro lit a cigarette and took a long drag. "Poor girl." Cigarette smoke escaped with the words. He handed the pack back to Father Joe. "Nunzio must have been devastated. You all, just kids, must have been—"

"It was the only time I ever saw Nunzio cry. Ever. It was the most heart-rending, profound sadness I ever witnessed. Nunzio dropped to his knees and touched her face. Meanwhile, the Bear was standing over Sylvia with his two buddies, one on either side of him, and he said to Stan, 'The girl's trash; nobody's gonna miss her. So, you and your wife keep your mouths shut.' He reached down and grabbed his shirt off Fiora and started to put it on.

He continued, "That was when I noticed that Nunzio was missing. And then I heard the scream. It didn't sound human. It was pain and fury. It was Nunzio, and he was in midair—he jumped from the top of the bar behind the Bear. In each hand, he gripped a baling hook—he had taken them off the wall. He looked like an eagle screaming in for the kill. The Bear's arms were halfway in his shirt sleeves when the points of the heavy hooks pierced his deltoid muscles from behind. The hooks hit both shoulders and sunk behind his collarbone."

"Dear God," Father Casimiro shivered as he imagined the pain of a thick steel hook sinking into his shoulder muscle.

"The Bear roared and swung from side to side. Nunzio held on tight to the hooks, his legs flying from left to right, back and forth. The Bear's arms were pinned halfway in his shirt. He kept trying to grab Nunzio's legs. But with each movement, the hooks sank deeper."

Father Casimiro was no longer aware of the people pushing past him, some smiling and nodding. The musty beer and sawdust of the Baling Hook filled his senses. He imagined the blood spurting from the hooks, and a thirteen-year-old boy hanging on—fortified by rage. Father Casimiro smoked and listened. "What about the Bear's friends?"

"The two of them grabbed at Nunzio, and that's when we—all four of us—jumped in. I was a pretty good boxer by then, and- Pompeo was always a strong kid. Nick pulled a knife, and George grabbed another baling hook off the wall. The Bear's buddies ran out of the place; they weren't up for the fight. After that, the only ones in the Hook were Stan, Sylvia, the Bear, Fiora, and us. The Bear started spinning and coughing up blood. Nunzio just held on. We were trying to get them apart. But the Bear kept spinning, knocking over tables. And Nunzio was like a cape flying from the Bear's shoulders.

"Then, finally, the Bear dropped to his knees, straight down, his arms dead, draped at his sides. As the Bear fell forward, Nunzio pulled on the hooks. The Bear growled and then whimpered as his face cracked the wooden floor. All the time, Nunzio held onto the hooks—pulling. He let go when the Bear rolled over on his back—hooks still buried in his shoulders. He looked straight up at Nunzio."

"He was still alive?" Father Casimiro gasped.

"Only for a moment or two. Nunzio wasn't finished, but Stan grabbed him and said, 'He's gone. You kids get out of here so we can clean up.' Nunzio never fell in love again."

"Did she have any family?" Father Casimiro asked, flicking his cigarette into the gutter. "I mean, Fiora."

"Fiora was fifteen and pregnant with Natale when she arrived in New York from Genoa. The Cherry Street Settlement took her in and after Natale was born, they got her a room with Sylvia and Stan, who hired Fiora to tend bar and dance on Tuesday nights. Fiora Ventosa was born on the third Tuesday in March and seventeen years later died on the third Tuesday in January, and her only family was two-year-old Natale Ventosa. No one ever knew who the father was. Natale was raised by Sylvia and Stan."

"What about the police and the Bear's friends?"

"No police—Stan fixed that. But the Bear's pals came after Nunzio. The five of us were inseparable. Nunzio was, is, a born leader. Battle after battle, victory after victory, we quickly gained a reputation. Eventually other guys wanted to join our gang. By sixteen, Nunzio was the most powerful gang leader in the city. When he was twenty, he bought the Baling Hook."

"He bought it?"

"Stan had passed away a couple of years earlier, so Nunzio turned it into a pretty good restaurant—no dancing—and re-named it Caffè Fiora. He sent Sylvia money every month to cover Natale's financial needs. He paid Sylvia more than she ever dreamed to run the restaurant. When Sylvia died in '51, Nunzio gave the restaurant to Natale."

"So, you became a priest to ..."

"The battles we won were hard fought and people were killed. We all...I killed," Father Joe confessed. "At nineteen, I decided to become a priest and devote my life to saving as many kids in these neighborhoods as I could in return for God's forgiveness. We have an uneasy relationship—I'm certain God doesn't always agree with my methods, and I have some questions for Him as well. But I'm sticking to the deal."

"What about the other kids? Did they stay in the gang?"

"No. Pompeo is a foreman at the meat market, Nick became a cop, and George is a foreman on the docks. But on the third Tuesday of each month, the five of us go back there, just like when we were thirteen, but now it's the Caffè Fiora—and we play poker in the back room and talk about how fast time passes."

"Does Natale know?"

"Sylvia told her the whole story. Natale loves Nunzio like a father," Father Joe said as he and Father Casimiro passed Columbus Park and made a left from Mulberry Street onto Worth Street. "This is the end of Little Italy."

As they reached St. Joachim's, Father Casimiro said, "I think I'll walk over to the Settlement. You want to come with?"

"Come with?" Father Joe teased. "Sure, I can use the exercise."

"Does Nunzio ever worry about some ambitious hooligan wanting to take over? Or is that just in the movies?"

"Hooligan?" Father Joe smiled. "Nunzio is the top lion. He is constantly watched by the ambitious and the aggrieved. He can't show weakness. He can't let a single insult—especially a public one—go unchecked. Continued leadership requires constant vigilance and no margin of error. None."

"Sounds stressful."

"It is. The only time Nunzio can relax—really be himself, joke around—is with us, the kids who grew up with him, on the third Tuesday of the month."

CHAPTER ONE

"The right four people"

"**P**al, in this city, you can have anything you want if you kill the right four people."

"Nunzio, we don't have to kill –"

"We? Me and you, De?" Nunzio leaned back, a gesture as intimidating as a knife to the throat when it came from Nunzio Sabino, the most powerful crime boss in the city.

Nunzio sat at his private table with his attorney, Declan Ardan, in the dusk-lit Caffè Fiora on Grand Street in Little Italy. On the walls, ropes, hooks, and paintings of Genoa's seaport, honored the birthplace of the owner's mother, Fiora, her dark eyes still vigilant from the portrait above Nunzio's table. The Caffè was quiet on this rainy St. Patrick's Day. Two of Nunzio's men sat at a nearby table. The guy who had come with Declan sat hunched over coffee near the entrance.

"No, I mean, nobody has to get killed; talk to your guys at Tammany. They respect –"

"You still got that scar," Nunzio said. *It's bad enough in court; there, I do what he says. But not at my table. Since we were kids, this mameluke was a bully. I can't give him an inch. Not an inch.* "What about my guys?"

De touched the scar above his left eye. "Doolin said the Italians run everything now. He said, 'If anyone can pull strings...'"

"Before you start pinning medals on my ass," Nunzio signaled to a waiter. "Arturo, bring me and 'Deadshot' here a couple of espressos and Natale's little cakes."

"All I'm saying is–"

"*Marone*, you're still talkin'?"

"All I want – "

"I know what you want. You wanna be mayor." Nunzio lit a Camel and tossed the pack on the table while exhaling through his nose like a dragon. "Listen to me, Brian Doolin is a *piantagrane*, a troublemaker. For an upfront payment he sells you a dream. Then when it doesn't come true it was always somebody else's fault. Like you, that time when we were kids, and you told me Eddie Fialco sounded on my mother. It was bullshit, you just wanted me to beat him up. You're a *piantagrane*, like Doolin. It works for you in court, but Doolin just likes to cause trouble. Look, you got a kid who wants to go to college for a grand, your kid's in. But mayor, *forse si forse no?*"

"So, maybe a chance?"

"Maybe."

De stroked his scar absent-mindedly. "You gave me this when we were kids."

"It makes you look like a tough guy."

"I once asked Joe why you hit me with that rock."

"It was a brick," Nunzio said.

"Joe said it was to save my life. I still don't get it."

"You don't have to."

"But Joe was there."

"Joe was with Pompeo and me and a bunch of us. What were we, ten years old? We were cutting through the empty lot to school, and you – "

"Okay, so I was taking kid's lunch money. They all gave it up except you. You were the smallest kid, and you just said 'No'."

"And what did you say to me?"

"That's what I don't get; I just said, 'okay, maybe next time' and you hit me hard with a brick. I swear I was knocked out for a couple of minutes."

"You said 'maybe next time.'"

"Yeah, that's all."

"But you never asked me again."

"I thought you were crazy. I followed you home one day. I figured if I saw where you lived, I would get a better read on you. I trailed you into the cellar of 57 Canon Street. I saw a little bed in one corner and a pile of banana crates by the door – the only things in that dirt floor cavernous space. You were shoveling coal into the furnace, which explained why you always had soot on you. I was about to say something when a spider the size of my face jumped out at me from the crates, and I beat it the hell out of there."

"You followed me?"

"How could you have lived in that cellar?"

"Instead of where?"

"I don't know. Maybe in...I don't know. Didn't some family take you in?"

"Yeah, the Sas family. Good people."

"Anyway, I never asked you for money again."

"If you had, I would've killed you. So, the brick saved your life."

Declan nodded. "Yeah. Got it."

Three years later, a hulking longshoreman people called "The Bear" wouldn't be so lucky. He was the first man Nunzio killed. At the ripe age of 13, his life and the lives of four of his friends, changed forever.

Nunzio drifted back to his childhood. He was six years old when his mother and he moved from Naples to the Lower East Side. Alone after his mother died, he learned to survive in one of the most notorious neighborhoods in the city. Where the narrow, trash-lined streets and alleys weaved together decaying brownstone tenements with common toilets, one per floor. He shoveled coal and guarded the produce stored there by the ships docked off South Street, to pay for living in the cellar.

After school, Nunzio mostly walked the streets. He recalled the putrid smell of decomposing cats and dogs covered with a trembling blanket of insects, rats, and things he didn't recognize. Lying in the gutter against the sidewalk on Pike Street was a horse, with old and fresh whip wounds, shrouded in a cloak of flying and crawling insects. Plenty of other horrors and hardships confronted him throughout his life, but when he closed his eyes, Nunzio saw the horse.

"I know you're not here to talk about old times. Whadaya need?"

"Nunzio, no one is better than you with –"

"Christ, without the bullshit."

De lowered his voice, "Tammany Hall is on the outs with the mayor, and they're scrambling to find a candidate to run against him. So, if you would tell them that you would be grateful if they would pick me..."

"You tellin' me what to tell them? Forget about it. Anyway, I like the deputy mayor; he postponed the Brooklyn Bridge deal as a favor to me back in '57.

"Nunzio, did I do something to piss you off? Is that why your guys searched us when we came in today?"

Chinatown was pushing towards Canal Street; the Russians were gaining a footprint in Brighten Beach. And Pepe, Nunzio's driver, bodyguard, and right hand since forever, told him there were rumbles of a hit on Nunzio. Someone or some group was always waiting and watching. He knew, like bosses everywhere, that everyone under him thought they could do a better job and thought the boss never did enough for them. This felt different. Pepe had heard it from one of his spies in Satan's Knights. Pepe would get more information.

But all Nunzio said was, "I'm a little cautious these days. You know how it is."

"I'm your lawyer; you call me when you need help. Right?"

"I pay you top dollar. You complainin'?"

"No, I'm saying we help each other. We knew growing up here, the only choice was to be a gangster or a victim. No offense."

"You believe that crap?" Nunzio shook his head.

"What?"

"You can be whatever you wanna be."

"I try to be straight, but you know – "

"Who you kiddin'?"

"The point is, we have to trust each other." De took a long breath and looked wistful as his eyes landed on the painting of Fiora. "I came here with you to see her dance. She was 16 back then, with a two-year-old kid."

"Seventeen," Nunzio said, "and the kid's name is Natale."

"And you were 13 and asked Fiora to marry you in this Caffè. Am I right?"

"I never got the chance."

"Oh, yeah. Sorry," De said. "It was 'The Hook' back then?"

"'The Baling Hook,' and you hung out with us until the trouble started."

"Before she...died."

"Was murdered. Right where you're sittin'." Nunzio wrapped his knuckles on the table. His mouth was dry. He didn't like De any better now than he did back when they were in school. But he was a good lawyer.

"The Bear. It was the guy they called 'The Bear' who killed her. I remember. Then you, you – " De gazed at the floor for a long moment, as if looking for a chalk outline. "I always tried to avoid trouble."

"Yeah, 'De Dodgeball.' We all knew." The scent of coffee and pastry reached Nunzio.

Arturo brought two cups, with three coffee beans in each, a pot of espresso, and a plate of cakes.

"*Grazie,* Arturo, *verserò l'espresso.*" Nunzio filled a cup and pushed it to De, then filled his own. One final drag on his Camel and he crushed it in the ashtray.

De picked up a cookie. "Are these from Ferrara's?"

"Natale makes them right here every day."

De nodded as he helped the last corner of cake into his mouth with a finger. "How's she doing?"

"Terrific."

"She's, what...42? You're 54. Twelve years difference isn't much. I always figured you two would tie the knot."

"De, Natale is my daughter."

"I know, adopted, not blood."

"*Tu sei cazzo*, what's wrong with you? I'm her father, period. It's good you never had kids."

"I just mean – "

"Never talk to me about my daughter again. *Capisci?* Let's get back to what you want."

"Sorry. Nunzio, it's 1960, I only have a year and a few months. I need you –"

"I'll help you –"

De's shoulders visibly loosened. "That's terrific. Talk to Tammany. They'll listen to –"

"*Jadrool*, either you're stupid, or you think I'm stupid; either way, you're stupid. I ain't gonna ask them for nothin'."

De's shoulders tightened, "You...you said you'd help."

"Yeah. You decide how you wanna go; I'll decide how to help."

"How I want to go?"

"My advice? Throw your hat in and run. You're a tall, good-lookin' Irish lawyer. A few months ago, they were sayin' no Catholic could have a shot at president. Nixon still has the odds, but I'm tellin' you Kennedy is a lock. You can do the same thing. Kiss Brian Doolin's fat Irish ass and give him the money he wants to fix it with the Tammany boys. Then you kiss every ass they put in front of you until they give you the nod, which I will make sure they do. In addition, I'll get you the unions, and –"

"I can't be sure I'll win that way," De said.

"No? Too bad." Nunzio shook his head. "Okay, then you gotta be what you uptown lawyers call innovative."

"I take it you mean cheat?"

"What're you, 12? You're already cheating. If you wanna be sure, then you gotta steal the election. The trials you won, you ever bribe or threaten a witness, a juror, a judge?"

"You know I did. I like having an edge."

"And you want an edge to win the election?"

"I think I'd be a good mayor."

"Not the point I'm making here. Like I said, De, you can have anything you want if you kill the right four people."

"Killing? You mean the guys running against me?"

"Jesus, no De, killing the competition would be stupid. Knowing who the right four people are, is the hard part. Think of it like a trial. You want an edge, what do you do?"

"If it's the wrong judge, I bribe a couple of jurors, a witness."

"And if the bribe doesn't work, you find a way to threaten one or two of them, right?"

"Sure, if that's what it takes."

"But you don't threaten or kill the prosecutor, right?"

"Right."

"Same thing, De. You need to own those self-important gavones managing the frontrunners, not the candidates themselves, at the exact right moments. If you can buy them, nobody dies. If not, you scare the shit out of them. And nothin' does that better than killin' someone right in front of them. But do it without it coming back to you, or worse, to me."

"So, maybe a threat first or – "

"Forget about it; I'll take care of that end. And I'll get you the unions and some others. But first, you get on the ballot and campaign your Irish ass off."

"Right. I will."

"I need you to commit to that. We do this my way. Understood?"

"Understood."

Nunzio leaned forward. "And in return, you'll owe me whatever I want, whenever I want it, *capisci?*"

"No problem. What does Kennedy owe you? You can tell me...wait, Cuba?"

"This and that," Nunzio said with a hint of a smile.

Nunzio raised his head and looked past De at the priest coming into the coffeeshop. De turned and stood when he saw the man headed toward them.

Father Joseph Bonifiacio was 55 years old, five-foot-eight, and built like a fire hydrant. His scars memorialized the Golden Glove championship he'd won in his youth. He still carried a matter-of-fact edge that served him well in the Two Bridges neighborhood.

"Am I interrupting, Boss?" Father Joe asked as he walked over to Nunzio.

"No, we're done," said Nunzio, as the old friends automatically hugged.

"Joe, I mean Father Joe, always a pleasure to see you," De said. "You look well."

"You too, De," he said as they shook hands.

"Well." De ran a hand down each arm to be rid of any crimps that might mar his crisp suit. "I have to go to the St. Patty's Day parade. This is the first time I can remember it raining on St. Patty's." He walked toward the door. "Let's go, knucklehead." The young man hustled to his feet, opened the door, and raised an umbrella for his employer as they stepped out onto the street. The bell on the door confirmed their departure when it shut.

"I know he's your lawyer, Boss, but I never trusted that guy." Father Joe sat down and pulled a cigarette out of Nunzio's pack.

He still called Nunzio "Boss," a carryover from their street gang days, when Nunzio led Joe, Pomp, and other kids barely in their teens, to victory after victory, on unforgiving streets with long memories. They would meet, hide out, and sometimes attend Mass, at Saint Joachim's on Roosevelt Street, so they called themselves the Roosevelt Street Boys.

"What's he gonna do? He's my lawyer. He can't say nothin'."

"Yes, he can, he'll just lose his law license. A coward would do that in a pinch."

Nunzio slowly nodded. *He'd lose more than just his license.*

CHAPTER TWO

"My mother sends you to hell"

Lanzo Basso, part wild boar, part man, oversaw his domain from a corner table in the Trattoria di Mario, on Via San Biagio. The trattoria wasn't open yet, but because he owned a piece of it, and as part of Camorra, in Naples, his access was unlimited. Nonetheless, life was not easy for him. Ulcers burned his stomach. The map of scars and deep lines on his face chronicled his childhood of survival on the streets and in the donkey stables of Naples. Each night when he returned to the stables, the donkeys expressed their joy and made room for him. On cold nights, they would cuddle-up with Lanzo to keep him warm.

His world softened with love only once in his life when he met Rosa in this very trattoria 30 years ago. But his reprieve was short-lived. She was moving to America with her parents. He proposed. She would've married him if he moved to America with them. She begged him. But he was moving up in the ranks of the Camorra and, in the ignorance of youth, he chose Naples over Rosa.

Today, on his 50th birthday, the idea of Rosa would not leave him. Yesterday, in a letter to his friend Nunzio Sabino, he asked if his friend could find her. Maybe if she wasn't married, he thought, maybe now, maybe.... After breakfast, he would buy a new pair of eyeglasses and spend the day alone with his music, some good wine, and thoughts of Rosa.

For now, Lanzo enjoyed starting his day here as he had for the last 30 years. It was the one place he could relax, read the paper and savor an uninterrupted meal while the kitchen and dining room staff prepared for the day. The smell of olive oil, garlic and spices filled the air as a sizzling symphony escaped from the kitchen. Chairs were arranged around tables. The bartender opened a box and began counting cash and receipts. It was a ritual performance that comforted Lanzo, like Mass.

A young woman with red hair backed out of the swinging kitchen door carrying a silver platter with Lanzo's warm, wet towels on it. Her flame lipstick wasn't wasted when she smiled.

Lanzo grinned back, transfixed by her undulating hips as she crossed the room. Does she always walk like that? Or was it for him? Perhaps the owner remembered his birthday.

Standing next to him, her white blouse unbuttoned lower than it should be, she held the tray in front of him, "*Asciugamani caldi, Signore* Basso."

Lanzo's mouth was dry, but he was able to squeeze out, "You are a *bellissima cerbiatta celeste.*"

"*Grazie.*" She dropped her eyes.

"You the new girl, from England, yes?"

"*Sì, ne ho iniziati tre –* "

"Speak English; I know some. Maybe I go to America soon. So, I practice, yes?"

"Yes, I started three weeks ago, Signor Basso."

He placed the warm towel over his face, both hands pressing it soothingly on his eyes, and sighed. "*Come ti...*

eh, what is your name"? he asked without removing the towel.

"Angie Zara. I changed it to Heather Potter, but no one here knows that, so promise me you won't tell." She smiled.

"Why did you change your name?"

"So you wouldn't find me." She leaned in, pressed the dry towel concealing a silenced .32 Beretta against his ear, and whispered, "My mother sends you to hell. *Addio.*"

Lanzo only had time to stutter, "Z-Zara?" And never heard the thub of her Beretta.

Heather looked around. No one had noticed. She propped the newspaper up as a screen in front of Lanzo, slipped the gun in the pocket of her skirt, and covered the bloody fragments on the table with a towel. Concentrating on walking casually, she carried the silver tray back to the kitchen and placed it on a stack. *Calm yourself; don't rush.* She glided as if indifferent, nose in the air, past the out-sized pots of simmering tomato gravy and sizzling pans of meats, poultry, and fish—all familiar and comforting smells. Her hands were shaking as she moved toward the back service door past the clanging utensils, running water, and voices. She thought she felt someone touch her arm.

Suddenly, she was in the alley. No memory of pushing through the heavy back door. *Keep going...keep going.* A few steps and she merged onto the street. Back inside, the staff continued readying Trattoria di Mario for the day. Heather vanished among the workers, shoppers, and tourists on Via San Biagio. She felt nothing but relief. The question of feeling guilty came and went without pause. She thought she might be haunted by remorse, never having killed a man before. But that, too, failed to take hold. The sole feeling that accompanied her down the street was pride. "For you, Mama."

CHAPTER THREE

"I know how to swim to PS-1"

Anna Pastamadeo was 34 years old and lived with her husband and their two sons in the Al Smith Projects on Manhattan's Lower East Side.

It was late, and Mac was drunk again. Anna had hoped that he had changed when he came back from Italy. For a while, he was the Mac she married, and then eight months ago, he started drinking more heavily and getting angry more often. Mac yelled at Anna for not having another bottle of whiskey, as he finished the last drops in his glass.

"Mac, I think you've had enough to drink and lower your voice. Angelo and Adam are in their room and can hear you."

"You don't tell me what to drink or how much. I'm the boss here, not you. You hear me?"

"The whole building can hear you."

Mac shoved Anna. She crashed into a chair and fell to the floor. The shouts and sounds brought Angelo and Adam into the kitchen. Anna was bruised and tangled in the chair. Mac was standing over her. Angelo grabbed a bread knife off the table and stood facing his father.

"Don't you hit my mother," Angelo said.

"Look at you, a punk, just like your father. I'll stick that knife up your ass and knock you through the wall."

Anna was getting up. "Hang on. Stop! Mac, get out."

Eight-year-old Adam grabbed a fork and stood next to Angelo.

This seemed to surprise Mac, who turned and stormed out of the apartment.

"Thanks for having my back, Adam." Angelo smiled.

"He's gonna be really mad when he gets home, huh?" Adam said.

"He's not gonna remember any of this," Anna said.

The next morning, Anna poured herself a second cup of coffee while Angelo and Adam ate Cheerios at their kitchen table. Mac put on a jacket and grabbed his baling hook for work.

"Mac, try to get home on time tonight. Your brother and Father Joe are coming for dinner," Anna said. "And please pick up a loaf of Italian bread on your way home."

"Angelo will pick up the bread after school. I gotta go. I'm running late. I work so you, and the two boys, can eat."

"You mean your sons."

"Yeah, and whoever else you invite. I'll be home when I get home."

"I'll get the bread, Mom," Angelo said.

"Hey, it's not up to you, big shot," Mac said, arm outstretched, pointing his finger at Angelo. "I told you to get the bread. It's an order. Got it?"

"Got it." Angelo continued to stare down at his cereal.

"Mac, what's wrong?" Anna said. "It's Johnny and Father Joe."

"I don't care if it's Jesus and Mary. This apartment is MY ship, and I'M the captain. You're the first mate, and the boys, my sons, are just sailors. I say who comes to dinner and does what. Period."

"Mac!" Anna said, as he turned and walked out of their apartment.

After Mac left, Angelo said, "You okay, Mom?"

"I'm fine," Anna said. "Listen, walk your brother to school on your way – "

"Ma, I'm eight-years-old," Adam said. "And I know how to swim to PS-1 by myself."

"Swim?" Anna said.

"Yeah, Dad said the apartment is a ship," Adam said.

"That's funny," Angelo said. "Good one, Adam."

Anna and her sons giggled.

* * *

Anna made fusilli with Italian sausage, leeks, and parmi-giana Reggiano. Angelo supplied the crusty Italian bread. Father Joe arrived with pastries, and Johnny brought Chianti and cream soda. They waited for Mac until 6:30 and decided to start without him.

"Mac, held up at work?" Father Joe asked Anna.

"Probably."

"He's the captain of the apartment ship," Adam said. "He is home when he is – "

"Adam, you're getting quite a mouth on you," Anna said.

"Mom, this is really good." Angelo hoped to change the conversation.

"This is delicious, Anna." Father Joe poured the wine in all glasses and added cream soda to the wine for Angelo and Adam. He held up his glass and said, 'Saluti.'"

Everyone joined the toast.

"Is my brother catting around again, Anna?" Johnny asked.

"I don't think so." Anna shook her head. "The last eight months or so, he'd been hittin' the bottle pretty heavy again. I don't know, Johnny."

"What's catting around?" Adam asked.

"Going out with girls," Angelo said.

"He's married to Mom," Adam said. "Is Dad gonna go away 'cause of Angelo again?"

"What?" Anna said. "Who said he went away because of Angelo?"

"The Knights," Adam said.

"Your father did not go away because of Angelo or anybody else," Anna said. "Some very bad people took your dad away."

"How did he get home?" Adam asked.

"Father Joe brought him back," Anna said.

"I'll talk to Mac," Johnny said.

"Let me have the tough talk with him first," said Father Joe. "Then you can have the brother talk."

"Whoa, Father Joe. Are you tough like Uncle Nunzio?" Adam asked.

"No one is as tough as your Uncle Nunzio." Father Joe smiled at the boys.

"Good plan," Johnny said. "Let me know when."

"We should change the subject." Anna's eyes shifted quickly between her sons.

"Father Joe, can you tell us one of your stories about when you and Uncle Nunzio were tough kids growing up here?" Angelo said.

"Were you and Uncle Nunzio in a gang when you were kids, like Angelo?" Adam asked.

"The Weepers aren't a gang," Anna said. "They're a social club."

"When can I join the Weepers?"

"You have to be 13," Angelo said.

"You're the leader, Angelo. Just tell them to let me join."

"When you're 13, I will," Angelo said.

"Boys, please. That's enough," Anna said. "Father Joe, we love your stories."

"Okay, here's the most courageous and toughest Nunzio story I know," Father Joe said.

"Cool," Angelo said.

"What's the name of the story?" Adam asked.

"Hmmm, how about 'Nunzio, Joey, Hank, and a damned good cop'?"

"Are you, Joey?" Angelo asked.

"I am," said Father Joe.

"Who's Hank?" Adam asked.

"You'll have to hear the story to find out."

"Were you and Uncle Nunzio in a gang?" Adam asked.

"Boys, let him tell the story." Anna smiled. "I don't think I've heard this one."

Father Joe gave his mouth a perfunctory wipe and leaned forward on his muscular forearms. "It was late afternoon in August, back when me and Nunzio were ten years old. We came across a horse with old and fresh whip wounds, lying in the gutter against the sidewalk on Pike Street. The horse was shrouded in a cloak of flying and crawling insects. The rats had not arrived yet. We stood still and stared down at the horse. And then Nunzio sat down on the edge of the sidewalk and lifted the horse's head into his lap."

"With all the bugs on it?" asked Adam.

"Yep, bugs, ants, and all."

"What did you do?" Adam asked.

"I asked, 'Whatcha doin' Nunzio?'"

"He blinked," Nunzio said. "'He ain't dead yet.'"

"So, I sat on the curb next to Nunzio. He brushed the flies away from the horse's eyes, and then gently rubbed its face. The horse opened his eyes and looked at Nunzio. 'It's okay, boy, you can go to sleep now,' Nunzio said to the horse. 'We're gonna stay right here with you.' A small crowd gathered. Me and Nunzio expected to see sympathy and sadness in their eyes, but when we looked up, we saw only disgust."

"Did anyone offer to help or say anything?" Anna asked.

"One woman said, 'That horse is filled with disease, boys. You need to get away from it, boys, and wash up good.' Somebody got on the callbox a few feet away, and pretty soon, a policeman walked over. He looked at us for a few seconds and then told the crowd to move on, shooing them away with a wave of his hands. To our surprise, he plopped down next to me on the curb, and said, 'What's the plan, boys?'"

"The policeman sat down on the sidewalk next to you guys?" Angelo said.

"Yes, he did. He said his name was William Cavallo. I'll never forget it. And, then he asked us again what our plan was."

"What'd you say?" Angelo asked, fork paused mid-air.

"Nunzio said, 'He ain't dead yet, Officer Cavallo. I promised him we're stayin with him. So if you're gonna arrest me, you gonna have to drag me away with a fight.'"

"Whoa, what did the cop do?" Angelo asked.

"Officer Cavallo said, 'I'll stay with you.' And then he said, 'That horse's name is Hank. He was Jocko the Junkman's horse.'"

"Wow, good cop" Anna said. "What did Nunzio do?"

"Nunzio looked down at the horse and said, 'You're a good boy, Hank,' and continued to stroke Hank's face and neck. After a couple of minutes, Hank slowly closed his eyes and snorted a peaceful burst of serenity. Nunzio said, 'Hank smiled.'"

"Officer Cavallo stood up and walked over to Hank. He lifted Hank's eyelids, and then placed his hands on Hank's neck and chest. He looked at us and said, 'You fellas did a brave and wonderful thing. Most pet owners don't show up when their dog, or cat, or horse is dying. Some because they don't care; some because it would make them sad. But that's when they need you most. Hank was scared, alone, and defenseless. You boys gave him courage and love when he needed it most. He's gone now. Sanitation is on the way to pick him up; you shouldn't witness that. Your last memory of Hank should be his smile. I promise I'll stay right here with Hank until they take him away.'"

"Nunzio asked Cavallo, 'Why'd the junkman whip Hank so much?'"

"'Hank just wanted to be a horse,' Cavallo said. 'Jocko wanted him to be a one-horse-power engine and nothing else.'"

"I said, 'Can't you arrest Jocko?' 'I wish I could," Cavallo said. 'I like animals a lot more than people.'"

"Me too," Angelo said.

Everyone at the table nodded, even Father Joe.

CHAPTER FOUR

"The torpedo's a girl"

Angelo Pastamadeo and his friends huddled together on the top steps of PS-65, a junior high school on Manhattan's Lower East Side. It was a chilly March morning. The boys wore their Weepers jackets collars up, smoking and talking as they shuffled in place against the cold.

It had been three years since Angelo defeated "The Razor" in the Cherry Street Park, opening the door to Weepers' fights with Satan's Knights and several other local gangs. Each time, Angelo led the Weepers to victory. By 1959, Angelo's reputation was more of a threat than he was.

His Uncle Nunzio had told Angelo, "Power is not only what you have, but what your enemy thinks you have. And they think you and Merlin, your button-knife, have some kinda magic." For the last year and a half, no one had challenged the Weepers. But Satan's Knights were getting edgy.

Members of the Knights, gathered on lower steps, shoved and dared each other to grab a smoke on the top step. One Knight started walking up when three other Knights pulled him back.

"Sooner or later, they're gonna come at us again." Howie looked down at the restless Knights. "We need a plan."

"Howie's right, Angelo. We graduate in a couple of months," Tate said, "then the Knights will be standing back on top here. We gotta think about our younger guys."

"Yeah, we need a plan." Angelo watched a seventh-grade boy start up the stairs. *He looks so young. That was me when I almost got into a fight with the Knights.* He watched the Knights demand lunch money as younger kids tried to pass. They shoved one kid who dropped his books and fell to the ground. The Knights howled.

Audrey stopped to help pick up the kid and his books. "Come on."

"Hey, yo, wait-up," Vinny, one of the Knights, said to Audrey.

Angelo started down.

Another Knight pulled Vinny back and held up his hand to Angelo. "He's new," and then to Audrey, he said, "No problem, doll, g'head and take the little fella to his homeroom."

Angelo stepped back up, remembering that Jimmy had knocked Audrey down when she had tried to help Liz three years ago. *The Knights are still the same.* Angelo looked across the street at the tenement roof where Jimmy had fallen. *I'm glad Jimmy's dead.*

Through a volley of whistles, calls, and a few boos from the Knights, the girls made their way up to the Weepers.

"Hey, Angelo," Audrey said, "I saw your Uncle Johnny at the bakery on Monroe this morning."

"Yeah, he's been getting out a lot more." Angelo took Audrey's hand.

"Angelo, you goin' to Boston?" Tate asked.

"No, they're sayin' I'm too young and not family. But Father Joe is going."

"Boston?" Liz said.

"Sage is doing time up there for a fight that went bad."

"He should come back here when he gets out. Tell Father Joe to tell him," Howie said.

"I will."

"Angelo, we need to talk later," Audrey said as the bell signaled time for class.

"About what?"

"Later, Angelo."

Cigarettes were tossed and flicked as the horde of students shuffled and shoved their way into PS-65.

* * *

Angelo sat next to Audrey in Miss Coluthia's English class. This was the last class on Friday, and it went on forever. Several students read their "A" essays, and a couple other students read their "A" poems. The school day was coming to an end.

"Well, look at all of you. In less than three months, you will all be heading to high school as sophomores. My, my, I will miss some of you."

The class broke out into laughter. With students saying "What" and "Me" and "Hey."

Their teacher chuckled and said, "No, no, no, I'm kidding, I will truly miss all of you."

Her students stood and applauded.

"Thank you." She smiled. "So, March has been an important month for literature and freedom. Who can tell me why?"

"Elvis is out of the Army," a student shouted.

"That's true. And I join you in being happy about that," said Miss Coluthia. "However, I was referring to the court ruling yesterday that *Lady Chatterley's Lover* by D.H. Lawrence is not obscene."

The class broke out in cheers again.

"I'm not saying you should read it; all I'm saying is that the freedom - "

"You said we should read everything," Audrey said. "Right in this class, you - "

"I did say that...but you do get the significance of this ruling, don't you?" Miss Coluthia said to a nodding class as the bell rang. "Wait, wait, um, Angelo, Carl, Dennis, and Audrey. Please stay for just a minute."

When the others had left, Miss Coluthia said, "I have some wonderful news. You will each be getting a letter, but I just couldn't wait to tell you. Carl, Angelo, Dennis, you three have been accepted to the High School of Art and Design. And Audrey, you have been accepted to both Stuyvesant High School and Art and Design. You get to decide. My advice, if you want it, is Stuyvesant."

"Wow" and "Cool" came from the four students as they flew out of her classroom. *I bet this is what Audrey wanted to tell me. Angelo thought. I bet she thinks I'll be pissed that we won't be going to the same school.*

Angelo put his arm around Audrey's shoulder as they walked home. "So that's what you wanted to tell me?"

"What?"

"You're going to Stuyvesant. Ya gotta be smart to get in. It would have been nice to go to high school together. But it's cool."

"No, not that."

"So, what?"

"My father is sending me upstate."

"What? Where upstate?"

"Ithaca. To live with my cousins, Morley and Stella. They're really neat, and smart, and they have a dog named Lucy. And my aunt is – "

"You sound like you want to go. You got into Stuyvesant!"

"I don't want to go, Angelo. My father says it is too dangerous for me here."

"When?"

"Right after graduation. So, we still have a couple of months."

"I'll pick you up tonight for the dance, and I'll tell him I can keep you safe here."

"I think he's made up his mind."

"I'll take a shot."

* * *

Rico Cruz had been the leader of Satan's Knights since the death of his brothers in 1957. He sat with the five top Knights in their first-floor, two-bedroom apartment in the Al Smith Projects. Over the past two years, Rico had orchestrated the transformation of the Knights from street-bullies to a money-making enterprise. He dreamed of buying a small business in Brewster, New York, maybe a diner, where he and his wife could live quietly away from the projects. He was anxious to make that happen before all the plates he kept spinning in the air came tumbling down on him. He had a plan.

"Rico," Andy said, "we got guys going to PS-65 now who don't know we used to be on the top step."

"Again, with the step?" Rico rubbed his eyes with the palms of his hands. "We run the Smith projects, we're back to making good dough doin' jobs for Nunzio, so who gives a shit where we smoke?"

"The point is, our guys want our rep back," Dom said.

"Dom's right," Domingo said.

"What's our future?" Mike said, arms outstretched with palms up and a shoulder shrug. "What're we doin', Rico? You gotta tell us something."

"Okay, this stays in this room," Rico said. "We made inroads into Nunzio's organization so that if something happened to Nunzio, we got a shot – "

"Hold up, Rico. That shit's what got your brothers offed." Derick said.

"No, no, we're not doing anything, guys. An assassin's comin' from England to hit Nunzio, Angelo's old man, and a couple of other guys. There's also a guy runnin' for mayor who wants our help. I don't have all the who, what, and when yet, but just keep it cool for now."

"Who's the torpedo?" Andy asked.

"I said I wouldn't tell anyone, so don't repeat this, not even to each other. You guys remember hearing about the Zara brothers?"

"Sure. They started the Knights with your brother before he went to Korea, God bless his soul."

"Right. So, after Mac killed the Zara brothers in '43, their mother and sister Angie moved to Italy. Three years ago, a hit man killed Angie's mother and stepfather. He thought he had killed Angie too, but it was a family friend who was visiting them. Bad luck for her. Angie's stepfather had been worried about a hit, so he had already set Angie up with a new name, money, and a job in London. The mother and stepfather had planned to follow, also with new identities, after they sold their estate. They thought they had more time. Anyway, Nunzio ordered the hit."

"The torpedo's a girl?" Dom said.

"Angie's new name is Heather Potter," Rico nodded. "She wants her revenge. I'll pick her up at the airport and we'll help her. When she's done, we take out the Weepers."

Chapter Five

"I'm gonna catch a beatin'"

After school, Angelo dropped into Mo-Mo's pizza place on Madison Street for a slice. Two of the seven booths were occupied, one with three men and the other held two couples sharing a whole pie. The Pastels serenaded customers with "Been So Long" on the jukebox. Angelo stood at the counter. "Hi, Morgan. Three slices and cherry cokes for here."

"Sure thing. Who you meetin'?"

"Tate and Howie."

"Good boys." Morgan tossed three slices in the oven to warm up and slid the drinks across the counter. Angelo carried the sodas to the nearest booth, lost in thoughts of Audrey, high school, and the warm pizza smell.

Morgan, known as Mo-Mo in the neighborhood, was 32 years old. His rich, deep-chocolate skin made the polished indigo marbles that were his eyes even more striking. From his neck to his thighs, he was all muscle, but everything from there down he'd left behind somewhere in Korea long ago. Now Morgan traveled perched on his scooter, a thick slab of oak wrapped in black leather and mounted on four swivel wheels. Push blocks dangled from a hook on one side and a metal basket attached in the front held things he might want to carry along.

In the restaurant, a ramp served as a highway to the waist-high, level spot at the takeout counter where, underneath, the cash drawer and an Army .45 automatic were within his reach.

"Slices ready, Angelo. Careful, son, they real hot."

Morgan pivoted, rolled down the ramp and up a second one to the sink on the other side to tend to a stack of dirty dishes.

Angelo came back and grabbed the small tray with the pizza and slid back into the booth as three guys walked over to him. "Tate what – "

"I ain't Tate, *estúpido.*" said Domingo wearing a Knight's jacket. "You here all alone?"

"Wadda you guys want?" Angelo said.

"This booth," said Eddie.

"You hear him, punk?" said Charlie.

The three men at the other booth got up and left. The two couples followed, one of the girls shouted over her shoulder, "Morgan, some trouble here," as they headed out.

Angelo looked toward the counter. Morgan had his back to them.

Angelo was scared. Merlin, the name of his button knife, was in his pocket. He would use it if he had to. *Take a deep, slow breath, don't shake or cry. I'm the leader of the Weepers; I can't let them push me around. Whatever happens here, everybody will know. I'd be a punk if I called Morgan. There're three of them, so I'm gonna catch a beatin'. No big deal, as long as I put up a good fight. Like Uncle Johnny said, throw the first punch and make it good. Wait for the moment.* "Forget about it; I ain't movin'."

"How's the pizza?" Eddie snatched a slice from under Angelo's nose and sank his teeth in for a bite. "Oh, hot, hot."

Shit, here I go. Angelo pushed the hot slice into Eddie's face and swiveled both feet out from the booth to kick him, screaming, into the other two Knights.

Morgan swung around, down one ramp, up the other, and grabbed the .45 off the hook, "All ya'll, hold it!"

By then, Tate and Howie had arrived and were running toward the pile-up. Tate grabbed Domingo around the neck from behind, and Domingo went limp. Howie yanked Charlie to the ground, kneeled hard into his chest, and dug his thumbs into Charlie's eyes. Charlie froze. Angelo stood above Eddie, who was on the floor, covering his face and whimpering.

"I said hold it," came Morgan's voice suddenly only a foot away. "Everybody up and still. It's okay, boys. Let go of them Knights now. Any move from them and my war buddy here will shoot their little dicks off." Everyone stood up.

"Angelo, Howie, and Tate, go sit in another booth. Now you three Knights, or as my Italian friends like to call you, *jambronis*—time to clean up that mess. When you're done, you can pay me for three slices and three drinks."

"Bullshit," said Domingo. "We ain't cleaning or payin' nothin'. What are you gonna do? Shoot us in the back for leavin'?"

"Oh..." Morgan sighed, shaking his head. "Wouldn't I truly love to? Don't you never come back in here, or I'll shoot you before your dumb asses clear the door. You tell Rico, from now on, no Knights allowed."

"Yo, shithead." Domingo pointed at Angelo. "Once your babysitter is gone, I'm gonna mess you up bad."

Angelo brushed his hand under his chin and flicked his fingers toward Domingo, "*Vafanculo jabroni*," as the Knights walked out.

"We got this, Morgan." Angelo and friends cleaned up the mess, while Morgan fixed them another round of pizza.

* * *

It was Friday night and that meant a dance at the Cherry Street Settlement. Angelo usually met Audrey at the dance, but tonight, he was picking her up. He was already at the apartment. He had arrived early so that while he waited, he could convince her father that he loved Audrey and that he could and would protect her in their neighborhood. He knocked, hoping Audrey would answer the door so he wouldn't have to shake hands with her father. No such luck. He was wiping his sweaty hands on his pants when Audrey's father, Aldo Vadunka, opened the door.

The man stared at Angelo with dispirited eyes for a long minute. "What are you doin' here?"

"Hi, Mr. Vadunka, I'm Angelo." He reached out to shake hands.

Mr. Vadunka glanced down but ignored Angelo's hand. "I know who you are. Why are you here?"

"I'm picking up Audrey for the dance, and I wanted to talk to you, sir."

"She must've told you she's leaving." Mr. Vadunka turned and walked into his apartment.

Angelo followed without an invitation, still confident. "Yes, sir. She did."

Mr. Vadunka sat down at the yellowing Formica kitchen table. An open bottle of vodka, a small glass, and brown bag of peanuts were surrounded by peanut shells. A dirty ashtray and a book were in front of him, "You want drink? A smoke?"

"Ah, no thanks." Angelo was surprised by the book. He didn't know many men who read books. "What are you reading? I like books. My Uncle Johnny said –"

"*Doctor Zhivago*. It's new…about the Russian Revolution." Mr. Vadunka lifted a burning cigarette off the edge of the ashtray. He took a long, slow drag then allowed the smoke to find its own way out of his mouth and nose. "But that ain't why you're here. What you want? Get to it."

Audrey suddenly appeared at the kitchen doorway, "I'll be with you in a minute, Angelo," and was gone again.

Angelo smiled and returned his attention to her father. He thought this was going pretty good so far. "Mr. Vadunka, I know you're worried about Audrey's safety in this neighborhood. But I promise you I can protect her. Plus, she got into the best high school in the city. You have to let her go to Stuyvesant. It would be a shame for her – "

"You, protect her? Ha. You're the reason I'm sending her away."

Angelo hoped he hadn't gasped out loud at the jab. "Mr. Vadunka, I love Audrey. I would never let her get – "

"Of course, you love her. She's beautiful."

"Yeah, and smart."

"Go look in that big mirror over the couch. Go ahead, look."

Angelo obediently got up and stood in front of the mirror. "What am I looking for?"

"What do you see?"

"Me."

"You see your dark, greasy, guinea skin? And pimples. Don't you wash?"

"I wash every day." Angelo said.

"You're short and you're scrawny," Mr. Vadunka spit out in Angelo's direction. "My daughter is a beauty with alabaster skin and blue eyes. She will marry a doctor, or a banker, or lawyer. They'll live in a big house upstate with a room for me."

Angelo hadn't prepared for this. But he thought fast. "My father can get me a job as a longshoreman – "

"Ha, longshoreman, that's what I do, *Ty slishkom khudoy, chtoby byt' gruzchikom.*

"What?"

"It's Russian, a beautiful language. I said you're too skinny and sickly to be a longshoreman."

"I'm not sickly. Mr. Vadunka, I...I...thought, we – "

Mr. Vadunka said something in Russian, and waved a dismissive hand.

"I don't understand what you're sayin'."

"It's because you're too stupid to understand Russian."

"But what did you say?"

"You wanna know what I said?

"Yeah."

"I said, 'you're a fuckin' Italian monkey,' that's what I said. You ain't good enough for my daughter. Period." Mr. Vadunka stood up and gestured toward the door. "Now get out of my house and wait on the street where you belong, *ty kusok der'ma.*"

Angelo didn't want a translation. His eyes began to tear. He walked quickly to the apartment door, then stopped.

"What? You forget something?"

Angelo's fists were tight at his side. "*Vai a farti fottere.*"

"What did you say to me?"

Mr. Vadunka's shouting was muffled as Angelo pulled the door shut behind him. He paced in small circles grumbling to the sidewalk in front of Audrey's building. "I shouldn't have said anything. I should've just taken it." He wiped his eyes with his shirt. Sidewalks were habitual recipients of Angelo's venting. Time had proven the pavement to be his most convenient and trustworthy confidant. "What was I gonna do, fight Audrey's father? Not a chance. But I just left. At least I didn't run." And so, it went between Angelo and the pavement as Liz, Gina, Judy, and Jane walked up to him.

"What happened, Angelo?" Gina asked. "Where's Audrey?"

"Ah, she's coming. I just wanted to wait out here."

"What did her father say about her leaving?" asked Judy.

"She has to leave."

"Here she comes," Gina said.

"Angelo, what did my father say to you?"

"I was just saying that you were right about him having his mind made up."

"Not about that," Audrey said. "What did he say that made you leave?"

"'Get out,'" Angelo said.

"What?"

"No big deal. It's his house. I don't wanna talk about it. Let's walk over to the dance."

"He gets angry when he's drinking," Audrey gently touched Angelo's arm. "Whatever he said – "

"I don't wanna talk about it." Angelo moved slightly out of her reach.

* * *

Since the Settlement House opened three years ago, all the gangs considered it a safe zone, except the Knights. They never showed up anyway. Angelo, Tate, and Howie walked into the large, bright room filled with teens, snacks, and music. Angelo looked at the adult table behind it all. Father Cas and Father Joe sat with Uncle Nunzio, Pompa, and for the first time, Uncle Johnny, though he looked a little uneasy.

Angelo's father had stopped coming a few months ago. Weepers gathered in one corner as other gang members and non-gang members stood in clumps around the dance floor. The "Theme from a Summer Place" drifted over the chatter and the dancing couples.

"I think it's so cool that your Uncle Johnny is here," Audrey said.

"His two war buddies, Ben and Henry, asked him to join their agency. They do detective work, bodyguarding, stuff like that. He said he's gonna join them."

"Neat."

"One Summer Night" brought almost everyone to the dance floor.

"Let's dance forever," Angelo said. "I want to hold you."

Audrey dropped her head on Angelo's shoulder, "Yeah, just hold me."

Angelo and Audrey danced tenderly, as they had every Friday night for the past three years.

After "One Summer Night," Audrey and Angelo danced to "Maybe." But when the needle dropped on "Get A Job," they returned to the Weepers. Howie talked about Angelo pushing the slice of hot pizza in Eddie's face.

"No big deal," Angelo said. "But, if Howie and Tate hadn't gotten there when they did, I probably would've caught a beatin'.'"

"No way," Howie said. "Old Morgan was there like *Gunsmoke*."

"Yeah, with the biggest gun I ever saw," Tate said.

"What's going on with the Knights?" Audrey asked.

"They're getting restless," Gerard said.

"Angelo, please tell me what my father said to you."

"He said I wasn't good enough for you. Which is true. And he said I was an Italian monkey. No big deal."

At that precise moment, Angelo's mother walked past. "What? Who called you an Italian monkey?"

"My father was drunk." Audrey quickly jumped in. "He gets mean when he drinks."

"Ma, please," Angelo said. "I didn't know you were standing there."

"When did he say this to you?"

"Ma, please. This is between me and Audrey."

"When?" Angelo's mother said.

"Today, Mrs. Pastamadeo. I will talk to my father when I get home."

"Ma, please go away so we can dance. Please."

Angelo's mother turned with clenched fists and stiffly walked to the adult table.

"I'm sorry about my mom. I didn't know she was there."

"No, I'm sorry my father said that stuff to you. None of it's true. None of it."

"My dad says mean stuff too when he's drunk. Let's just dance."

"Lovers Never Say Goodbye" played as Angelo and Audrey returned to the dance floor.

"Audrey, we've been going steady for three years. I want to go all the way with you."

"You still just say what pops into your head."

"You're going leave and I want you to be my first, and maybe my only."

"I know. Me too." Audrey said.

A silent moment passed as they swayed to the music.

"How about now?" Angelo said.

"Now?" Audrey sounded a little panicked, but then... "Where?"

"Father Cas's office is just past the girl's bathroom. He keeps the key under a statue outside his door. I've talked to him in there a few times. He has a couch and – "

"Ha, Angelo," Audrey giggled. "How long have you been planning this?"

"No planning, but I been thinking about it for three years. Now seems right."

"What do we do?"

"I'll go first, unlock the door, and wait for you. Then you just pretend to head to the bathroom. Everyone is paying attention to the gangs and dancing. No one will notice."

"Okay," she said, and smiled.

"We're going to do this?" Angelo said as they left the dance floor and headed to Father Cas's office together, forgetting all about his brilliant and surreptitious plan.

"I want to," Audrey said.

"Me too." Angelo loved Audrey and often dreamed about this moment in enthralling and adoring images. But this was different. Angelo's passion was born of anger.

This moment was more about Audrey's father than Audrey.

Angelo found the key under the statue. He and Audrey walked into Father Cas's office and locked the door behind them.

CHAPTER SIX

"Past love has wings"

On an overcast April day, Rico, Dom, and Domingo walked along Madison Street after enjoying a lunch of scungilli in hot sauce and hard biscuits at Vincent's.

"Walk me over to the shoe store. I need new heels." Rico pulled a pack of Cavaliers from the pocket of his white, short-sleeved shirt. His shoes were highly polished, and his black pants pressed. He wore his shirt unbuttoned and untucked, a white, sleeveless T-shirt underneath. Around his neck, on a thin chain, hung a gold half-dollar-sized medallion with Saint Justus and Saint Pastor on the front, his name and birthdate on the back.

Rico smoked as they walked along, silver taps on their shoes clicking in triplicate. The three Knights crossed Madison and made a right on Catherine. They stopped in front of Scarpa's Shoe Repair. Rico remembered when this was Bookman's. He looked over at Linda's Luncheonette. He missed his brothers.

Hector had liked getting his coffee there and breaking people's shoes. They were difficult to have as brothers. Hector had beaten the shit outta Ernesto in the handball courts right across the street in the projects. Right in plain view. Even so, they were always brothers, and they would die for each other.

Who would die for me now? Not these two tirones. No one.

"You okay, Rico?" Dom said. "We goin' in or what?"

"Just thinking about when it was Bookman's."

"Did they ever find out who torched it?" Domingo offhandedly yanked a blanket off a bum sleeping against the stoop next door to Scarpa's and tossed it into the gutter.

"What the fuck is wrong with you?" Rico asked.

"What? I'm just messin' with him," Domingo said. "He's a bum. Who gives a shit?"

"Get the blanket and put it back on the guy."

"Eat shit. I ain't gettin' the bum's blanket," Domingo said.

"What did you say to me?" Rico said.

"I ain't doin' it."

"I'm only gonna say this once more. Get the blanket and cover the guy, or you're out of the Knights."

"Fine. What's wrong with you, Rico? Ernesto did shit like this all the time." Domingo grabbed the blanket and kicked an empty glass bottle that rested among the trash in the gutter. The bottle shattered against the curb, sending shards in all directions. A couple with two small children walking toward them stopped and crossed the street. Domingo threw the blanket on the bum. "Happy?"

"Not really." Rico recalled how his brother Hector loved the rain because it washed away all the broken beer bottles and trash in the street.

"So, who do they think torched Bookman's?" Domingo asked.

"They think you did it," Rico said.

"Me? Why me?"

"They think it was a crazy Knight, so you or Ernesto."

"Maybe your brother. I ain't that bent."

"I think Angelo did it," Rico said, opening the door to Scarpa's. "Ernesto and The Razor saw him that night."

Rico was greeted by the smell of shoe polish, leather, and Mr. Scarpa, the short, hunched man with large shoe-polish-stained hands. The store had a row of wooden booths. Each booth had a wooden bench where customers sat and waited. A knee-high door was in front of each booth.

"Heels and taps?" Mr. Scarpa asked Rico.

"Yeah, I'll wait." Rico placed his shoes on the counter.

The three Knights sat in adjoining booths.

"Our assassin gets here tomorrow and I have some shit I need to do for Nunzio. So, Dom, you need to pick her up at Idlewild. I have all the information you need and stuff to give her back at the club. Tell her I'll check in with her tomorrow."

"Will do."

"Now, Domingo, tell me how and why we are banned from Mo-Mo's because of a fight with Angelo right after I told everyone to leave off him?"

"It wasn't a fight, and anyway, he started it."

"You're telling me that Angelo started a fight with three Knights in Mo-Mo's?"

"We were just talking to him. Okay, you know Eddie likes to Bogart people. He picked up a piece of the kid's pizza and took a little bite...Big fuckin' deal. Angelo started everything by pushing the slice in Eddie's face. Next thing we know, a couple of Weepers jumped us. And crazy Morgan is pointing a gun and telling us to get out. That's it. They started it."

"And this all happened right after I fuckin' told everyone to leave Angelo alone. You were there when I said that, right?"

"Yeah, but he was the – "

"Shut the fuck up! Leave Angelo alone. Understand?"

"Yeah, but your brother Ernesto would've – "

"Ernesto is dead. Next time you violate one of my orders, you're out of the Knights. You got that? No warning, out. Got it?"

"What're you getting so pissed off about?" Domingo said.

"Domingo, knock it off," Dom said.

"You knock it off," Domingo said back.

"You don't get it, Domingo. You'll never get it." Rico shook his head and lit a Cavalier. "I'll tell you what. I just decided this right here. It came to me like a bolt of lightning. You, you Domingo, you've convinced me. We got Knights who are still in their teens, and we got guys over 21. Even on our counsel, Dom, Michael, and I are in our twenties. You, Derick, and Andy are all 18 or 19 years old. Here's the plan."

"When the Nunzio thing is over, me and any senior Knights that want to be part of my money-making crew will join me. We'll call ourselves 'Rico's Crew.' Domingo, you can be in charge of Satan's Knights; you can keep the name. And you and your Knights can start smoking on whatever fuckin' step you want at PS-65, or anyplace else. I don't give a shit what you do. But until then, you do what I say, or you're out. Got it?"

"Got it. But I don't – "

"Got it?"

"Yeah, got it."

CHAPTER SEVEN

"You're such a romantic"

The young, red-haired woman stepped off Pan Am's brilliant star of the stratosphere, the DC-8 Jet Clipper, after a six-and-a-half-hour flight from London. She walked into the Worldport Terminal at New York's Idlewild Airport. Inside, the glass walls leaned away from her, giving the uneasy illusion that she was looking out of a plane. The porter who collected her suitcase followed behind as she walked through the terminal and directly to the young man with the sign, "Heather Potter."

"I'm Heather. You're not Rico."

"No, I'm Dominick, Dom. Gimme the bag."

Heather tipped the porter. To Dom, she said, "Dump the sign."

"Follow me. The car's right out here." Dom said and stuffed the cardboard with her name on it in the trash can by the door.

Dom threw Heather's bag on the '58 Chevy's backseat, held the passenger door open for her, then climbed in behind the wheel. They followed the evening traffic out of Idlewild.

"Good to see you, Angie. Hey, here's today's newspaper in case you wanna catch up."

"What did you call me?"

"Angie, it's okay; I knew you and your brothers and Hector from back when —"

"Who else knows my real name?"

"It's no big deal. We're the Knights. We're on your side."

"Who else?"

"Rico, my brother Derick, and, ah, the other three Knights on the council. But that's all. It's cool, doll. Dom is gonna take good care of you."

"Is this your car, Dom?"

"Ah, actually, no. I lifted it just to pick you up in style."

"This is stolen?"

"Yeah. You mad?"

"No. It's exciting."

"Hey, doll, if you like exciting, how about we park and I'll—"

"Do you know someplace nice and quiet?"

Dom couldn't believe his ears. He sat up straight behind the wheel. "The best. My favorite spot is around Central Park off 79th."

"Let's see it."

"On our way." Dom reached under the seat and took out a large yellow envelope and handed it to Heather. "In there is your New York driver's license, the key to your apartment in Knickerbocker Village, keys to your car, some cash, a bankbook, Social Security card, blah, blah, blah. Everything you need in your name...I mean in Heather Potter's name."

"Thanks." Heather tossed the envelope on top of her suitcase.

"Ain't ya gonna check?"

"I trust you, Dom. Tell me everything you know about Nunzio Sabino, Angelo Pastamadeo, and Angelo's whole family, his mother, his uncles, everything."

Dom smiled and drove with renewed energy as he regaled her with stories glorifying himself and the Knights. He also shared information about Nunzio, Mac, his family, and Anna and her family. And only afterward, as they drove into Manhattan, asked, "Why do you want to know all this stuff? "Mac's the one that killed your brothers."

"You think I don't know that?"

"Sorry, I just – "

"So, Mac is living at home now."

"Yeah. And, his crazy brother Johnny has a one-bedroom next door to them."

"I heard he never goes out." Heather said.

"He goes out sometimes."

"Anna's family?"

"Don't know much about her parents, except they're friends with Nunzio."

"Her brothers?"

"Danny is in the Army. Frank owns a liquor store on Catherine and lives in Knickerbocker. In the same building as you, 10 Monroe Street." Dom said.

"That's not all. He used to be a cop, right?"

"Yeah, right after the Army."

"The Army?"

"Yeah, he doesn't talk about it, but he has a frame above the counter with his Army medals and patches and shit. Anyway, after the Army, he was a cop for about ten minutes and – "

"Why are we stopping?"

"This is it, doll; my secret spot in the park."

The Chevy pulled into a secluded space under a large ash tree.

"This is perfect, Dom."

"How about I put your bag in the trunk? There's plenty of room on that backseat."

"Not yet. I'm going to freshen up in the backseat, so you stay right there; and no peeking."

Heather climbed into the backseat, opened her suitcase, and removed the Beretta .32 caliber pistol. She attached the silencer. "No peeking, Dom." Anna flirted.

"You gotta hurry up, babe. I'm dying here."

"That's funny."

"Okay, Dom, don't turn around and do everything I tell you. Lie down on the front seat facing the glove compartment."

"What? Why? What?"

"Just do it."

Dom lay down on his right side. "Okay, now what?"

From the backseat, she placed the newspaper on Dom's head. "Just stay still."

"Wait, no, no," Dom started to get up.

She nudged him back down with her Beretta. "Don't be a big baby, Dom. I like my men strong. Be brave."

"What? Look, Angie, I mean Heather...We don't have to do this."

"Dom, you are such a romantic. I'm going to kill you, and you are going to die, and you make it sound like something we're doing together; 'We don't have to do this.' How lovely."

"Shit, why?"

"For practice and to see." Heather said.

"See what? Wait, please."

"Shhh. Don't whine, Dom. Tell me what you hear."

Dom didn't hear the *thub*.

Her hand didn't shake this time. Again, she felt nothing. Lanzo had killed her mother and stepfather. That's why she didn't feel remorse, she told herself. But Dom was a nice guy. Helpful. Even sweet. She wanted to feel something. Some normal reaction. So she killed him to see if she had normal feelings. And for practice. She felt nothing.

Heather wiped anything she might have touched. She tucked the yellow envelope into her suitcase, placed the gun in her right coat pocket, locked the car doors, and threw the keys into the bushes. She walked east along 79th Street in the park. As she neared Fifth Avenue, a sudden movement to her left caught her attention. Two boys pulled her into the dark shadow of several trees. In an instant, she went from startled to intrigued.

"Did you come into the park to play?" the smaller boy asked as he shoved her against a tree. "Look in her suitcase, Tank."

Now she felt almost amused. These were teenagers… kids. Tank pulled the suitcase from her left hand. "Got it, Dillon."

Heather looked to the sky. "Are you kidding me?"

"Does this look like we're kidding?" Dillon pulled out a knife.

"I wasn't talking to you." Heather didn't like knives and removed the Barretta from her pocket.

"That don't even look real." Tank said.

Heather smiled. "Maybe it's not. Come touch it."

"It's got a silencer on it." Dillon grabbed Tank's arm. "Who carries a gun with a silencer?"

"Me." Heather raised the Barretta. "Now, run or die. I dare you to be brave and not run."

The boys froze for a brief second, then vanished into the shadows.

Heather slipped the Barretta back into her right pocket, picked up her suitcase, straightened her clothes, and headed on to Fifth Avenue.

As Heather turned right, she heard laughter and loud talking from two couples crossing the Avenue together about a block and a half in front of her. They, one other couple, and a police officer, walked toward her. She spotted a stopped taxi dropping off passengers two blocks ahead. Several other couples chatted on the sidewalk. The police officer said something to them as he passed, and they smiled as they responded.

This was stupid. I need to plan better. What do I tell the cop if he asks how I got here? Where do you live, young lady? Where are you walking from? What's your name? And then tomorrow, when they find the dead guy in the car, the cop will remember a woman walking along Fifth Avenue with a suitcase. Stupid, stupid. Think.

The police officer was getting closer. The couples were walking behind him, chatting and laughing.

Good Lord, if I shoot the cop, I'll have to shoot his happy little following. I think the cop just smiled at me. He's going to want to talk. If I cross the street now, it would be suspicious. What was I thinking? I wasn't.

Heather and the police officer were now within talking distance.

The officer stopped walking, "Good evening, Miss. May I help you with something?"

"Ah, good evening, Officer."

One of the men in the happy little following waved to a taxi.

"Oh, no, Jim. It's such a lovely night. Let's walk," said one of the women in the happy following as the taxi pulled up to them and stopped. And then to Heather, she said, "Dear, did you want a taxi?"

"Yes, I do."

"Marge, it isn't advisable to walk through the park at this hour," Jim said.

"Well, I'll bet this nice officer will walk with us," Marge said.

"I would be happy to," the policeman responded.

"Jim, help the girl with her suitcase. You have such lovely red hair, dear."

"Thank you."

The taxi driver opened the trunk and Jim put Heather's suitcase inside.

The police officer held the back door open for Heather. "Are you okay, Miss?"

Yes, Officer, thank you, I'm fine. A bit tired, but okay." And then, once the taxi pulled away, she said to the driver, "Ten Monroe Street in Knickerbocker Village, please."

I need a drink.

CHAPTER EIGHT

"Lilly's Spirits"

Heather walked into her one-bedroom apartment in Knickerbocker Village. Rico had furnished it. Even the bed was made. Dishes, glasses, some food in the fridge and a bottle of wine, but she wanted something stronger. She put her suitcase on the kitchen table and tossed her coat on it.

Who else might have a key?

She tucked her gun under the mattress, left the apartment, and walked along Catherine Street toward the liquor store that Dom told her Frank owned. Just before reaching Lilly's Spirits, she passed in front of the Weepers club. Two boys sat in chairs tilted back against the wall, a white dog curled between them on the pavement.

"You takin' a walk all alone, babe?"

Heather stopped. "I'm going to the liquor store."

"It ain't safe for a chick to be out all alone in this neighborhood."

"I'm not alone; I have two tough guys and a dog watching over me. What's his name?"

"Who?"

"The dog."

"Sammy. He lives here in the club with us. What's your name, sweetheart?"

"I like dogs." Heather walked away and into Lilly's Spirits.

Frank Terenzio was just finishing with a customer, who held the door open for Heather as he left. Three other men sat at a round table. The youngest wore a priest's collar. All talking stopped when she walked in.

"I'm sorry, am I interrupting – "

"Not at all," Frank said. "Can I help you?"

"Do you have White Heather Whiskey?"

"I do." Frank took a bottle of White Heather off a shelf behind the counter and wiped the dust off with a rag. "You're the first person to buy a bottle of this in a long time. Are you visiting someone?"

"No. I just moved into Knickerbocker."

"Well, welcome to the neighborhood. I'm Frank; I own this joint. The old guy at the table is my father, Pompeo."

"Call me Pomp." Pomp and the other two men stood up.

"The young, good-lookin' guy is Father Casimiro." said Frank.

"Please call me Cas."

"And the other guy is Jokes. He's hilarious and helps out at the store."

"I'm Heather. It's lovely meeting you, gentlemen."

"Where didcha move from?" Pomp asked.

"London."

"Well, that explains the White Heather. Is it good?" Frank asked.

"I like it. Maybe because of my name."

"What building are you living in?" Jokes asked.

"Ten Monroe."

"That's my building," Frank said.

"Yours?" Heather asked.

"No, I mean I live in 10 Monroe, too. We're neighbors. I have an idea. How about I open this bottle of Heather, and we all toast to you and your arrival in the good old USA. The bottle is on the house. Whadaya say?"

"Brilliant, but I'll pay for – "

"Not a chance." Frank opened the bottle, filled five shot glasses, and passed them to the other men, who were now standing at the counter with Frank and Heather. "Father Cas, do the honors."

"Welcome to your new home, Heather, and may your future here be blessed."

After they finished, the four men put their glasses upside-down on the counter. Heather wasn't sure why, but she nodded and did the same.

"That's an American Army patch." Heather pointed to the frame above the counter.

"It is," Frank said. "How do you know that?"

"My husband was an American soldier I met at home."

"Was?"

"He was in the Korean War and had same patch. He came home mentally ill."

"I'm sorry to hear that," Pomp said. "Where is he?"

"The short of it is, he was in an Army hospital. He was being transferred to work at a recruiting station here in New York."

"Probably Whitehall Street," Frank said. "Sorry, I interrupted you."

"Whitehall is right," Heather said. "The London Bank gave me a transfer to its branch on Canal Street and even helped get us an apartment. But a couple of weeks ago, he killed himself."

"Good God, my dear woman." Father Cas said. "I am so sorry. How can I help?"

"Oh, no, no, we hadn't seen each other for over a year, and even then, he didn't know who I was. So it is not as terrible for me as it sounds. But too late to cancel my work transfer, so here I am."

Father Cas handed her a card with his phone number. "Call if you need anything."

"I'm sorry," Heather said. "This is a happy occasion meeting you lovely gentlemen. The eagle patch brought back fresh memories."

"Lots of guys came back pretty rattled, as they do from every war." Pomp said.

"Anyway, thank you so much, gentlemen. I hope I see you again."

"You will if you come back, and I hope you do, even if you just need to talk."

"You okay there, Frankie?" Jokes chuckled.

"I will." Heather smiled as she headed back to her apartment. *Perfect. Flirty Frank is Anna's brother. It will be easy to play him. Maybe I'll kill him, so Anna knows what it's like to lose a brother.*

CHAPTER NINE

"Give Dom a scolding"

"I'm coming; I'm coming," Heather said to the knocking at her door, "Who is it?"

"Rico. It's Rico. Didn't Dom tell you I'd check on you today?"

Heather opened her door and invited Rico in. "Jesus, you knock like a cop. It's only ten in the morning and I have jet lag. I'm having coffee; you want some?"

"Sure. Is Dom here?"

"Dom? The guy who was supposed to be you at the airport? That Dom?" She handed Rico a cup of coffee. "Check with his girlfriend."

"Who? Which girl?"

"He dropped me off, said he had a date. Didn't even offer to carry my suitcase up."

"Well, no one, not even his brother, has heard from him."

"I'm sure this is all very troubling for you, but I don't care. What I do care about is you telling people who I am and why I'm here. I thought you understood that. And then you pop into my apartment without even a call. Suppose Frank was here, what would I say? 'Oh, this is my friend, the leader of Satan's Knights, just checking on how I'm doing.'"

"Frank who? From the liquor store? Why would he be here?"

"Oh Lord, do you get my point, or are you as dim as that Dom guy?"

"I get your point. I'll call next time and say it's the bank or something. We'll decide."

"And, quit telling everyone!"

"I just told my top guys because I needed a little help."

"Who are they?"

"Dom, his brother, Derick, Domingo, Mike, and Andy. Just my top guys."

"Christ, and who did they tell? They'd better not act like they know me if they see me taking a walk or something."

"No. They're cool. So, why would Frank be here?"

"I went to buy liquor from his store last night, and he was very flattering."

"Did he ask about you? Don't underestimate him, he's a pretty sharp guy, a former cop."

"They bought my bollocks army husband story."

"They?"

"A young priest, Frank, his father, and some guy named Jokes. "They were terribly sympathetic."

"Okay, all good."

"What do you want, besides looking for your friend?"

"Cool. Your blue-and-white '56 Chevy Bel Air is parked on Market Street across from the A&P. I can walk you over."

"We don't know each other, Rico."

"Yeah, right, sorry. Okay, you need anything, here's my number. Call anytime."

Heather enjoyed Rico's being jealous of Frank, but she needed to own him. "Thank you for all the furniture, car, money, everything. I do appreciate it, Rico."

"Hey, your husband is paying for all this with a nice bonus for me, right into my account, no questions asked. So, whatever you want, you got it, doll."

"It's Heather. And remember, you'll get a big reward from my husband if I get home safely."

"You will. I'm just surprised your husband is letting you do this shit."

"Letting me?" No one lets me do anything. I make my own decisions. Phillip loves me and pays the bills. But no one owns me."

"Cool. He must be a lot older than you. I know he's very rich."

"He's older, kind, rich, and he'll do anything for me." "He also has powerful friends in Russia. Anything else you want to know?"

"No, no, just curious."

"Fine. You need to go now. Oh, and give Dom a scolding for not carrying my suitcase."

"Okay." Rico put his cup on the table and left.

* * *

Pomp walked into Lilly's. Frank was sitting at the table with Johnny.

"What's up, Pop? You look lost," Frank asked his father.

"Lost is a good word, Frankie. How ya doin', Johnny?"

"Should I leave?" Johnny asked.

"No, no, stay," Pomp said. "Frankie, we got a letter from the Army sayin' your brother Danny is being transferred to Fort Benning, and then to Walter Reed, before his discharge. We don't know what that means. What the hell? Why don't he just come home if he's being discharged?"

"You got the letter?" Johnny asked.

"Yeah, right here." Pomp handed the letter to Frankie, who skimmed it and passed it to Johnny."

"You got a clue, Johnny?" Frank asked.

"Let me hang on to it for a couple of days. Ben and Henry have a good connection in the military. I won't tell you not to worry. You will. But it could be nothing. I'm on it. If you have any letters, postcards, anything from Danny, or anything else from the Army, leave whatever you have with Frankie, and I'll pick them up," Johnny said.

"Whaddya need that stuff for, Johnny?" Pomp asked.

"Probably don't." Johnny shrugged. "Just in case... maybe there's info in there to help track down answers if we need 'em."

"Does Anna know about the letter, Pop?"

"Your mother was on the phone with her when I left."

"I'll drop in on her on my way home." Johnny headed for the door energized by the familiar surge of a mission, letter in hand.

"Thanks, Johnny." Pomp yelled after him as the door closed. "Geez, Frankie, I hope it's nothing."

* * *

Rico, Mike, Domingo, and Andy were sitting in the Knights' apartment watching "The DuPont Show" when Derick burst in. "They found my brother."

"Who found your brother?" Domingo asked.

"The cops. He's dead."

"Dom is dead?" What happened?" Rico was on his feet.

"I don't kn…know." Derick burst into tears.

"I know a reporter with the *Journal*." Rico dialed the phone. "Turn off the TV."

After the phone call, Rico sat on the couch, shaking his head. "My guy said it would be in the morning papers. The cops found Dom shot dead in a stolen car. The car was parked on 79th and Central Park. The cops think it was a rival gang but no suspects yet."

"Which gang?" Mike said. "We gotta find out which gang."

"No way the Weepers or any gang from around here would do that," Domingo said. "What gangs are up in Central Park?"

"What was Dom doing uptown anyway?" Mike asked.

"Heather told me that when he dropped her off, he said he had a date. Derick, you know anyone he was seeing uptown?"

"No, but he has a favorite make-out place up on 79th."

"That's where they found him," Mike said. "Rico, we got a gang coming at us, and we need to end them now."

"Don't nobody jump crazy. Let's see what the cops come up with," Rico said. "I'll talk to Heather again and see if she can remember anything else Dom might have said."

"Maybe she did it," Derick said.

"And then, what … walk back downtown, take a cab, or hitch a ride?" Mike said. "I don't think so. If she was going to kill him, she's probably smart enough to do it closer to where she lives. And anyway, why would she kill Dom? No,

I think it's an uptown gang. Telling us not to come on their territory."

"Maybe," Rico said. "Maybe."

"My brother had an assassin in his car last night who came here to kill Nunzio. So she's got to be around the bend," Derick said. "All I'm sayin' is don't be too quick to cross her off."

"We're on her side." Mike said. "It's gotta be a gang hit."

"Let's see what the news says," Rico said. "I have a contact with the cops uptown, and the reporter said he'd call back when he has more info."

CHAPTER TEN

"Mussels and Mugs"

Heather walked into Lilly's. Frank was at the round table to the left of the entrance with Jokes writing in a ledger. Both were drinking coffee.

"Hey, Red! Welcome back." Frank dropped his pen on the table.

"Heather works."

"Heather it is. What can I get for you?"

"A decent bottle of red. You choose."

"Sure thing." Frank rose and walked to the wine collection behind the counter. He immediately pulled a bottle from the shelf with no hesitation. "This is one of my favorites. Any occasion?"

"No, just a mood. Can you recommend a lunch place?"

"What kinda place?"

"Something with character."

"Frank's a character; take him with you." Jokes smiled.

"Jokes, you're putting her on the spot."

"I'd love your company, Frank, if you can get away."

"I got the store, Frankie," Jokes said.

"I'll pick up the wine after lunch."

"If you need me, Jokes, we'll be at Mussels and Mugs."

"Now, that sounds interesting," Heather said as they left Lilly's.

"I like the joint—great seafood on an old tugboat.

"Is it always tied up there?"

"It's permanently moored off a South Street dock. The owners are sisters, Syd and Kate. The best seafood chowder anywhere. I guarantee it."

"Sounds like a tough business in a tough neighborhood. Just the two girls run it?"

"And no one ever messes with them." Frank led Heather down Catherine Street, then right on South Street. "My sister Anna and her family live in that building." Frank pointed to 20 Catherine Slip as they passed. "It's part of the Al Smith projects...I'm sorry, am I boring you with this tour guide routine?"

"No, not at all. I appreciate it. Tell me about your sister and her family."

"Oh, just typical stuff. Anna works part-time at the *Journal American*; her husband Mac is a longshoreman and a mean drunk. They have two boys; Angelo is 15 and Adam is eight. Terrific kids, despite Mac. Anna is a great mom. How about you? Brothers or sisters?"

"No, only me. My parents died several years ago. So, just me."

"Were they good people?"

"Odd question. My mom was. My stepfather beat us. He would hit my mother with a belt. I would scrunch up and hide under the sink. My mother never told him where I was."

"I'm so sorry. That must've been rough."

"Oh, I think we need to be drinking and know each other better, before I bore you with my long sad tale."

"Well, both work for me." Frank smiled.

"Me too."

"Let's cross here. Mussels and Mugs is right across the street."

Heather took Frank's arm as they crossed South Street.

A couple of Popeyes were coming out, "Looking good, Frankie," a Popeye held the door open.

Frank smiled and nodded.

"You know them?" she asked as they walked in.

"They're South Street Boys, better known as the Popeyes."

"A gang?"

"A gang." Frank walked up to the bar with Heather on his arm."

"Frankie, love, good to see you," said the tall woman wearing a big hat, standing behind the bar. "And who you got with you?"

"Hi, Kate. This is Heather."

"Hello, Heather, nice to meetcha. Stay here a second." Kate turned to the cracked door at the far end of the bar and shouted, "Syd, get out here."

A tall, conservatively dressed, blond-haired woman came out of the room carrying a prehistoric meat cleaver. She walked up to them. "Hey, Frankie! Nice to see ya. What's up? Wait, is she with you?" gesturing toward Heather.

"She is. Heather, this is Syd, Kate's sister."

"Pleased to meet you, Syd. I'm guessing Frank is popular here?"

"Frankie is popular everywhere, sweetheart," Kate said. "But Frankie with a woman on his arm. Well, now that's somethin' ya gotta stand and salute."

"Okay, okay, it's not like I never –"

"No, Frankie, you never. Now you two take table three at the window over there before the lunchtime goons get here," Kate said. "I'll bring ya a bowl of bouillabaisse and some bread. And a couple of beers. Anything but Rheingold, 'cause you're still pissed about the Miss Rheingold thing, eh, Frankie?"

"Is that good with you?" Frank asked Heather.

"Certainly."

"Will you look at that? He asked her if it was okay." Syd shook her head as she walked back to her office, cleaver in hand.

"Perfect, Kate." Frank said.

On the way to their table, Heather noticed a large photo hanging on a wide post in the middle of the dining room. They stopped. It was a picture of the back of an attractive woman wearing a low-cut black dress. A note was attached: "To Syd and Kate, keep a walkaway dress at hand, 'cause knowin' when ta walk away is more important than knowin' when ta stay – Gammy." Underneath the note was a short poem that read:

Listen to Gammy's lesson
as a looker in my day.
A looker gets to look a lot,
so, she might go astray.
Look each boy over closely
before pickin' one ta stay.
And, when one isn't nice,
slip on your "walk away,"
a special dress ta wear
with low cut back ta there!
Show 'im what he's missin'
by seein' what ya bare.

"I love this, I'm guessing Gammy is Kate's and Syd's grandmother," Heather said.

"Right, but more than just a grandma." Frank and Heather sat down and welcomed the mugs of beer and bouillabaisse Kate set before them.

They pulled apart pieces of the crusty bread and dunked those into the stew.

"Back in the day, Gammy was a fixer. She knew everyone you needed to know to get things done. Her nickname was Sas. She took in Nunzio Sabino when he was 12 and raised him along with own her kids."

"Who is Nunzio Sabino?" Heather asked, even though she knew exactly who he was.

"Nunzio is like the neighborhood boss. He's connected. So, when Gammy's granddaughters wanted to open a restaurant, Nunzio bought the tugboat and made sure it included permanent mooring rights. The rest, Kate and Syd did. In the early days, there was some trouble, but Syd and Kate mostly handled it themselves.

"They're not to be messed with, these two. Three years ago, when the city demolished Roosevelt Street, Saint Joachim's church, and several tenements, the Roosevelt Street Boys—kind of an older gang—needed a new place to hang out. They made a deal with Syd and Kate to be the bouncers here in exchange for two tables in the back corner, over there." Frank pointed and five men at one of the tables waved.

"They just hang around? Do they get free food or beer?"

"Nope, they own those tables, that's it. They pay for their food and drink. They're good customers and they're good for the other customers."

"Brilliant," she said as she lifted a spoonful in her mouth. Then swallowed. "This bouillabaisse is the best I've ever had."

Mussels and Mugs was now almost at capacity with the lunch crowd. Behind Heather and across the room, Frank spotted a table with seven Knights. They seemed to be drinking heavily and it looked like two were a little agitated.

Frank could always read a room, even before he became a cop. He noticed they had also caught the attention of the Roosevelt Street Boys. One of the Knights started to get up but was pulled back by another Knight. *What the hell is going on at that table? Whatever it is, it can't be good.*

"Are you okay, Frank? You seem distracted," Heather said.

"Sorry. At a table behind you in the back are a group of Knights, a bad-news gang from the projects. But you know what? It's none of my business. I'm out with my girl."

"Am I your girl?" Heather smiled as she turned to look at the Knights for a moment. "Bad boys and booze, never a good mix." She shook her head.

Frank smiled. "Would you like a piece of pie or anything else?"

"I couldn't eat another thing. This was perfect."

Now one of the Knights walked toward them. A second Knight was trailing and trying to stop the first one. Frank pushed his chair away from the table as he stood. Two Roosevelt Boys were also heading toward Frank. The other three Roosevelt Boys walked to the table with the Knights, who were now all standing.

Syd appeared with her prehistoric meat cleaver in hand and walked toward the two Knights approaching Frank and Heather.

"What's going on?" Heather turned to see Syd and the two Knights coming toward her.

The three Roosevelt Boys had reached the Knights' table in the corner. All the Knights sat down.

"Frank, what do you think the Roosevelt Street Boys said to make the Knights sit down?"

"Sit," Frank said, "They said, 'Sit.'"

Frank stood facing the two Knights who were only a foot from his table.

"Hey, Frankie, I'm Derick. How you doin'?" Derick was unsteady and slurring his words. "Whatcha doin' with her?"

Heather stood up.

Frank stepped between the Knights and Heather. "Shut up and leave. Now!"

"She's with you?" asked Derick.

"C'mon, Derick, let's go back," said Domingo, the other Knight who was slightly behind Derick. "Sorry, everybody."

"Fuck this, Domingo. What's she doin'?" Derick said.

Suddenly two Roosevelt Boys were between Frank and the Knights. "We got this, Syd. Okay with you, Frankie?"

"Thanks, guys," Frank said.

Syd headed back to her office.

"Boys, I'm Daddy-Bruce," said the taller of the two Roosevelt Street Boys. "My buddy here is Nicky Two-Bridges. Empty your pockets of all cash. You will leave it here for a tip, because that would be the right thing to do after making Syd come out to check on youse."

Domingo looked over at their table and saw his fellow Knights sitting still while three Roosevelt Street Boys stood behind them. Without another word, Derick and Domingo emptied their pockets and gave their cash to Daddy-Bruce, who put it on Frank's table.

The pub was stone silent.

"Good, let's cop a breeze," Nicky-Two-Bridges said.

"I ain't goin' nowhere with you, you dumb freak." Derick said.

"Ho!" Daddy-Bruce said, mockingly widening his eyes and tucking his chin. "Nicky, I believe he just called you a dumb freak."

"Freak is cool," Nicky said. "And, I do confess I have been unnewsworthy lately. But dumb? Hmm."

"Shall I kill this nosebleed or just pity him?" Bruce didn't take his eyes off Derick.

"Let's pity him for now," Nicky said.

"At least I ain't no – " Derick said.

"Shut the fuck up. You ain't nothin' but a skell." Daddy -Bruce grabbed Derick's hair, bent him sideways, and walked him to the door.

Nicky-Two-Bridges grabbed Domingo's neck and pushed him toward the door.

"You don't need to put your hands on me, I'm goin'," Domingo said.

"Do you know me?" Nicky said.

"Yeah, everybody does."

"Then you know...fuck with me and I'll kill you."

"I know. You got it. No nothin'."

The area around their table suddenly cleared. Frank and Heather sat back down.

The Roosevelt Street Boys at the Knight's table herded the remaining Knights out of the pub.

Heather looked at Frank. "You weren't joking when you said a place with character."

"Well, there you have it. Bouncers, when necessary."

"Interesting nicknames, Daddy-Bruce and Nicky-Two-Bridges."

"Daddy-Bruce because he became a father when he was 14. And Nicky-Two-Bridges because he lived on the street in the Two-Bridges neighborhood until he was 16 and then joined the Army. He and Daddy-Bruce met in Korea. They were Rangers. So was my sister's brother-in-law, Johnny, and a few other guys from the neighborhood. These are real tough guys.

Bruce and Nicky came back in and walked past Frank.

"Sorry for all that, Frankie," Nicky said over his shoulder.

"Thanks," Frank said to them.

"No problem," Bruce said.

"Why did that boy call Nicky a freak?"

"Korea screwed Nicky up. Add that to growing-up on the streets, and you got something...not a freak, but something dangerous."

"I get it. This has been the most brilliant lunch I've ever had."

"Oh yeah. So this hasn't turned you off me?"

"Quite the contrary, Frankie." Heather smiled.

CHAPTER ELEVEN

"Get off my roof or we'll throw you off"

R ico was sitting back, shirt off, catching rays on the roof of 10 Catherine Slip. This is where he lived and where the Knights had their club apartment in the Al Smith projects. He sipped coffee, absorbing the early morning sun and the peace of tar beach. Rico heard footsteps approaching him. "No, no, no, this better be important," he said to the unknown intruders.

"It kinda is, Rico," Mike said.

Rico opened his eyes, took a sip of coffee, and looked at Mike, Domingo, and Derick. "If this is about yesterday, I already heard. They threw you out of Mussels and Mugs. Too much booze for lunch, boys?"

"We need to kick the shit outta the Roosevelt Street Boys," Derick said. "And you need to ask your girlfriend why she was hanging out with Frank."

"Mike, what is he talking about?"

Derick said, "I'm telling you what happened."

"Shut the fuck up, Derick." Rico said. "Mike. What happened yesterday?"

"Frank and Heather were having lunch at M&M's," Mike said.

"So what?" Rico said. "She wants to get close to Angelo's family."

"Derick and Domingo went up and asked her why she was with Frank."

"I was just trying to stop Derick," Domingo said. "That's the only reason I was with him."

"Wait. You guys went up to her and Frank like you knew who she was and asked what they were doing together?" Rico stood up. "You guys did that?"

"Not me," said Domingo. "Just Derick."

Mike said, "Derick was upset about his brother being found dead in the park and all, he had a couple of drinks and – "

Rico's head was exploding. He had to hold the Knights together, at least until Heather killed Nunzio. But his control was slipping and time was running out. "Mike, this all happened in front of Heather and Frank?"

"In front of the whole place," Mike said. "Frank and Heather were on their feet."

"That's when the Roosevelt Street Boys made us look like punks, throwing us out," Derick said. "We gotta kick their asses."

"You are punks!" Rico said.

"Not me," Derick said. "I called Nicky a freak. Domingo didn't say anything. I ain't a punk. I ain't scared of them."

"Then you're a stupid punk," Rico said. "But I'd be more afraid of Heather if I was you. You're out of the Knights."

"Wait? What?" Derick asked. "You're taking her side against one of your own Knights?"

"You ain't a Knight anymore," Rico said. "Get off my roof or we'll throw you off."

"Fuck all of you! I'm gonna start my own gang," Derick shouted and stomped away.

"I will talk to Heather. You two let the others know Derick is out," Rico said.

"He'll try to take some Knights with him," Mike said.

"Fine," Rico said. "Domingo, you got anything to say?"

"Derick ain't all wrong. Why should you let the Roosevelt Street Boys treat us like that?" asked Domingo. "We can stand up to them."

"They wouldn't fight us; they would kill every last one of us." Rico said. "You don't know them. My brother Danilo was a Roosevelt Street Boy before the Zara brothers talked him into starting the Knights. Frank and Danny were Roosevelt Street Boys. Remember Johnny, the ghost in the window; he was one of them. Nunzio started the Roosevelt Street Boys back when he was a kid with Father Joe. They are not a gang. They are something else. Anyone with half a brain is smart enough to fear them. You don't mess with the Roosevelt Street Boys."

* * *

After spending the day at Coney Island, Angelo, Audrey, Tate, and Gina rode the subway home. Audrey and Gina sat near the exit doors chatting about remaining long distance friends. Angelo and Tate stood looking through the front window as the train screeched into City Hall station.

"Angelo I really think we need guns."

"Tate, you were the one that said it would change us."

"That was three years ago, after you beat the Razor."

"So, all the fights we had since then, two with the Knights and one with the Falcons, we won without guns."

"I know, Angelo, but it's different now. The other day I gave a couple of Knights the finger and one of them pointed a gun right at me and laughed."

"Who?"

"Derick. You know the one whose brother was shot?"

"You worried they're gonna come at us with guns this time."

"Angelo, you're my best friend, I'd take a bullet for you. I ain't worried about me. I'm worried there's a storm coming your way, and I won't be able to stop it. We need guns."

"I'll talk to my Uncle Nunzio about getting us a couple."

"Cool. Here's our stop."

The four friends walked along Madison Street. Tate had his arm around Gina and Angelo held Audrey's hand.

"Ain't there any way I can talk you out of leaving, Audrey?" Angelo said.

"I'm afraid not. We'll keep in touch."

"It's not about keeping in touch. I love you, Audrey."

They all stopped in front of Audrey's building.

"I know, Angelo," Andrey nodded, and then to Gina, she said, "Can you come in for a minute?"

"Sure," Gina said.

Angelo and Tate walked to their club.

"I don't know what to say to her to make her stay. Has Gina said anything to you about Audrey?"

"A little. Like you need to stop asking her to stay."

"What? I just said I loved her, and she just said, 'I know.' What the hell?"

"I heard."

"So, what's goin' on? How do I get her to stay?"

"You can't, Angelo. Look, think about a girl you don't like, if she keeps telling you she loves you and wants to go out with you, whadaya think?"

"I think she's annoying."

"Right. All them love songs are bullshit. When it's over, it's over."

"Did Audrey tell Gina it's over? That I'm annoying?"

"No. I'm just sayin' you need to stop bugging her. Be cool. Cool makes you more attractive to girls. It's your only shot."

"She said I'm annoying?"

"No, I'm just saying it's annoying to keep asking and asking."

"I'm annoying? Me, I'm annoying?"

"Angelo, I'm saying don't be annoying, be cool."

"Maybe if I ask her to marry me, she'll know how much I love her."

"No way. Don't do that. It ain't about you loving her, she already knows that. Be cool."

"I don't know, Tate. Maybe I gotta ask her."

"No way, Angelo don't...hey, there's your uncle's car in front of Lilly's. Go ask him."

"Wait here."

Angelo ran over to the Cadillac. He talked for less than a minute and returned to Tate.

"So?" Tate said.

"He shrugged and said he'd think about it."

"Cool."

Angelo and Tate joined Carl, Bobby, and Howie in chairs in front of the Weeper's club, and Sammy, the dog, curled at their feet.

"How's things going with your old man, Angelo?" Howie said.

"He was great when he came home three years ago, but lately he's back to being an asshole."

"How come?" Carl asked.

"I don't know. Probably drinking and remembering that he doesn't like me."

"Sorry, pal," Tate said. "Why don't you talk to his brother or Father Joe?"

"Yeah, maybe."

CHAPTER TWELVE

"Mine is bigger"

Heather felt safe but confined in her apartment. She was thinking about Frank. *Good lord, can I be falling for him? How would that work?*

Rico called. He said they had to talk and suggested dinner at 7:00 at the East Harlem Diner uptown. He said he would pick her up. Instead, she said she would meet him there. Heather didn't want to go, but knew she still needed Rico. She took her silenced gun.

She walked along Market Street to her Chevy. She got in, moved her seat forward, rolled down her window and saw Derick leaning against the burgundy brick walls of Knickerbocker Village, staring at her. He walked toward her, arms limp at his sides, but in his right hand was a gun. She smiled. Her gun was now in her lap. "Why Derick, it's nice to see you again," she said as he appeared on the sidewalk next to her car.

"It ain't nice to see you. I'm out of the Knights because of you."

"How long have you been standing there waiting for me?"

"A while."

"I'm flattered." Heather continued to smile.

"I knew Rico would want to meet you so I waited by your car."

"You're a clever little wanker, aren't you?"

Derick was now near her window. "What's a wanker?"

"Is that a gun in your hand?"

"It was my brother's gun."

"It's a tiny gun. May I see it?" Heather said.

"It's a .25 automatic. You can see it from there." Derick took several steps back and held the gun up sideways. "It has a pearl handle my brother put on."

"I see. A pearl handle is pretty, but if your hand sweats, it's slippery. Anyway, mine is bigger." Heather pointed her silenced Beretta at Derick.

"Whoa. You killed my brother, didn't you?"

"Ask him." She shot Derick once in the chest.

Derick fell back against the brick wall and slid down into a sitting position. He was stunned. His gun lay on the sidewalk next to him.

"You should shoot me back with your tiny gun."

"It burns and hurts." Derick looked surprised. He took his bloody hand off his chest and reached for his gun.

"Ta ta, wanker." Heather aimed for a second, then shot him in his forehead. Derick fell sideways, dead still. She needed to put a new silencer on her gun. Her second shot was too loud. Heather looked up and down the street. It was clear. She took one more look at Derick. She felt nothing but accurate, and drove away.

* * *

Rico was seated at a booth in the rear of the East Harlem Diner. Heather walked up to the booth and sat down.

"The burgers here are the best in the city," Rico said.

"How do you know?"

"I know the owner."

"Well then, of course, they must be the best." Heather smirked.

"You two ready to order or what?" asked the waitress walking up to them.

"Sadie, ain't these the best burgers in the City?" Rico said.

"Yeah," Sadie said. "I checked yesterday with every place and these are the best. So, what do you want?"

"Cheeseburger, fries, and coffee," Rico said.

"Two eggs over hard, bacon, toast, and coffee," Heather said.

"I'll bring the coffee now." Sadie walked away.

"Breakfast for dinner?"

"Is that okay with you?"

"It's fine; I'm just breaking your shoes a little. Just playing."

"Brilliant." Heather shook her head.

"Listen, we need to talk about Derick," Rico said. "What he did yesterday will never happen again. I promise."

"I know. He's dead."

"What?"

"He's dead on the sidewalk where my car was parked. He had a gun but was too slow."

"He had a gun?"

"A .25 automatic."

"A .25 automatic?"

"Are you just going to repeat what I say?" Heather said. "Yes, with a pearl handle."

"I think that was his brother's gun."

"That's what he said."

"What else did he say?"

"He said it burns and hurts." Heather smiled as the coffee arrived.

"I'll make a call," Rico said. "To get some of the guys to pick up his body."

"Rico, the cops will find the body and think it was the Roosevelt Street Boys."

"But the Knights will want more. They will want to do something."

"That's something their leader could handle, isn't it?" Heather said.

CHAPTER THIRTEEN

"Shoot the rock off the guy's shoulder"

Nunzio and Father Joe sat on a wooden bench in City Hall Park, each feeding pigeons from small, brown paper bags as they had done so many times as kids. Three of Nunzio's men sat on benches across the footpath.

"So, Lanzo is dead." Nunzio said. "Shot dead on his birthday, at his favorite trattoria."

"I'm sorry, my friend."

"Do the cops know who did it?" Nunzio asked as he tossed peanuts to the birds at their feet.

"The police think there were two witnesses, the bartender and a waitress. The bartender told the cops that he opened the trattoria and saw Lanzo with his newspaper, but not his breakfast. The waitress serving Lanzo was gone. Now, the bartender skipped too, and the police are looking for both."

"You can bet Lanzo's Cammora are looking for them, too. Makes no sense. Lanzo was high-up Camorra, but not a boss, and he was leaving."

"I'll try to find out more," Father Joe said.

"No, Joe, this is my business, not for you, my friend." Nunzio said. "That poor waitress must be scared to death."

"You okay?"

"It's all part of my business. It is what I do," Nunzio said. I've got some tickets for *Bye Bye Birdie* at the Shubert for Frank and his family. Ride over there with me."

"Sure, Boss."

"Pepe, let's go to Lilly's," he said to his driver on the bench across the way.

* * *

Angelo and Tate sat in chairs in front of the Weepers' storefront, watching as Satan's Knights gathered in the projects across Catherine Street. Domingo and another Knight crossed the street and walked toward them. Domingo put a small rock on his own shoulder and walked right up to Angelo.

"Go ahead. Knock the rock off my shoulder, punk," Domingo said.

Angelo took the rock off Domingo's shoulder, looked at it, and handed it back to Domingo. "Here."

"Are you stupid or what?" Domingo said as he put the rock back on his shoulder. "You know what to do."

Before Angelo could respond, a 1961 black Cadillac Fleetwood sedan stopped in front of the Weepers' clubhouse. Uncle Nunzio and Father Joe stepped out with Pepe and two other men.

"What's going on, Angelo?" Uncle Nunzio said.

"Domingo wants me to knock the rock off his shoulder."

"Oh, yeah? Pepe...do this guy a favor and shoot the rock off his shoulder," Nunzio said.

"Sure, Boss." Pepe pulled out a .38 Colt Special and pointed it at Domingo.

"Wait up!" Domingo knocked the rock off his own shoulder.

"Didn't I tell you punks to leave Angelo alone?" Nunzio said, taking a step toward them.

"Yeah, sorry, Mr. Sabino. We're gone." The two Knights crossed the street back to the projects.

Frank and Heather walked out of Lilly's to see what was going on.

"Whoa, you're the babysitter," Angelo said to Uncle Nunzio.

"Babysitter?" Uncle Nunzio said. "Whadda you talkin' about?"

"I had a fight with some Knights in Mo-Mo's a couple of weeks ago. No big deal," Angelo said. "But when Domingo was leavin' he said something like, 'once your babysitter is gone, I'm gonna mess you up bad.' I didn't think nothin' of it. But just now, I don't know, do you think the Knights are planning to kill you, Uncle Nunzio?"

"Good thinking, kid," Uncle Nunzio said. "Pepe, pick up that Domingo kid tomorrow. Maybe he's just blowing smoke, or maybe...who knows."

"Will do, Boss."

"Why would the Knights want to kill you?" Heather asked.

"Who are you?" Uncle Nunzio said.

"Boss, this is my girl, Heather," Frank said.

"Nice to meet you." Uncle Nunzio handed an envelope to Frank. "Here's a dozen good seats for *Bye Bye Birdie* for you, your girlfriend, your sister, whoever else you want."

"Speaking of girlfriends, Angelo," Tate said. "Here comes Audrey and her father."

"You and Audrey should come to the play with us, Angelo," Frank said.

"That would be cool."

"Hi Angelo." Audrey gave him a hug. "My dad wants to tell you something."

"Angelo, I am sorry for what I said to you." Mr. Vadunka held out his hand to Angelo. "I was drunk. None of what I said was true. You're a fine young man and my daughter is lucky to be dating you."

Angelo shook his hand, surprised but pleased.

Mr. Vadunka turned to Uncle Nunzio and bowed.

"Good," said Uncle Nunzio. "Show up for work tomorrow."

"Thank you, Mr. Sabino." Mr. Vadunka turned and walked away alone.

"Does this mean you're gonna stay?" Angelo asked Audrey.

"No. I'm leaving tomorrow morning. It just means he gets his job back. He lost his job because of what he said to you."

Angelo panicked. "Audrey, we can get married and live with my parents, until I...."

Audrey's eyes emptied. "Stop, Angelo! It's settled. I'm leaving tomorrow morning. Let's just try to enjoy tonight."

Chapter Fourteen

"Submarine Races"

Rico and Heather drove separately to Battery Park in Lower Manhattan. Rico parked his car and joined Heather in her car. Heather didn't like these meetings, but it was clear Rico needed close and constant supervision. And this was important.

"Domingo told Angelo your Knights are planning to kill Nunzio."

"What? How do you know that?"

"I heard Angelo tell Nunzio."

"He told Nunzio?"

"You're repeating me again."

"When did he tell him?"

"Yesterday."

"Holy shit! What did Nunzio say?"

"He told his guys to pick up Domingo."

"They'll beat everything out of Domingo," Rico said. "We gotta get him out of the state, maybe even out of the country."

"Let's talk about that, but first tell me what you found out about Mac. Where does he go after work?"

"Mac has a girlfriend. They watch the submarine races on Thursday nights under the East River Drive."

"So, tonight?"

"Yeah, I guess so," Rico said.

"Okay. Good. Then tonight," Heather said. "This is brilliant. Domingo steals a car, and he drives, while I'm in the shotgun seat. You follow us in your car. Domingo pulls alongside Mac and his girlfriend, my window facing the driver. I kill Mac, his girlfriend, and then Domingo. We leave in your car. Mac is dead and the Domingo problem is gone."

"Ah, shit, Heather. We can't kill another Knight. This is getting crazy," Rico said. "There has to be another way."

"This is the way. The cops will think it's the same gang at war with your guys."

* * *

Johnny, and Frank's sister, Anna, walked into Lilly's and sat at the small table with Frank, Pomp, and Jokes.

"All good news," Johnny said. "Danny is fine. He even got a couple of medals and was promoted to sergeant."

"So, what was all the mystery?" Pomp asked. "Fort Benning, Walter Reed, all that stuff?"

"Danny and one of his buddies were sheep-dipped into Cambodia. Sorry, it just means since the military can't be in Cambodia, they kinda unofficially transfer the soldiers to the Agency."

"Sheep-dipped?" Jokes asked.

"Yeah, sheep farmers dipped their sheep in a special bath to kill fungus, insects, anything else. They come out clean," Johnny said. "Danny and his buddy are back in the Army. They will first go to Fort Benning for a briefing, then to Walter Reed for a medical check and a briefing by the Agency. And then home. Probably next month."

"Geez, Johnny," Pomp smiled. "Great news. Thanks."

"No problem."

Anna sighed and relaxed. "Frankie, can I meet your girlfriend before Danny does"?

"She's a doll," Jokes said. "Plus, her ex was in the 101 Airborne, like Frank."

"Oh, yeah?" Anna said. "So, another WWII old guy?"

"No, in Korea," Jokes said.

Johnny shook his head. "101st wasn't in Korea."

"She recognized my Screaming Eagle patch over the counter," Frank said. "She told me that her ex wore the same patch in Korea."

"Not for nothin', Frank, but they were not there," Johnny said.

"You sure?" Frank asked.

"I was with the Eighth Army Rangers. We bumped shoulders with the 187th Airborne in Korea. They were it," Johnny said. And they didn't wear the eagle patch."

"Why the hell would she lie about that?" Frank said.

"Easy, Frank," Jokes said. "We're all made up of who we are, who we want to be, and who we're hiding."

"Jokes, have you been reading again?" Anna smiled. "She probably just liked you and made up something to get your interest. It's called flirting, Frankie."

"Anna's right," Johnny said. "Who cares if her ex was a paratrooper, a leg, or a nothin'? You like her. She likes you. Enjoy."

"As your protective sister, I say run," Anna said. "As your loving-nice-to-see-you-happy sister, I'm with Johnny. Enjoy."

* * *

Rico, Heather, and Domingo sat in Rico's car. A stolen black 1955 Chevy sedan was parked behind them.

"You're sure this is their spot?" Heather pointed at the East River across South Street.

"I'm sure. I'm payin' a couple of Popeyes for this info," Rico said. "Mac and his girl will be in a Tampico Red 1960 Buick. Her car."

"Nice ride," Domingo said. "Can I keep the Buick when you're done?"

"You can keep the Buick and the Chevy when I'm done," Heather said.

"Cool."

"There it is." Rico pointed.

"Let it park," Heather said. "Give me your map, Rico."

Rico handed her the large paper map as the Buick cut its engine.

Heather looked at Domingo. "Let's go."

Domingo got behind the wheel of the Chevy. Heather opened the large map in the shotgun seat and readied her silenced Barretta. Domingo pulled within inches alongside the Buick.

"Holy hell, Domingo. You're a little close. I can't even open my door."

"Want me to pull out and –"

"No. Cut the engine." Heather turned in her seat to get a better right-handed shot. She rolled down her window and called to the couple who seemed startled. Heather waved the map. Mac's girlfriend rolled down the driver's window.

"Hi, where are we?" Heather thought Mac would be driving but this would work.

She had to shoot Mac first, or he might jump out of the car. His girlfriend, pinned in the driver's seat, would wait. Mac leaned forward and turned toward Heather. Her shot split the bridge of his nose. Mac's girlfriend screamed and froze. Heather's second shot was in the girl's temple.

"Holy shit! Are you done? We'd better beat it." Domingo said.

Heather turned in her seat and shot Domingo in his right cheek and then in his ear. She sat there for a couple of seconds. There was a ton on blood on Domingo, who leaned against the driver's door. Heather climbed over the front seat and left by the backdoor. She walked around the Buick. Mac's head was resting on the passenger-side window.

"For my brothers." She put the gun against the window and fired an insurance shot. Mac dropped into his girl-friend's lap.

Heather walked to Rico's car and got in. "Did you see how close that wanker parked to the Buick?" Heather said. "I had to climb into the backseat to get out."

"Yeah, I'll be sure to scold him about that." Rico shook his head. "You know, like you told me to scold Dom after you killed him. I know it was you."

"Well, aren't we clever and pouty?" Heather said. "Take me home."

CHAPTER FIFTEEN

"We need to own Clarke"

N YPD Detective Hartz walked into Lilly's and found Frank alone behind the counter pouring a cup of coffee.

"Can I get one of those?" Hartz said.

"Hartz, great to see you," Frank said. "Here you go and there are donuts on the table. I'll join you."

"Thanks. Sorry about your brother-in-law. How are your sister and the boys doing?"

"Life with Mac has been hard for Anna. She didn't know Mac was cheating on her again, so she's angry and sad for the boys, and, well everything," Frank said. "Angelo's girlfriend just moved upstate, and then this. So, he's pretty beat-up and angry. And little Adam is devastated."

"How's Mac's brother Johnny doing?"

"Johnny, as you can imagine, is pissed and focused," Frank said. "He recently joined a security agency run by two of his war buddies, Ben, and Henry. They're determined to find out who did it."

"Me, too," Hartz said.

"Yeah, but you want to arrest the killer."

"Are you talking about Nunzio Sabino or Johnny?" Hartz nodded in understanding.

"Both, but Johnny is unstoppable," Frank said. "So, what brings you here?"

"Mac," Hartz said. "But I was coming anyway to look into the recent shootings of Satan's Knights. Ever since the '57 Knights killings, I'm the go-to guy when it comes to them."

"Lucky you."

"Yeah, right."

"I know there was a dead Knight parked next to Mac, but I figured the girlfriend's husband for Mac's killing," Frank said. "You look like you doubt that. You think the killings are all related?"

"I do. But the husband is still at the top of my list. He's Oliver Macallan, a rich Wall Street guy who wanted a divorce, but didn't want to pay a lot for it. His wife probably took up with Mac to make him jealous," Hartz said. "Sorry. We can talk about this at another time. Now's your time for grieving."

"No, I welcome the distraction," Frank said.

"You were the best NYPD ever had, Frank. Sure wish you'd stayed," Hartz said. "I'd love to get your take if you're up for it."

"Talk to me."

"We found that Knight shot in the head in a stolen car in Central Park a couple of weeks ago."

"Right," Frank said. "Dom something. The news said it was a rival gang."

"He was shot with a .32 that left tiny metal fragments from a silencer."

"A silencer?"

"Yeah, a silencer," Hartz said. "Then Dom's brother was shot on Market Street a few nights later, also with a .32."

"There was a rumor about the Roosevelt Street Boys, but I don't see them good for this."

"You're right," Hartz said. "It's not them."

"Was Mac killed with a .32?"

"A silenced .32. I'm guessing a Barretta," Hartz said. "So was Mac's girlfriend, and the Knight, Domingo, who was in the Chevy next to the car Mac was in. And get this. Domingo was shot from the passenger seat of the Chevy."

"The killer was in the Chevy?"

"Pretty sure," Hartz said. "Domingo was shot from his right, and close enough that metal fragments from the silencer adhered to the right side of his face. The Chevy was too close to the Buick for anyone outside the cars to reach in and shoot Domingo.

"So, the husband hired a killer who used a .32," Frank said.

"It's possible. But why kill the Knight? And him hiring the Knights' killer, or another killer with the same M.O? Too much of a coincidence for me. Most likely one killer."

"Let's step back a minute," Frank said. "The way I figure it, the Buick got there first because Mac and his girlfriend wouldn't park that close to another car. Then the Chevy pulls up next to them. The killer is in the passenger seat and shoots the girl who is closest. No, wait, if he shoots the driver, Mac will jump out of the Buick. He shoots Mac first. Then the girl. Then Domingo. And then he leaves by the backdoor."

"Good," Hartz said. "After the killer leaves the Chevy, he walks around to the passenger side of the Buick and fires another shot through the closed window into Mac's head. We found silencer fragments on the passenger window."

"Two shooters?"

"Possible, but then they wouldn't need Domingo, and the Chevy would be gone."

"You need to grab Rico," Frank said. "He has—or had—five top guys running the Knights with him. Three of them are dead. That leaves Andy and Mike. Rico must have some idea."

"I'll pick him up," Hartz said. "Maybe Andy and Mike, too."

"Listen, Hartz, my mom's having a small gathering at her place on Sunday," Frank said. "Come by. You know everyone, and they'd love to see you're on the case."

"Thanks. Maybe I will."

* * *

Nunzio Sabino lived in a large suite in Park Avenue's Drake Hotel. At times, when threats were certain, Pepe and a couple of bodyguards would spend days and nights with him. Mostly, Nunzio liked being there alone. Each morning, he enjoyed his breakfast at a window table in the lobby restaurant. Even now, as he thought about his friend Lanzo Basso, who had been shot while having breakfast in Naples, Nunzio remained unafraid. This was his church, his quiet moment.

The only company he looked forward to was when, his daughter, Natale, joined him for breakfast. On those occasions, three pieces of Fauchon chocolates were always delivered to her by the owner of the chocolate shop on the ground floor. Natale would say, "That's why I come here, Papa," and they would chuckle.

Pepe always parked and waited for Nunzio in front of the Drake. On rare occasions, when there was something pressing to discuss, Pepe would join Nunzio for breakfast. This was one of those occasions.

"Sorry, Boss," Pepe said. "I gotta thing."

The waiter appeared immediately at Nunzio's table. "Breakfast, sir?"

Nunzio said to Pepe, "You want some breakfast? I recommend the Swiss omelet."

"Just black coffee and a pastry, please," Pepe said to the waiter.

"Whaddya got?" Nunzio concentrated on continuing to work the fork through his omelet.

"Deputy Mayor Clarke wants to ask you for a favor, in person."

"This is good news. We need to own Clarke," Nunzio said. "I'm goin' to Pomp's place on Sunday evening for Mac's memorial dinner. Let's meet Clarke at the Caffè, Sunday afternoon around one."

"Done."

"Is Father Joe all set?"

"All set. The warden asked him to talk to a couple of other inmates. Father Joe said he'll talk to the whole prison if he gets some real time with Sage. The warden is thrilled. No problem," Pepe said. "Jimmy Knuckles and Bobby Moe are driving him to Boston in the Fleetwood. He's got a suite at the Fairmont Plaza on the Back Bay, and tickets for the Orioles-Red Socks game."

"Geez, they may never come back," Nunzio said. "Good work."

"Thanks, Boss."

"Any news from Naples?"

"Not yet. I'll stay on it."

"Good," Nunzio said. "*Grazie.*"

CHAPTER SIXTEEN

"You will never hear from them again"

Anna sat with her two sons and her parents as Father Joe dedicated Sunday's Mass to Mac. She stared at the priest but heard nothing. She knew he was talking about Mac but was lost in a seesaw of emotions: of anger and sadness; of self-pity; of concern for her sons; of fear of being alone again... and relief.

After Mass, Anna, Angelo, and Adam went to Pompa and Nonna's for dinner. Angelo and Adam joined Pompa in the living room. Anna went into the kitchen to be with her mother. They pulled out pans, pots, and spices.

"What are we cooking, Mama?"

"Your father's boss at the meat market gave him some nice tenderloin for tonight's dinner. I have fresh escarole we can cook with olive oil, onions, and tomatoes. And Italian bread still hot out of the oven."

"Sounds perfect."

"How you doin', Annabella?"

"I'm doing okay. Getting better," Anna said. "I'm mostly concerned about the boys. But they seem to be coming along. This is hard, Mama."

"I know, and time doesn't make it go away. It will get easier. We are all here for you, my beautiful daughter."

"I know you are."

"Good. Now, let's cook for those boys."

"How should we prepare the tenderloin?" Anna said.

"My father would say, '*con carne di prima scelta usate tre vini*' – with top beef, use three wines. I have Barbareco red, Benanti Etna white, and Marsala. Add some garlic, olive oil, red wine vinegar, fresh rosemary, and black pepper. And you have *deliziosa magia* – delicious magic."

"And cheesecake for dessert?"

"The way you like it, baked with no crust, and just cinnamon sugar sprinkled on top."

"Mmm, where is it?"

"In the icebox."

"Fridge, Mama," Anna said. "You have a refrigerator now."

"To me, it's an icebox, but '*un po 'meglio*'."

"A little better?" Anna said. "Ha."

* * *

Deputy Mayor Raymond Clarke walked into the Caffè Fiora at exactly 1:00 p.m. Pepe met him at the door and walked him to Nunzio's table while Nunzio still was talking with Natale at the small bar. He acknowledged Clarke, squeezed Natale's hand, and walked to his table.

"Deputy Mayor Clarke, good afternoon. Natale will be bringing us some coffee unless you want something stronger."

"Coffee's good," Clarke said. "Please, call me Ray or Clarke."

"Clarke it is."

"Mr. Sabino, thank you for seeing me. I don't know —"

"Here's your coffee gentlemen, and some pastries," Natale said. "I will make sure you're not disturbed."

As Pepe pulled out a chair at the table, Nunzio told Clarke, "Pepe is joining us. I trust him, and whatever favor you need, Pepe will help make that happen."

"That's fine, but I'm embarrassed and nervous."

"Whadaya need, my friend?" Nunzio asked.

"Money. A big loan just for a year," Clarke said.

"Clarke, if you're coming to me instead of a bank for a loan, you have bigger problems than money," Nunzio said. "Tell me what's going on."

"You're really going to hate me, or worse, laugh at me," Clarke said. "I like men."

"You like men, so what?"

"No one knows, not my wife, not the mayor, nobody. And nobody can know."

"I get the feeling somebody does knows. Am I right?" Nunzio lit a cigarette and tossed the pack on the table toward Clarke.

Clarke lit one of Nunzio's Camels, took a long drag, and said, "A few months ago, I met a guy at a party, and we hit it off. You understand?"

"Yeah, go on."

"Two weeks later he turned up at my office. He showed me some pictures. He said if I gave him a hundred bucks, he would give me the pictures and I would never see him again. Or else everyone would see them."

"So, you gave him the money," Nunzio said. "But he came back, and he wants more."

"Worse, he never left," Clarke said. "One hundred every week. Now he wants a thousand a month. He said I can take it out of the campaign funds. I did it once. If I keep doing that, someone will certainly find out. I need to borrow enough money to pay him off, just until after the election, then I'll tell everyone I'm a queer and he will have no power over me."

Nunzio paused for a sip of coffee, and then looked directly across the table into Clarke's frightened eyes. "You can't afford to borrow that kind of money from me. How about I tell him to give you the pictures, notes, whatever he has about you, and to leave you alone?"

"You... you would do that for me?"

"Sure, and it won't cost you a penny. We might even get your money back," Nunzio said with a slight hunch of his shoulder. "Do you know where this guy lives?"

"Yeah, the East Village. He wants me to bring the money to him there."

"Any kids?"

"No, just him and his wife. He let it slip that she took the pictures."

"Do you know if they are home now?"

"I think so."

"Pepe, remember the Carson job in Vegas?"

"Yeah, Boss. I got this."

"Hold Clarke's hand and take the Sicario brothers with you."

"I have to be there?" Clarke asked.

"You do, my friend," Nunzio said. "They have to know you are with us, and you have to make sure they give over everything they have about you. You will never hear from them again."

"Jesus Christ," Clarke's face turned ashen. "When?"

"As soon as Pepe says so," Nunzio said.

"Finish your coffee, call them to make sure they're home and tell them you're coming over with the money." Pepe said. "I'll call the Sicario boys, and we can pick them up on the way. Relax, Mr. Clarke. You ain't gotta do or say nothin'. We got this for you."

CHAPTER SEVENTEEN

"The Guys"

Heather met Frank at Lilly's and they walked to Nonna's apartment. Heather was caught up in the moment. *Meeting the family of my boyfriend. What am I doing?* She was fully into the role play, and she liked it.

"I'm sorry you're meeting everyone under these circumstances," Frank said.

"It's fine, Frankie."

They met Father Joe and Father Cas outside the door of the apartment. The four of them walked in without knocking.

"I picked up a couple of priests lurking outside your door," Frank said to everyone.

"Oh, *stai zitto*, Frankie," Nonna said. "Father Joe, Father Cas, thank you for coming. Johnny just got here. All the boys are in the living room."

"Mama, Anna, this is Heather. I think everyone else has met her."

"Not me," said Adam.

"And not me," said Johnny.

"Heather, this is my nephew, Adam. You met his big brother, Angelo, the other day," Frank said. "And over there is Johnny. He's my brother-in-law, but more like a brother."

"It is a pleasure to meet you all."

"Please call me Nonna. It is a pleasure to meet you, too, Heather. What beautiful red hair you have."

"Thank you."

"You look familiar," Anna said. "Is it possible we've met?"

"I don't think so." *Maybe I look like Angelo, my nephew. Maybe that's it, Anna.* "I guess I have one of those familiar faces."

"No, you don't," Anna said.

"I am so sorry for your loss," Heather said. "How awful and sad."

"Thank you," Anna said.

"Please, dear, make yourself at home," Nonna said.

"How can I help?" Heather asked.

"You can bring this beautiful antipasti and plates out to the savages in the living room," Nonna said.

"Of course." Heather smiled, then walked into the living room with the antipasti and plates. She placed them on the coffee table, and then sat next to Frank on the sofa.

Pompa stood up, walked over to Father Joe, hugged, and kissed him. "That was a beautiful homily you gave today. Thank you, my friend."

"Father Joe, whatever happened to Jocko the Junkman?" Angelo asked. "Mom didn't know."

"You told them about the horse?" asked Pompa.

"You know about that, Pompa?" Angelo asked.

"He was there," Father Joe said.

"Whatever became of Jocko after the poor horse died from his beatings?" Anna asked.

"Jocko pushed his junk wagon around himself, saving what little he could to buy a new horse," Father Joe said. "It took him about five years before he purchased a beautiful chestnut Morgan with a red mane."

"Oh, my lord. He got another horse?" asked Anna.

"He did," Father Joe said. "But he was quickly told he could not have a horse."

"Who told him that?" asked Johnny.

"Nunzio."

"But Nunzio must have only been 14 or 15," Anna said.

"Fifteen, but he was already becoming 'Nunzio.' And, back when Nunzio was 10 years old, and living in the cellar at 57 Canon Street, a 14-year-old named Benny "Bugsy" Siegel lived in the same tenement, and befriended him. Nunzio would run errands for Bugsy, bang on the pipes if trouble was coming, and be a lookout for Bugsy and 'the guys,' as Nunzio called them. They'd give Nunzio a couple of bucks, buy him clothes, some food, stuff like that. Anyway, when Nunzio told Jocko he could never own another horse, me and Pomp were standing with him, and so was Bugsy, and 'the guys,' who were Meyer Lansky, Frank Costello, and Vito Genovese," Father Joe said. "Jocko the Junkman pushed his own cart around from then on."

"So, it was mostly 'the guys' who convinced Jocko?" Johnny said.

"No, no. It was Nunzio," Pompa said. "Vito told me 'the guys' thought they were tomcats protecting a kitten, but it turned out that the kitten was a young lion. There is a children's story from Naples about a kitten with the shadow of a lion. Eventually, the kitten becomes this huge, beautiful lion. The kitten's name is *Gattino*. For a couple of years after that night, they called Nunzio *Gattino*. And then, like the rest of us, they called him 'Boss'."

"Uncle Nunzio calls me *Gattino*," Angelo said.

"That is a high honor," Pompa said.

"What happened to the new horse?" Angelo said.

"Officer William Cavallo retired from the NYPD that same year and wanted to borrow some money to buy an old farm in Jersey and turn it into a retirement home for old police horses and other hard-working horses. Nunzio borrowed the money from Bugsy, bought the farm, and sold it to Cavallo for one dollar," Father Joe said. "Nunzio repaid Bugsy in seven months; and the chestnut Morgan was Cavallo's first resident. He named the horse Hank."

* * *

Pepe made everyone—even Clarke—wear gloves. He stood against the wall to the right of James' and Paige's apartment door, the Sicario brothers stood to the left. Clarke stood in front of the door and knocked.

Paige opened the door a crack, with the chain still attached, and looked at Clarke. "Do you have the money?"

"Yes."

"Pass it to me."

"Bullshit!" Pepe kicked the door open, breaking the chain and knocking Paige to the floor.

"What the fuck!" James squawked.

Pepe, Clarke, and the Sicario brothers were now inside the apartment. Pepe closed the door. "Everybody relax!"

"What're doing, Clarke?" James said. "I thought we had a deal."

"Don't talk to him," Pepe said. "Right now, you're going to give me everything you have about my friend, Mr. Clarke, and all your cash."

"What?" Paige yelled. "We're not giving you shit."

"Do it now," Pepe said with a dark look.

"You think you can scare us, Clarke, with your punk friends?" Paige shouted in a high, nasal voice. "We grew up here and we ain't scared. Leave your money and get the fuck out of our apartment. You want us to call the cops and your wife, shit for brains."

"Paige, these are serious men, please calm -" Clarke said.

"Mr. Clarke, we got this," Pepe said.

"Who the hell are you?" Paige said.

"I'm Pepe."

"Well, fuck you, Pepe!"

"Hold up. Are you the Pepe who works for Nunzio Sabino?" James asked.

"That's right, James," Clarke said.

"Mr. Clarke, please don't say anything else," Pepe said.

"You know these mooks?" Paige asked James. "Well, I don't give a shit about Nunzio, whoever, or anybody else they work for. Are you a man, or what, James?"

"Paige, please. Calm down," James said to his wife in a shaky voice.

Paige walked up to Tommaso Sicario, her nose an inch away from his, and yelled "Maybe you scare my husband, but not me. So, take your goombahs, Clarke the queer, and get out of my apartment."

Tommaso took a step back and punched Paige in the face. Paige slumped to the floor, her face splashed with blood. She moaned.

James dashed to his wife. "What the fuck?"

Clarke yelped. "Is this necessary?"

"Tommaso," Pepe said.

"Sorry, Pepe, she was so loud and kept on and on," Tommaso shrugged.

"James, I am only gonna repeat this once," Pepe said. "Give me everything you have about my friend, Mr. Clarke, and all the cash you have. Now."

"In the bedroom." James walked into the bedroom, followed closely by Tommaso. They returned with a two-drawer metal file cabinet and a cigar box.

Tommaso began rifling through papers in the first cabinet drawer. "Pepe, they're blackmailing half the city. This cabinet is full of people payin' this guy." Tommaso handed the cigar box to Clarke. "Here's your money back."

"Clarke, go through the files and take out everything about you," Pepe said.

Clarke searched through both drawers and removed pictures, notes, and anything else that could be incriminating. "Got it," Clarke said. "We'd better go now."

"Is that all of it?" Pepe asked James.

"Yes, I swear. Please leave the rest of our files, so we can make a living." James was kneeling over his wife and holding a handkerchief on her nose. "We won't say anything about this; I just need to get a doctor for my wife."

"She don't need no doctor." Pepe took out a pistol with a silencer attached, shot Paige in the forehead, and then shot James in the head as he was standing up. James collapsed on top of his wife.

Clarke's knees buckled. Lorenzo Sicario held him up. Tommaso looked around the kitchen and found a bottle of whiskey. He poured some into a glass and handed it to Clarke. Clarke drank it down.

"Mr. Clarke, pull yourself together. Put the money in your pocket and the cigar box back in the file cabinet,"

Pepe said. "We'll take the cabinet with us. Mr. Sabino might be interested in knowing who else they blackmailed."

"What about my files?" Clarke said.

"Burn every piece of paper before you throw the ashes down the incinerator," Pepe said. "Make sure they're nothin' but ash, *capisci*?"

"I thought Mr. Sabino would keep them to hold over my head."

"Did you see what happened here? Mr. Sabino doesn't need anything to hold over your head."

"Yes, of course. I just thought if Mr. Sabino needed something, he would want to have leverage, you know?"

"If Mr. Sabino asked you for somethin' and you said no, the Sicario brothers would visit you. You don't ever want them to visit you," Pepe said. "Do you understand?"

"Yes, I do. Completely. Please tell Mr. Sabino I will do whatever he wants, whenever he wants it done. Anything. No matter what. Please tell him that."

"Good. I will tell him," Pepe said. "Now you no longer have a blackmail problem, you have money in your pocket, and you have a powerful friend. All good?"

"Yes."

"Mr. Clarke, leave your gloves on until you're in the car," Pepe said. "Lorenzo, you and your brother put the file cabinet in the trunk. Let's go take Mr. Clarke home."

CHAPTER EIGHTEEN

"Men always underestimate women"

Heather felt overwhelmed by a conflict of emotions over dinner at Nonna's table. She was Italian, living in this neighborhood; this was Sundays at her home. Her two brothers, father, mother, grandmother, the Italian food, the conversations, and laughter. She missed it all. Even with Nunzio Sabino sitting right across from her, for the first time in years, she felt she was home. She had to kill Nunzio, but no matter how much vengeance she reaped, she would never feel this again. Unless...maybe...if she stopped after Nunzio.

I could marry Frank and have a couple of kids. Phillip doesn't want any more children, his ex-wife has their two grown daughters, who hate me. Life with Phillip is easy, servants, travel, opulent dinners, and parties. But not this, not warm passionate family. I couldn't just stay here. Phillip would look for me. I would have to kill Phillip first. I would be wealthy. I don't have to kill Pompa and Nonna. I should though. And Rico. I would have to kill Rico and the other Knights who know who I am. I would have to be clever. But what if Frank doesn't want to marry me? Of course, he does. He loves me. Does he? What's wrong with me? I have a mission, I need to do it without distraction, and get home. But what if...?

Heather was helping clear the table of dinner dishes when Detective Clarence Hartz arrived. He was immediately pulled into the dining room.

"Detective Hartz, I think you know everyone here," Frank said. "Except for this lovely young lady, Heather."

"Nice to meet you, Heather," Hartz said.

"My pleasure," Heather said. "Are you a real police detective? With NYPD?"

"I am."

"Excellent," Heather said.

"Detective Hartz, are you hungry? We have plenty of food here," Nonna said.

"I hear you made your cheesecake for dessert," Hartz said. "I'll just join you for that when you're ready."

"Oh, we're ready, my friend," Frank said.

"Anna, Johnny, all of you, I am so very sorry for your loss," Hartz said.

"Frank told us you were working the case," Pompa said, "We're all grateful for that."

"This guy is my favorite cop," Nunzio said. "Come sit with us."

Hartz joined everyone in the living room. "What a nice family."

Father Cas sat next to Anna and asked, "How are you and the boys doing?"

"Better and better, thank you," Anna said.

"So, Hartz, have you arrested the husband yet?" Johnny asked.

"We talked to him, but haven't made an arrest."

"Did he confess?" Angelo said.

"No. It was just routine questioning," Hartz said. "Are you sure you want to talk about the case with the kids and women here?"

"Anna, you okay with us talking about this?" Father Cas asked.

"Fine with me. I've come to terms with Mac gallivanting around. And I would have to tell the boys everything later if they left the room. So, yeah, what's up?"

"Frank filled us in on some stuff, like how the cars were parked, and that the husband wanted a divorce," Johnny said, then asked, "Do you think the husband is the shooter?"

"I don't. But I do think he hired the shooter. I'm still pulling that together," Hartz said. "Also, the cars being parked so close together is troubling."

"Why's that?" Pomp asked.

"Why so close? Hartz asked. "You couldn't open the Buick's driver's door or the Chevy's passenger door. Why did they have to be so close?"

"Amateurs, or at least the driver was," Nunzio said. "No good plan in doin' that."

"Why do you say that?" Johnny asked.

"The shooter, right-handed or left-handed, is gonna have to turn in his seat and practically stick the gun through the Buick's window," Nunzio said. "And, if for any reason the shooter needs to get out of the car fast, to return fire from the Buick, or whatever, he can't get out unless he climbs over the driver or into the back seat. Amateurs."

Nunzio is exactly right. This is so weird watching Nunzio and a detective solve my murder case. I love this, Heather thought. *I wonder if I'll be arrested after dessert, with shouts of "That's her, take her away."*

"Amateurs, maybe, but the shooter used a silencer and his shots were dead on," Hartz said.

"The shooter might be a pro who picked the wrong driver. The driver was that Knight, Domingo, right?" Nunzio said. "The husband hires the killer, or the Knights. No, Rico's not gonna let one of his top Knights take a bullet. More likely the killer hires Domingo without Rico knowing, a quick side job for a couple of bucks in his pocket. But the killer decides he don't want no witnesses, not even Domingo."

"The situation is becoming clearer to me," Hartz said. "This is good."

"What else bothers you about how close they were parked?" Johnny asked.

"It's where they were. Sorry, Anna, it's a lover's lane. Folks don't want their cars so close to each other," Hartz said. "So, who got there first? The Buick with Mac and the girl, or the Chevy with the shooter and driver, and whoever else might've been in the back seat? My working assumption is the Chevy had the driver and shooter but no one else."

"If the Chevy got there first, there is no way the girl driving the Buick would park that close to it," Johnny said. "Mac wouldn't let her. They would go someplace else."

"My thought exactly," Hartz said. "If the Buick was there first, and the Chevy with two guys in the front seat parks that close to them, what does Mac do?"

"No question. Mac is out of the Buick and gone," Johnny said. "I'm sure of it."

"There you have my troubling detail," Hartz said.

"What about the windows? Were they up or down?" Nunzio asked.

"Good question, Mr. Sabino," Hartz said. "That's one of my hold-backs."

"Call me Nunzio, Hartz."

"All the windows on both cars were closed except the one on the front passenger side of the Chevy and the driver's window of the Buick," Hartz said.

"So, the girl driving the Buick was not immediately frightened by the passenger in the Chevy, and since Mac did not jump out when she rolled down the window, he wasn't alarmed either. Am I right?" Nunzio said.

"Keep going," Hartz said.

"One possibility is that the shooter was in uniform—a cop, soldier, someone who would not alarm the Buick," Nunzio said.

"I hadn't thought of that," Hartz said. "That's a possibility."

"Cheesecake for everyone," Nonna announced as she entered the living room carrying the cake on large metal tray. "Who would like coffee?" The conversation switched quickly to the cheesecake.

"This is amazing," Heather said.

"It's Frank's favorite," Nonna said.

"Then I must have the recipe, please." Heather said.

"Recipe? You just have to know." Nonna dismissed the nonsense of a recipe. "You come over sometime and we'll make it together. It is *dolce magico*."

"Dessert magic," Heather said.

"*Brava*," Nonna said. "You speak a little Italian."

Everyone sat together eating cake, drinking coffee, and solving the Mac murder case. Heather loved every bit of it and was sucked into joining in.

"Were there any other clues or, what did you call them, '*hold backs*?'" Heather asked, sounding as innocent as she could, hoping to find out what the police knew.

"Okay, but just for this room," Hartz said. "There was a large, unfolded paper map on the floor of the front seat. It had Domingo's blood on it. Domingo is a neighborhood guy, a Knight. He doesn't need a map to find South Street. Even if the shooter is from out of town, why the map in the front seat on South Street? And if the shooter needed the map, why didn't he take it with him?"

"Because the map was a prop," Heather heard herself say. She could not resist being part of the give and take; she wanted to impress Frank and Hartz.

"A prop?" Hartz said.

"If the shooter wasn't in uniform, maybe he held up the map, pretending to be lost, and the Buick driver rolled down the window to help," Heather said.

"Yeah, but Mac wouldn't fall for that," Johnny said. "He sees these guys in the Chevy. Map or no map, he's out of the Buick."

"What if the shooter is a girl, lost, and in tears holding up the map," Heather said. "Now Mac—sorry, Anna—might get all flirty, wanting to help. He might even lean toward the open window. Some men underestimate women. We're smarter, stronger, and more capable than you think." *What in God's name am I doing? Shut up, Heather. Right now. Enough.*

"Some men?" Anna said. "All men."

"Maybe the shooter was a girl," Nunzio said. "Maybe a waitress?"

"Nonna, can we watch *Maverick* tonight?" Adam said.

"Sure," Nonna said. "Whatever you boys want."

"Heather, join me and my friend, Rosemarie, for a girls' night out?" Anna said.

"I'd love to," Heather said. "When?"

"Thursday night?"

"Perfect."

"This isn't gonna to be a grilling or some kind of test, is it?" Frank said.

"A test?" Anna said.

"C'mon, Sis," Frank said. "We're good here."

"Not for long, son." Pompa chuckled.

"Is Frankie always so protective?" Heather said.

"You have no idea," Anna said. "Let's meet at Lilly's at seven. Rosemarie will drive."

"Brilliant," Heather said. "I'll be there."

CHAPTER NINETEEN

"The kings of the street"

At noon on Thursday, Rico sat at a rear table in Linda's Luncheonette with Andy and Mike.

"Here ya go boys. Three burgers, two Cokes and one black coffee," the waitress said. "Anything else?"

"No, this is it." Rico took a burger and the coffee. "Thanks, Gloria."

"Enjoy your lunch, fellas," Gloria said.

"What's so important that we have to meet outside the clubhouse?" Rico asked.

"Rico, now don't jump crazy and kill the messenger," Mike said.

"Just get on with it," Rico said. "What's up?"

"Our guys are scared and jumpy, you know, about the killings of Knights," Mike said. "And we're not doing anything about it."

"You mean, I'm not doing anything about it," Rico said.

"Rico, me, you and Andy here are the last three Knight leaders still alive," Mike said. "And we look like we're playing marbles while our guys are getting whacked, one by one."

"What the fuck do they want?" Rico said.

"They want you to take action against the Weepers and the Roosevelt Street Boys, or step down as the leader of Satan's Knights," Mike said.

"The younger Knights feel the same way," Andy said. "Not me, or Mike, or even all the Knights—just most of them."

"Go to war against the Roosevelt Street Boys and the Weepers?" Rico said. "That's what they want?"

"It's not that nuts, Rico," Mike said. "We got the numbers. We got three times more guys than both those gangs put together. We could win everything. We could be the kings of the street again."

"The kings of the street," Rico said. "We don't know who's killing off our Knights, and whoever it is probably just killed Angelo's father. You think the Weepers killed Angelo's father?"

"If not them, then the Roosevelt Street Boys, or that girl assassin, Heather," Mike said.

"I know it's not her 'cause I was with her at the East Harlem Diner the night Derick got it, and I was with her the night Domingo got it," Rico said. "And why would the Roosevelt Street Boys want to start knocking off Knights? We gotta be smart about this, guys."

"Being smart ain't working," Andy said. "It don't matter who's doing it. The Knights need to see us go to war against the Weepers and the Roosevelt Street Boys to show some balls."

"Look, Rico, we get seven or eight Knights to jump two of the Roosevelt Street Boys and we do the same with a couple of Weepers," Mike said. "We give them a good beatin' and say, 'if another Knight dies, we'll kill three of your guys.'"

"That is stupid and dangerous," Rico said.

"It's what Hector and Ernesto would've done," Mike said. "Meanwhile, your girlfriend is gonna kill Nunzio, so we don't have to worry about him."

"Hector is dead. Ernesto is dead. You know why?" Rico asked. "Because of this kind of stupid bullshit. No. We are not gonna do any of this."

"Then you should step down," Andy said. "Because the Knights are gonna do it with or without us."

"No, they're not." Rico said. "You two knuckleheads already decided you're gonna lead them in this feel-good suicide mission. Am I right?"

"We told our guys we would. It cheered them up," Mike said. "You'll see, it'll work. No more Knights getting shot."

"Okay, your only chance, and it's a long shot, is if Nunzio is gone. So, give Heather time to hit Nunzio before you lead your cavalry to the Little Big Horn," Rico said. "And then I'll step down and out of the Knights."

"What's the Little Big Horn?" Andy said.

"We'll wait. You got our promise," Mike said. "But we would rather you stay and lead us to victory."

"As soon as Nunzio is gone, I'm quitting the Knights," Rico said. "You guys will be kings of the street. Good luck. I mean that."

CHAPTER TWENTY

"Rico wasn't there"

Heather was mostly quiet in the backseat of Rosemarie's car. She enjoyed the chatter of two women who had known each other since childhood. Friends through everything. Friends no matter what. Heather didn't have friends. Phillip's friends were gracious, but they weren't her friends. They wouldn't be there for her in a pinch. Rosemarie and Anna were true friends. Heather would have liked that.

Rosemarie found a parking spot near the Luna Blu in Greenwich Village. Guido Pappa, the owner of the restaurant, greeted the three women at the door. Ten years ago, Guido was an ambitious waiter with a head for business. He had needed Nunzio's help to get his own restaurant. He got it.

"Good evening and welcome, ladies. I have a nice window table reserved for you. Please follow me." Guido snapped his fingers at a waiter, who immediately followed the women. Once at the table, the waiter filled the water glasses. Guido collected the paper napkins from the table, handed them to the waiter, and said, *"Biancheria."* The waiter quickly returned with linen napkins.

"Porta asciugamani caldi per le donne," Guido said to the waiter. "Matteo will bring you warm towels. Can I get you wine or anything else to drink?"

"We decided in the car that we will start with Manhattans to welcome our new friend, Heather," Rosemarie said. "Can we see food menus?"

"Do you want to read or eat?" Guido smiled.

"Eat, of course." Anna smiled.

"Excellent. Matteo will bring your drinks," Guido said. "I will prepare a special dinner for you starting with a lovely antipasto."

"Um, respectfully, shouldn't we have a hint as to what this will cost?" Heather said.

"You are with Miss Anna. *Sono onorato della sua presenza* – I am honored by your presence. So please, you no pay for anything in my Luna Blu."

"I love going out with Anna," Rosemarie said to Heather.

"It's not really about me," Anna said. "Nunzio is my godfather, and he helped Guido get this restaurant. The last time I was here, I didn't mention it to Nunzio, and he gave me a hard time, so I promised I would tell Guido the next time I was coming. This is the next time."

"Was the last time with that young priest?" Heather asked. "What's his name, Cas?"

"No, I was with Mac," Anna said. "Why would you think that?"

"I saw the way he was looking at you at your mom's dinner. He has a crush on you."

Rosemarie howled, "I told you, Anna! I told you."

"He's a priest," Anna blushed. "Anyway, we should be talking about Heather."

"Ah, the test that Frankie feared," Heather laughed.

"Your warm towels, ladies," Matteo said, as another waiter stood behind him with the Manhattans and antipasto. After Matteo retrieved the used towels, he placed a cocktail and a small plate in front of each of the women and put the antipasto in the middle of the table. "Would you like me to serve you?"

"No, thank you, Matteo," Anna said. "We've got it from here."

"Welcome to Manhattan, Heather," Rosemarie said.

The three women said "cheers" and clicked their glasses together.

"Now. Tell us everything about you." Rosemarie said.

"I think you probably know all there is to know," Heather said. "I'm truly quite boring."

"I don't believe that for a minute," Anna said.

"How are you and your sons doing, Anna?" Heather asked.

"Better and better. Good change of subject, but back to you."

"Okay, Anna, what do you want to know?" Heather said.

"Why did you tell my brother your ex-husband was in the 101st Airborne in Korea?"

Heather took a long drink. *I need to double down on this, but if they know I lied, Frank knows. I need a better bullock's story.* "He was a soldier, but he never went to war. I picked the patch in your brother's store because I thought it might be a way to get to know him," Heather said. "Dumb, I know."

"Where's your ex now?" Rosemarie asked.

"He did kill himself at Walter Reed." Heather conjured up some tears and took another long drink. "He was hospitalized because he tried suicide. And, while there, he finished the job."

"Good Lord, I'm sorry." Rosemarie took a drink and signaled a waiter that they would need another round.

"I am so sorry, Heather," Anna said. "Do you have children?"

"Thankfully, no. I hope someday with the right man."

"You have plenty of time for that! What are you, twenty-one?" Rosemarie said.

"Twenty-two."

"How are things going with my brother?" Anna asked. "He tells me nothing."

"I hope good," Heather said. "I think I may have fallen for him."

"Don't be afraid. Frank's one of the good guys," Rosemarie winked.

"I think my brother has fallen for you, too." Anna said. "So, where has he taken you?"

"Well, our first kind of date was lunch on a tugboat," Heather said.

"I love Mussels and Mug," Rosemarie said.

"It was brilliant. Frank almost got into a fight with a gang of Knights."

"Satan's Knights are bad news, especially in a group and when they've been drinking," Anna said.

"There were about seven or eight of them, but only two came to our table."

"Rico needs to do a better job controlling his guys," Rosemarie said.

"Rico wasn't there," Heather said. "Frank was up like a shot. He was very impressive."

"What were the other Knights doing?" Rosemarie asked.

"They just stayed at their table," Heather said. "It all happened so fast. And these guys from Roosevelt Street tossed all the Knights out of the place."

"Yeah, no one messes with the Roosevelt Street Boys," Anna said. "They're cool. You must have been scared."

"No, I wasn't," Heather said. "Frank makes me feel safe."

"Frank has a way of doing that," Anna said.

"So, how about you and Cas?" Heather asked Anna.

"Again, he's a priest," Anna said a little too loudly, and took a final drink as another round arrived.

"He's a man," Heather said.

"Heather, my new friend, you're gonna fit right in," Rosemarie said.

"You do already," Anna said.

Guido, Matteo, and another waiter arrived at the table with a dinner of a porterhouse vitellone steak Florentine style, sauteed parmesan carrots with marsala, and porcini mashed potatoes. Guido sliced and served the porterhouse at the table while Matteo served the potatoes and carrots. The other waiter opened and poured a deep red Tuscan wine into three crystal glasses.

"Oh, my, I want to live in this restaurant," Heather said after tasting the steak.

"I think that should be our plan," Rosemarie said.

"The dinner is good?" Guido asked.

"*È celeste*, it is heavenly," Anna said.

"The best we've ever tasted," said Rosmarie.

"*Grazie mille*," Guido bowed. "I will leave you to enjoy your meal."

"Anna, I so enjoyed dinner at your mother's." said Heather. "You have a lovely family."

"Thank you. You're always welcome. Frank mentioned you don't have any family."

Frank tells you nothing, huh? Heather thought. *She asked if I had children, but already knew the answer. She's trying to catch me in a lie. I won't let her.*

"No, no one." Heather said. "Just me."

"Now you have us." Rosemarie sipped her wine.

"You two women are amazing," Heather said. "And Anna, you'd better capture that priest before some other woman less concerned about his calling does."

The three women laughed, ate, drank, and shared the chef's famous tiramisu as friends would do.

CHAPTER TWENTY-ONE

"There is a complication"

Sergeant Danny Terenzio and Sergeant Elwood Patterson, in class-A U.S. Army uniforms, stepped off the
airport shuttle in Cloven City, Georgia. Here they
would grab something to eat and catch a ride to Fort
Benning. It was early evening, raining, and hot. The soldiers were tired and hungry. The smell from Buford's Diner
and the rain drove them through the front door before
they saw the "Whites Only" sign.

Buford's had a long, light-colored Formica counter with
round red stools and twelve tables for four. Most of the
stools and half of the tables were occupied. Danny spotted
a staff sergeant and a private at a back table. Danny and
Elwood walked toward them.

"Are you our ride?" Danny asked the staff sergeant.

"I am." The sergeant looked at the two men and
wrapped the remainder of his sandwich in a paper napkin.
"We'd better go now."

"Do we have time to grab a burger or something to
go?"

"Buford," the staff sergeant said to the counter man.
"Can you fix a couple of burgers to go for these soldiers?"

"Not for the colored boy," said Buford. "Okay for the
white soldier though."

Danny felt someone grab his arm from behind. In an instinctive move, Danny twisted the man's wrist, Aikido style, and dropped him to the floor. A deputy sheriff hit Elwood in the back with a chair, causing him to tumble into the staff sergeant's table. The sheriff, his deputy, and three other men stood in front of Danny and Elwood.

"Whoa, whoa, Sheriff Forrest, hold it," the staff sergeant said. "These are the men I'm here to take to Fort Benning. They are combat veterans. American heroes. I got this."

"I see a colored boy and a Yankee soldier," the sheriff said. "And they both broke the law in my town. They will be our guests tonight, and Judge Jolly will decide when you can take them to your fort."

"Sheriff, I am here because my major wants to talk with these American heroes tonight," the staff sergeant said.

"I don't give a rat's nest about your major. This is a civilian matter and they belong to me. "Y'all come back tomorrow to collect them after the hearing."

"What time is the hearing?"

"10:30 a.m. sharp. Judge Jolly doesn't like delays."

"You're making a big mistake, Sheriff," the staff sergeant said.

* * *

A deuce-and-a-half Army truck, a Dodge WC-64 Army ambulance, and an Army jeep arrived at the sheriff's office in Cloven City, Georgia at 10:00 the following morning. Captain Gunther Reinart of the U.S. Army military police and First Lieutenant Arnold Sweet, an Army lawyer with

JAG, stepped out of the Jeep and into the sheriff's office with three MPs at their side.

The office was little more than a dusty cabin. On the wall above the sheriff's large wooden desk was an American flag, a Confederate flag, and between them hung a large painting of Confederate General Nathan Bedford Forrest on a white horse.

The sheriff, his deputy, and two men in white short-sleeved shirts sat around a small table and looked up at the military as they entered.

"Sheriff, I am Captain Reinart. With me is Lieutenant Sweet. Lieutenant Sweet is a military attorney who will be representing our two soldiers at this morning's hearing."

"Sheriff, I need to speak with our soldiers immediately," said Lieutenant Sweet. "I need to prepare them for the hearing."

"Well, gentlemen, there is a complication," Sheriff Forrest said as he tossed his pen on the table. He leaned back in his chair, both hands rested on the table's edge.

"A complication?" Lieutenant Sweet asked.

"We had the hearin' at 8:00 this morning." Deputy Lee Arsch smiled. "Your soldier boys were found guilty."

"Lee, no cause to be unkindly," Sheriff Forrest said. "Given the complication, Lieutenant Sweet, Judge Jolly thought it best to have the hearing first thing this morning."

"When did the judge decide to do that?" asked the lieutenant.

"Late last night."

"You could have notified us," said the lieutenant.

"I could have," said the sheriff. "Didn't have to and didn't want to."

"Bring me my two soldiers!" the captain said to the sheriff.

"That's the complication," said the sheriff.

The captain turned to one of the MPs. "Get my men out of the truck. Tell them to lock and load their weapons and stand at parade rest in front of the sheriff's office."

The MP turned and left.

One of the white short-sleeved men walked over to the window. "There are a whole lot of soldiers out there, Sheriff."

The sheriff walked over to the window. "Now hold on."

"My men will conduct an aggressive enemy-based search of every house, office, and stable in this sad town, starting with your home, Sheriff, in exactly one minute." Captain Reinart looked at his watch.

"I'll give you your boys. I'm just trying to explain the complication," said the sheriff.

"What's the complication, Sheriff?"

"Your boys committed several crimes, entering a whites-only establishment, causin' a disturbance, resisting arrest, and so on. Judge Jolly found them guilty on all counts. He also found that me, my deputy, and those brave citizens who assisted us in making the arrests, acted with reasonable force and within the law."

"You assholes beat my men?" said Captain Reinart.

"That is not how the judge saw it," said the sheriff. "Lee, go fetch the white soldier."

"That's a painting of Nathan Forrest, over your desk, isn't it?" Captain Reinart pointed.

"Yep. How do you know that?" asked the sheriff.

"Military history, West Point," said Captain Reinart. "Your last name is Forrest."

"He is my kin."

"He was a disgrace to even the Confederate uniform, and the first Grand Wizard of the Klan," the captain said.

"We honor him down here," said the sheriff.

"Of course, you do."

Danny walked into the room bent over and handcuffed with the deputy holding his arm. The left side of Danny's face was swollen. His uniform was torn and blood stained.

"Danny, I'm Captain Reinart. I've got medics here who'll look after you."

"I think broken ribs is the worst of it," Danny said. "You need to find Elwood. He wasn't at the hearing."

The captain nodded toward Danny, then glowered at the sheriff. "Take those cuffs off my man, Sheriff. "Where is Sergeant Patterson?"

"He's at Doc Damon's right across the street."

Captain Reinart said to one of his MPs, "Take five men and bring me Sergeant Patterson." And then to the sheriff, he said, "Will they need a stretcher?"

"Your colored boy seemed to have passed away during the night. So, take whatever y'all need," said the sheriff.

Captain Reinart took a long and deep breath. "Take a stretcher, a body bag, and a flag." The captain could barely contain his rage as he walked to the window. He stood looking out as the soldiers walked over to the doctor's office. He stood there, watching and waiting for the soldiers to return with the body.

Meanwhile, the sheriff went on and on about the judge and the medics tended to Danny. It seemed like a long time until the four soldiers returned with Elwood's body in a bag on the stretcher. The captain stepped outside, walked to the men, and unzipped the bag. One of the MPs threw up at seeing the body.

Captain Reinart shouted, "Attention!" All the soldiers snapped to attention. The captain gave a slow salute. Afterward, he zipped the bag closed and covered it with the American flag. "Now, put this hero in the ambulance."

The captain's face was twisted in wrath when he returned to the sheriff's office.

"Captain?" Danny said. "Elwood?"

The captain shook his head. "You ride with me to Benning, Sergeant."

"No offense, Captain. I'd like to ride with Elwood," Danny said.

"Me too," said the captain.

"Now, y'all need to holdup here a minute. There is a fine that was ordered by Judge Jolly," said the sheriff. "I'm afraid your boy can't leave until the fine and court costs are paid."

The captain drew his .45 automatic and pointed it at the sheriff. "Put your weapon in the trash can, Sheriff, or I swear to God, I will kill you as an enemy combatant, right here, right now."

The three MPs with the captain also pulled their weapons.

The shaken sheriff complied. "Now look here –"

"Shut up!" the captain said. "You too, Deputy."

Deputy Arsch looked at the sheriff.

"Just do it, Lee."

"You boys have any weapons?" the captain asked the two short-sleeved men.

"No, sir."

Captain Reinart turned to his MPs, "Lock all four men in a back cell and toss the keys in the trash can. Let's get out of this hell hole."

CHAPTER TWENTY-TWO

"Who's gonna kill me"

Rico sat alone at the bar in the Caffè Fiora, waiting to talk with Nunzio. He watched as men bowed to Nunzio. They gave him notes, envelopes, and some whispered secrets only for kings and gods. *That could have been me. I could do that better. I could've been a great leader.* Rico's thoughts were interrupted by Pepe standing next to him.

"Mr. Sabino is ready for you," Pepe said.

Rico followed Pepe to Nunzio's table. Pepe pointed to a chair, Rico sat, Pepe poured him an espresso, and left.

"Thank you for seeing me, Mr. Sabino."

"Whadaya need, Rico?"

"I wanted to tell you directly, sir, that I will be quitting the Knights."

"Oh, yeah? Why's that?"

"They no longer want what I want. They no longer respect my leadership." Rico took a gulp of espresso. "I wanted to tell you before you heard it from anybody else."

"You want something stronger?"

"No, thank you, Mr. Sabino. I'm okay. I'll be okay."

"Who's killing your Knights?" Nunzio asked. "You must have some idea."

"I wish I knew. That's part of the problem," Rico said. "My guys think it's the Weepers or the Roosevelt Street Boys."

"It ain't them. I'd know if it was," Nunzio said. "Who do you think it could be?"

"I don't have a clue. But the Knights are gonna go after the Roosevelt Street Boys and the Weepers. I tried to stop them, and they told me to retire so that Mike and Andy could lead them."

"That will be the end of the Knights," Nunzio said. "When is this supposed to happen?"

"In couple of weeks," Rico said. "They promised me they'd wait until I was gone."

"When you leave here, go to Lilly's and tell Frank what the Knights are planning for the Roosevelt Street Boys and the Weepers. He will let them know. You tell the Knights nothin'. Got it?"

"Yes, sir."

"Who's gonna kill me?" Nunzio said.

"The Knights have learned the lesson of '57, Mr. Sabino," Rico said. "Not a single Knight would dare plan to kill you. Not ever again."

"That's not what I asked you. Who is planning to hit me?"

"Um, look, Mr. Sabino, um, I don't -"

"You took too long to say you don't know," Nunzio said. "That tells me there is a hit on me and you know something about it. Are you gonna tell me or not?"

"Mr. Sabino, I don't -"

"Yes or no?"

Rico's mind was racing. He had to give Nunzio something and didn't want to give him Heather. He and the

Knights had been helping Declan Ardan with his campaign. But the Hell's Kitchen guys had been providing the muscle and keeping the lion's share of Declan's payments. He liked the idea of a wedge between Nunzio and his lawyer, Declan. He said, "Declan."

Nunzio immediately looked at Pepe. Pepe walked over to Nunzio and Rico.

"Tell me what you know," Pepe said to Rico.

"Declan asked me to have the Knights help with his election," Rico said. "He also hired guys from Hell's Kitchen to provide muscle. I don't know for sure, but if the Hell's Kitchen boys are gonna get rid of anyone who knows Declan cheated, you'd be on the list, Mr. Sabino."

"Whadaya think, Pepe?" Nunzio asked.

"I don't know, Boss," Pepe said. "I'll find out."

"Good. Stay with us," Nunzio said to Pepe, and then to Rico, "What else you got?"

"Nothing, sir," Rico said. "Thank you for your support over the last three years, Mr. Sabino. I regret leaving, but I assure you, I leave with silence and loyalty to you, sir."

"Okay, good, and try to find out more about the hit on me," Nunzio said. "Good luck with your future, Rico."

"Thank you, Mr. Sabino." Rico stood, bowed, and walked away.

* * *

Once Rico left, Nunzio said to Pepe, "Rico might be trying to cause trouble between me and Declan but look into it anyway."

"Will do, Boss."

"Also, I got a lesson in not underestimating women at Pomp's place last Sunday. Find out everything you can about the waitress who saw Lanzo bein' killed."

"The waitress, Boss?"

"I think she could be the shooter," Nunzio said.

* * *

Rico walked into Lilly's and found Frank and his sister sitting at the small table. He told them about his retirement and the planned attack on the Weepers and the Roosevelt Street Boys.

"Why are you telling me?" Frank asked.

"I told Mr. Sabino and he told me to tell you."

"Good. Thanks for the head's up," Frank said.

"What will you do, Rico?" Anna asked.

"My wife and I are moving upstate, maybe Brewster," Rico said. "I always wanted to own a business, you know car repair, hardware store, maybe a diner, something."

"Good for you," Anna said.

"Yeah, good luck, Rico. I mean that," Frank said.

"Thanks. And be careful."

Rico left Lilly's.

"Frankie, seeing Rico, reminded me of something," Anna said. "Did you tell Heather that Rico wasn't at Mussels and Mugs the night you almost got into a fight with the Knights?"

"No, why would I tell her that?"

"The question is, how would Heather know that?"

"I don't know," Frank said. "Maybe someone...I don't know."

"Did you tell her that Rico was the leader of the Knights?" Anna asked.

"I don't think so," Frank said. "Maybe, I mentioned it in passing. I can't think of any reason I would've. Maybe someone, Father Joe, maybe, at Mom's said something on Sunday?"

"I don't remember anyone talking about the Knights," Anna said.

"What's this about?"

"When I was having dinner with Heather and Rose-marie, we got to talking about that almost fight at Mussels and Mugs. Rosemarie said something like Rico needs to control his Knights better, and Heather said, 'Rico wasn't there.'"

"I can't think of any reason she would know who Rico was," Frank said. "But right now I'm thinking about Angelo and the Weepers. You gotta tell him right away to watch out for an attack by the Knights. I'll let the Roosevelt Boys know."

Chapter Twenty-Three

"I want to take your life"

Frank walked into Mussels and Mugs and went directly to the Roosevelt Street Boys. Four Roosevelts were sitting at one table and three at another. Frank sat down with the three Boys. The other four left their table and gathered around.

"What's the news, Frankie?" Daddy Bruce asked.

Frank told them about the Knights' plan. "Rico said you got a couple of weeks, but I wouldn't bet on that," Frank said. "My guess is it will be sooner, and a surprise."

"Do the Weepers know?" another Roosevelt asked.

"They do," Frank said. "You need anything from me, or even Nunzio, don't hesitate."

"Thanks, Frankie."

* * *

Johnny Pastamadeo sat in a leather martini chair in Oliver Macallan's palatial apartment overlooking Central Park. Johnny sat in the dark, sipping a glass of scotch, and waiting for Oliver to come home. Oliver would be surprised, and Johnny would kill him. Johnny was on his second drink when Oliver walked in.

"Welcome home," Johnny said.

Oliver jumped back and stumbled against the closed door. "What in God's name... Who are you? How did you get in here? Did the doorman let you...Who let you in? Who are you?"

"Shhh, so many questions," Johnny said "No one let me in. I came in by way of the roof and an open window. Now sit."

"Impossible. No one can get in here from the roof. Too far a climb."

"And yet, here I am." Johnny shrugged, arms out and palms up.

"Whatever you want, just take it and go."

"I want to take your life." Johnny attached a silencer to his .38 pistol. "Shall I take it and go?"

"No, no, wait, please." Who sent you? I can pay you –"

"Mac, the guy you killed, along with your wife in her car. I'm his brother. Now, sit. Or die where you stand."

Oliver sat down across from Johnny. "Please, I swear, I had nothing to do with your brother's or my wife's, death. Nothing."

"Convince me."

"I can do that. Let me do that."

"Calm down. Get yourself a drink."

"That would help. Can I?"

"Sure, it's your booze." Johnny watched the short, stout man as he walked to the small bar display, poured scotch into a glass, and returned to his chair, glass and bottle in hand. "Scotch has your name on it, Macallan. Your family, I'm guessing."

"I wish." Oliver drank the whole pour. He refilled his glass and Johnny's glass. "Just a coincidence."

"So, best I can figure, you hired a private dick and found out your wife was cheating on you. You're pissed and hire a guy to kill your wife and my brother," Johnny said. "You wanted out of the marriage anyway, and this way was less costly. Not a smart plan, but, like I said, you were pissed."

"That's what the cops think. Probably what most people think," Oliver said.

"So tell me your side of the story."

"My story? My story is sad and pretty pathetic. My wife was a bitch. She was pretty, in a Doris Day way, but she was mean. She had affairs before we were married and carried on all during our marriage. She cared nothing about other people. It was just all about her. I finally had enough and talked to a lawyer who told me I could only get a divorce in New York if I had proof of adultery, cruelty, or desertion. So, as you know, I hired a private eye. He gave me a complete report, including pictures. I gave them to my lawyer who was certain I would get a divorce on my terms."

"Do you have a copy of the dick's report?"

"I do." He walked across the room to his desk and returned with a folder that he handed to Johnny. "I wasn't jealous or angry. I was glad to have the evidence I needed for the divorce. I was relieved. I didn't want her dead. And I certainly didn't have anything against your brother; I didn't even know him. He was just the last in a long line of men my wife took up with. Your brother, actually, helped me get the divorce I wanted."

"Do the police have all this?" Johnny looked through the papers and photos in the folder.

"Not yet. My lawyer is putting together a package to give to a detective named Hartz, I think. It will include my statements, the information in that folder, and testimonies from a couple of other men she slept with. They should get it sometime this week. I also want to meet with the detective."

"I'll be honest. I don't know what to think right now," Johnny said.

"The other thing is, as bad as my wife was, I can't think of anyone who would want to kill her. Now, don't get angry, but I think the killer was after your brother. My wife was just in the wrong place at that moment."

"If you're lying to me –"

"It's the God's honest truth," Oliver said. "I'm sorry about your brother, and I'm sorry about my wife."

"Okay." Johnny paused briefly for another sip. "I won't kill you today."

Oliver's hand shook as he finished his glass. "Would you like something to eat with the scotch? I certainly would."

"Geez, that's pretty cool of you considering why I came here," Johnny said. "But I think I'll just leave."

"You can leave by the front door," Oliver said. "I'll not tell anyone you were here."

"Why?"

"This is the first time I told the truth about my wife to anyone, even though you were threatening to kill me. It actually felt good," he said. "And you, and your family, have had enough heartache."

CHAPTER TWENTY-FOUR

"It's Now or Never"

A t the Cherry Street Settlement dance, the Weepers gathered around Father Joe as he told them about his visit with Sage. It was all good news. Sage was doing well. He was starting high school classes, working in woodwork shop, and there was a chance for parole in a couple of years.

Angelo did not want to come to the dance. He was missing Audrey a lot and the dance brought back painfully lovely memories. But, given the threat from the Knights, his mother convinced him to stick close to his Weepers. He was their leader.

After talking with Father Joe, Angelo and the Weepers returned to their corner of the Settlement's dance hall. Tate and Gina danced to "Come Softly to Me" by The Fleetwoods.

"Dance with me, Angelo," Liz said.

"I can't, Liz," Angelo said. "I know I'm nuts. Maybe next time."

"Is Audrey still writing to you or calling?" Gerard asked.

"Not as much," Angelo said. "She kinda stopped calling. It's expensive."

"Do you write to her?" Judy asked.

"Yeah, we still write, but just sometimes," Angelo said.

"Sorry, Angelo," Judy said.

"Angelo, my girlfriend's high school is having a back-to-school dance," Bobby said. "And, she's got this real cute friend, name Joni. Whadaya say? Take a shot?"

"Yeah, maybe," Angelo said. "Why not?"

The song ended and Tate and Gina were back. Tate asked, "Any news about the Knights?"

"Nothing that I heard," Angelo said. "You got anything, Ju-Ju?"

"Andy keeps asking me when I'm gonna come back," Ju-Ju said. "When Rico left, they lost a bunch of guys, and I think that surprised them. They're recruiting hard."

"It's Now or Never" by Elvis Presley, came on, and as the dance floor filled, Liz said, "This is next time, Angelo. It's now or never, as the king says." Liz held her hand out to him.

Angelo smiled and went out to the dance floor with Liz.

* * *

Over dinner at the East Harlem Diner, Rico explained to Heather why he was leaving the Knights.

"I don't give a damn about the Knights," Heather said. "You're my contact here, and you're the one I'm counting on to get me home."

"I know. And I will," Rico said. "I bought a diner in Brewster; my wife is there and will manage it for now. I have an apartment on Water Street. You're the only one who knows that. I am here until you're safely out of the City."

"Good. Who's left in the Knights who knows who I am and why I'm here?"

"Andy and Mike."

"And whoever they told," Heather said. "We—or rather I—need to kill both of them now."

"No. No more killing Knights. They won't tell anyone."

"They're going to be a problem for you, Rico. They set the Knights against you. You should not quit the Knights; but you do need to get rid of disloyal ones. Let me kill Andy and Mike."

"Andy and Mike aren't going to do anything stupid," Rico said. "I know them. It's cool."

"No, it's not. You're not being smart. And I don't trust them."

"They wouldn't tell anyone about you. I told Nunzio that his lawyer is going to kill him. You're all good."

"All good? You're such a fool." Heather said.

"Look, it's my worry, so let's just change the subject."

"The hell with it. Fine. What's the name of your diner?"

"The Sunshine Diner."

"Why not Rico's Diner?"

"The Sunshine has loyal customers." Rico shrugged. "So why change the name?"

"I didn't know it was that easy to buy a diner."

"I got lucky. The owner wanted to retire. So, we made a cash deal with a one-page contract. He gave me the keys and all the inventory."

"You should still change the name."

"Why?"

"To make it yours. I bet they don't have a lot of choices in Brewster," Heather said. "And the customers might even like Rico's Diner better."

"I'll think about it," Rico said. "It seems to me that something else might be bugging you. Am I right?"

"Phillip wants me to come home right now," Heather said.

"So, kill Nunzio and go home. What're you waitin' for?"

"It's a little more complicated than that, Rico."

"You're not fallin' for Frank, are you?"

"Of course not."

"Bullshit. You are," Rico said.

"I might want to kill Anna's parents and brothers before Nunzio," Heather said. "So she knows what it feels like to lose her whole family, like I did."

"Why? Anna never did anything to hurt you. Mac killed your brothers, and Nunzio had the rest of your family killed."

"You don't think I know that?"

"Your brothers raped Anna. That's why you think Angelo is your nephew, your only remaining blood family. Why do you want to hurt Angelo and Anna?"

"I don't," Heather said. "I wanted...I don't know."

"You're an assassin and your target is Nunzio. Forget all the other shit. Complete your mission and go home," Rico said. "Do it now."

"That's probably good advice," Heather said.

* * *

Mike and Andy walked along Mott Street eating slices of pizza from Lombardi's and talking about the future of their Knights. Andy was anxious to start the war with the Weepers and the Roosevelt Street Boys, but Mike had become more cautious.

"Maybe we need Rico back," Mike said. "We lost too many guys when he left."

"We still outnumber both those gangs combined," Andy said. "We need to do this before they get wise to us. And the Knights are ready. Come on, Mike, let's do it."

"Okay. But we need a solid plan. We need to hit both gangs at the same time. It has to be perfect, so they never want to mess with us again."

"We're gonna be the kings of the streets again," Andy said. "Top step at PS65."

CHAPTER TWENTY-FIVE

"Merlin slipped into Angelo's right hand"

On Monday, September 12, 1960, Angelo sat in his first class at the High School of Art and Design. It was an art class, and the teacher told the students to remove something from their pockets or purses and draw it. Most kids pulled coins or keys. Angelo took out a closed combination lock. In case of a fight, he could slip the loop over his middle finger, the lock in his closed palm, and improve the power of a punch. Merlin, his button knife, was strapped to his right wrist under a long-sleeved shirt. He was ready for high school. When he completed his sketch, he scratched his name into his wooden desk.

Angelo's mornings were filled with various art classes, and his afternoons were all academics. This was an uptown school, with kids from all over the city. He liked the school, but he didn't know where he belonged. He was not an uptown kid. He was from the projects. During a 15-minute recess, he stepped outside and lit a cigarette. Several students were clumped together here and there along Second Avenue, laughing and talking. He looked for Carl and Dennis, but they were not outside.

"Can I bum one of those?" A kid walked up to him. "I'm Larry."

"Sure." Angelo handed a cigarette to Larry and held his out to light it. "I'm Angelo."

"Where you from?" Larry asked.

"Lower East Side," Angelo said. "You?"

"East Harlem."

"Cool," Angelo said. "You got a club?"

"Chick-a-Dee Social Club," Larry said. "You?"

"Weepers."

"I heard of you guys."

* * *

Angelo stood against the subway door leading to the next car as the train rumbled downtown. His classes had ended earlier than Dennis's or Carl's, so rather than waiting, he headed home alone. He regretted his decision as three older teenagers walked up to him.

"Whatcha got in that school bag, little man?" the largest teenager said.

"Just school stuff," Angelo said.

"What's in your pockets?" The large teenager held out both his hands palms up. "Empty your pockets into my hands."

"No. It's my stuff."

"Your stuff? We gonna beat the stuff outta you if you don't empty your pockets. You decide which it's gonna be, little man."

Angelo felt the loop that would release Merlin. His lock was in his left front pocket. *I have to stab the big guy in the neck, in and out quick as a lizard's tongue, then cut one guy, slip my lock on my left hand, and cut with my right hand. No one in the subway car is gonna help. They're gonna look away and see nothin'. This is just me. And, as Uncle Johnny said, go first and fast.*

"I got beat before," Angelo said. "But I ain't got no other stuff than what I got. So, I'll take the beatin'."

"Ain't no one ever said that before." The large teenager chuckled and looked at his two friends who were smiling and shaking their heads. "Where you from, little man?"

"Lower East Side." Merlin slipped into Angelo's right hand. "The projects."

"Which projects?"

"Al Smith," Angelo said.

"A couple of my boys live in those projects," the large teenager said. "You know Nathaniel?"

"I know a Nathaniel who has a brother named Melvin," Angelo said.

"Yeah, that's him."

"They live in my building," Angelo said. "Twenty Catherine."

"A'right. You say, 'I'm sorry, Mr. Romeo, for not giving you my stuff,' and we'll – "

Angelo laughed. "Mr. Romeo. Your name is Romeo?" Angelo continued to laugh.

Angelo knew his laughter was making the big guy angry. He knew it was a mistake. He tried to stop. But his nerves, relief, and surprise at the teenager's name, had hold of him, and he laughed. It became infectious, and the other two guys started to laugh. The large guy, who had been annoyed by the laughter at first, was having trouble holding back a chuckle or two.

"I gotta let you slide, little man. You're batshit crazy," the large teenager said. "You in a gang or club?"

"The Weepers," Angelo said.

"My man, Howie, is in the Weepers," one of the other teenagers said. "What's your name?"

"Angelo Pastamadeo. Howie's like my brother."

"Romeo, Angelo's the kid who beat The Razor back in '57," the other teenager said. "That was you, Angelo? Am I right?"

"Yeah. It was me."

CHAPTER TWENTY-SIX

"First a soldier, then a cop, then a liquor store"

anny Terenzio, in full uniform, was greeted with a big brother's bear-hug before he was completely through the door at Lilly's Liquor Store.

"Danny, look at you. Geez, kid, I'm glad you're home," Frank said. "You should've called. I would've picked you up."

"It was a last-minute military transport. No sweat," Danny said. "I heard about Mac. How's Anna doin'?"

"Not bad," Frank said. "Johnny's in the back, using the head. He's doing better too."

"Who the fuck is this good-looking soldier boy?" Johnny walked in from the backroom and hugged Danny.

"Johnny, so sorry about Mac," Danny said. "I heard they busted the girlfriend's husband."

"Johnny doesn't figure him for the murder," Frank said.

"I talked to the guy," Johnny said. "I would have killed him if I thought it was him."

"The cops got anything?" Danny asked

"There's a good detective on the case, Clarence Hartz," Frank said. "I know he'll get to the bottom of it."

"I remember him from before I left," Danny said. "Good guy."

"What about you?" Johnny asked. "I heard Cambodia was hell."

"You okay, Danny?" Frank said. "Whatever you need, little brother."

"I'm good," Danny said. "Taking the test for NYPD next week."

"So, you're not going to partner with me in this magnificent liquor store?"

"First a soldier, then a cop, then a liquor store." Danny smiled. "I want to be just like you when I grow up, brother."

"How was Benning and Walter Reed?" Johnny asked.

Danny told them about Elwood and the sheriff. He stopped several times to hold back tears and catch his breath. Frank poured three glasses of bourbon. The three men sat at the small table. Danny talked. Frank and Johnny listened.

"Is the military going to follow up?" Frank asked.

"The captain said he would push it," Danny said.

"What's the captain's name?" Johnny asked.

"Gunther Reinart, Military Police," Danny said. "Seemed like a good guy."

"Among officers, captains are on the low end of the officer pool. They mostly just drive Jeeps for the generals," Johnny said. "I'll look into how the follow-up is going."

"Thanks, Johnny. Keep me in the loop. I need to be there when the sheriff goes down," Danny said. "Elwood's from Newark. I know the Army talked to his folks already. I want to be able to tell them the Army hasn't let this go."

"You got it," Johnny said.

Angelo looked through the window of Lilly's and darted in. Danny spotted him in time to stand as Angelo leaped into Danny's arms. Danny hugged him for a solid minute before he lowered him to his feet.

"Whoa, look at all those medals," Angelo said.

"You can have them," Danny said. "From what I hear, you deserve them more than me."

"No way. When did you get home?" Angelo asked.

"Just now. How're you doin'?"

"Okay." Angelo sat at the table with his three uncles.

"Last letter I got from you said your girlfriend moved upstate."

"Yeah, but I just met another girl who's pretty cool."

"Good for you," Danny said. "What's her name?"

"Joni Varese." Angelo said.

"Is she Italian?" Frank asked.

"I don't know. Why?"

"Varese is a small town in Italy, just north of Milan," Frank said. "Is she from the neighborhood?"

"No, she lives in Stuyvesant Town. Her father's a lawyer," Angelo said.

"How did you meet her?" Johnny asked.

"My friend Bobby has a girlfriend who goes to PA with Joni, and he fixed us up."

"What's PA?" Danny asked.

"That's what they call the High School of Performing Arts," Angelo said. "Joni goes there. She wants to be a dancer, singer, actress...you know."

"You like this girl?" Frank said.

"Yeah, kinda, I think."

"You want a couple of tickets to *Bye Bye Birdie*?'" Frank asked.

"That would be cool," Angelo said. "I'm bringing her to the Settlement dance tomorrow night. Will you be there, Uncle Danny?"

"I wouldn't miss it, kid."

CHAPTER TWENTY-SEVEN

"The tumbling of bodies into the East River"

O n Friday night, Angelo introduced Joni to his mom, uncles, grandfather, Father Joe, and Father Cas at the adult table in the back of the dance floor. Afterwards they joined the other Weepers.

"Bobby, you know Joni," Angelo said. "Tate, Howie, Gerard, guys...this is Joni."

"Hi, everyone," Joni said. "Thanks for inviting me to your dance."

"So, Joni, how do you like PA?" Gina asked.

"Oh, it's really cool, but I just started."

"How did you two meet?" Liz said.

"Bobby fixed us up." Joni smiled at Bobby.

"Nice going, Bobby." Liz glared at him.

Bobby raised both hands, palms out.

Angelo said, "Let's dance," as "Sleep Walk" by Santo and Johnny played.

"Okay. So that girl Liz is definitely not happy about my being here," Joni said.

"Everyone else is," Angelo said. "Especially me."

"You're sweet." Joni put her head on Angelo's shoulder.

Angelo's thoughts drifted off to Audrey for a moment, but then back to Joni. The next song was "Lonely Boy," by

Paul Anka, and Angelo and Joni stayed on the dance floor. He thought he saw his mother smile.

* * *

Nicky-Two-Bridges sat alone on a six-by-six beam and looked out at the East River. He was taking a short break from the Friday night crowd at Mussels and Mugs, which was directly behind him. The night breeze was comforting, and he drifted into a daydream. The Roosevelt Street Boys were on heightened alert for Knights, so they took turns walking the outside perimeter of the tugboat.

That's what Nicky was doing when he decided to sit for a moment and gaze at the river. He did not hear the Knights approach from behind. He took a sudden painful blow to his head. Instinctively, his hands turned into fists and covered his face, drawing his elbows together in front of his body while bringing up his knees. The next swing slammed against his ribs. The following one caught his left shoulder. He whimpered as a bat hammered across his fists. And then the beating stopped.

"Don't nobody move an inch," Daddy Bruce said. "Nicky, what the fuck, man? Did you get lost in your head? Shit man, look at you. Can you hear me, brother?"

"C'mon, Nicky. Let's sit you up," another Roosevelt Street Boy said.

They lifted Nicky into a sitting position. He threw up. He was in a fog, dizzy, but he started to remember. Through blurry vision, he saw seven Knights kneeling in front of him, and four Roosevelt Street Boys standing behind them with shotguns. Daddy Bruce also had a shotgun and was leaning over Nicky.

"Nicky, say something." Daddy Bruce said.

"They got me good, brother. I think I have a concussion. Ow! Maybe a couple of broken ribs," Nicky said. "Dumb. This is on me. Looking out at the river. Fuckin' punks. They get anyone else?"

"No, brother." Daddy Bruce held Nicky tight. "Go easy now. But don't fall asleep."

"Whadaya wanna do with these skells?" a Roosevelt Boy asked.

"Line them up at the edge of the dock, facing the river." Daddy Bruce stood up and shifted his shotgun to his other hand. "You stay right here, Nicky."

Nicky heard the blasts of shotguns, the tumbling of bodies into the East River, and the splash of guns hitting the water. He thought he heard Daddy Bruce cry.

* * *

After the dance, Angelo and Joni took the First Avenue bus to Stuyvesant Town. They kissed goodnight and promised to see each other again and again. When Angelo got back to his neighborhood, he sat in front of the Weepers Club with Tate. They talked about their girlfriends, movies, and plans. It was a nice night and Sammy the dog curled up next to them. From the corner of his eye, Angelo saw a car speeding up Catherine Street.

"Tate, check this out." Angelo pointed at the red '57 Plymouth Fury as it picked up speed.

"What the hell?" Tate said as the car swerved toward them.

"That's Andy driving. They're Knights. Get inside!" Angelo shouted.

Angelo and Tate dove for the door of the Weepers Club as a shower of bullets rained from the Fury. The Plymouth hit two parked cars as it flew down Catherine Street toward the East River. Frank burst out of Lilly's, looked around. Sammy chased the car for block or so and then came back.

Angelo came out of the Weepers Club with blood on his face and shirt. "They shot Tate."

"They shot you, too, right above your ear. Let me see it." Frank examined Angelo's ear, face, and neck. "Looks like a too- close miss. But it will leave a scar. You hit anywhere else?"

"No, I'm fine, but Tate's bad."

"You got a phone in the club, right?"

"Yeah. Who should I call?"

"You call Jokes or Danny to come watch Lilly's," Frank said. "I'll call an ambulance. Then I'll call your mom and tell her to bring Tate's mom to Lilly's. I'll drive everyone to the hospital. You too, pal. I think that's just a bullet graze, but let's be sure. After you call, wash the blood off your face and I'll bandage your cut. Meanwhile, I'll patch up Tate best I can."

Frank lifted Tate off the floor and followed Angelo into the Weepers club. He placed Tate on the sofa and bent over, checking him up and down.

"Is Tate gonna make it?"

"I don't know, pal. He's pretty bad." Frank pulled gauze from a first-aid kit and pressed hard on Tate's worst wound, trying to stop the flow of blood. "Do you know who the shooters were?"

"Satan's Knights."

"You sure?"

"Andy was driving, two in the back, one in the shotgun seat, all Knights. I'm sure," Angelo said. "In a red '57 Fury."

Chapter Twenty-Eight

"You have an army now"

Angelo stood in the vestibule of the funeral home looking out of the Madison Street window. Father Joe's Mass and eulogy for Tate and Nicky-Two-Bridges was sad but also comforting. Tate's family and friends were gathered in one of the parlor rooms, and Nicky's friends were gathered in another. Angelo needed a break from the sadness, the sobbing, the whys. It did not feel real.

"You okay, kid?" Daddy Bruce asked as he walked up to Angelo.

"I don't know."

"You're Angelo, right? I'm Bruce. Everybody calls me Daddy Bruce."

"Yeah, I know," Angelo said. "Tate was my best friend. Was Nicky yours?"

"He was. They died on the same night. That makes us close friends."

"My Nonna said time will heal my wounds. You buy that?"

"Nah. I had a lot of friends die in the war. Nothing heals. Nothing makes you stronger. It's all bullshit. I still miss them. I still carry the pain of loss, and I will forever. But now when I think of them, I mostly think about the good times, the fun times, instead of the sorrow. I smile more."

"Tate always repeated what I said. It annoyed me. Maybe in time, when I think about him doing that, it will make me smile."

"You got it," Daddy Bruce said. "I think right now, my friend is putting his hand on your friend's shoulder and saying, 'Don't worry, Tate. This ain't nothin' but a thing. I gotcha, pal.' I believe that."

"Yeah, me too," Angelo said. "Cool."

"I'll tell you a secret. Sometimes I talk to my shadow."

"Whoa. I do that too," Angelo said.

"Well, from now on, I'm gonna talk to Nicky instead," Daddy Bruce said. "I don't have to believe he's dead if I don't wanna. It's like he's in another country and we talk long distance. I don't have to see him to talk with him and feel him."

"Yeah, I'm gonna talk to Tate from now on. I'm gonna do that, too."

"I'm gonna go back in," Daddy Bruce said. "You should too."

"I need to find Andy before he skips," Angelo said.

"Andy?"

"Him and the three Knights that killed Tate," Angelo said. "I need to make things right."

"No, you don't. You have an army now."

"An army? My Uncle Nunzio said something like that back in '57 when I... never mind. Who's my army?"

"Us. The Roosevelt Street Boys. And today we are gonna put an end to Satan's Knights."

"I should be with you."

"You're the leader of the Weepers, right? A good leader takes care of his guys. They need you right now, so go be with them. And tell them your army's got this."

* * *

Rico walked out of his apartment on Sunday afternoon, straight into the arms of four Roosevelt Street Boys.

"We were just comin' up to getcha," said one of the Boys.

"How do you guys know where I live?" Rico said.

"You kiddin'?"

"Where we going?" Rico said.

"Andy called an emergency meeting of the Knights at their club," said one of the Boys. "You need to be there."

"I'm out of the Knights," Rico said.

"You still need to be there."

"Who said?"

"Me."

"Do I have a choice?"

"Yeah. I really want to kill you right now, so there's that," the Roosevelt Boy said. "Or you can come with us."

"Why?" said Rico as someone from behind shoved him toward a waiting car at the curb. "Calm down. I'm comin'."

"You know about last night?" another Roosevelt Boy asked.

"No. What about last night?"

CHAPTER TWENTY-NINE

"This will not take long or end well"

Twenty-two Knights and 12 Roosevelt Street Boys were already there when Rico and his escort arrived at the Knights' club apartment. Andy sat at the head of the long table with a couple of his top guys seated on either side of him.

"Rico, the Roosevelt Street Boys said you invited them to this meeting. Why?" Andy asked. "What are you doin' here, anyway? Are you comin' back in?"

"No, I'm not comin' back," Rico said. "What happened last night?"

"We're waiting for Mike and some of his guys to get here before we start," Andy said.

"Mike's not coming." Daddy Bruce walked into the apartment with six more Roosevelt Street Boys."

"I know you," Andy said. "What do you know about Mike?"

"He's face down in the East River with a bullet in his back." Daddy Bruce fitted a silencer to his handgun. "And six of his guys are swimming with him. So, we can start."

"What happened last night?" Rico asked again, sounding urgent. He was worried.

"Your Knights killed my friend," Daddy Bruce said. "They also killed Tate, one of the Weepers, and shot

Angelo, the Weepers' leader. Angelo is also a friend of mine."

"What! No, no, no! Killed? Andy, what the fuck?" Rico rushed towards Andy but several Roosevelt Street Boys held him back.

"Andy, did you want to have your little meeting first or should we just go on with why we're here today?" Daddy Bruce asked.

"Look, no one was supposed to get killed last night. We just wanted to give you and the Weepers a warning," Andy said. "Since you're here, this is the warning. From now on, if a Knight gets shot, we will kill three Roosevelt Street Boys and three Weepers. That's the warning. That's it."

"You done?" Daddy Bruce said.

"Yeah. That's it. You've been warned," Andy said.

"You're out of your mind, Andy." Rico shook his head. "You are clueless, way too far around the bend."

"Okay, my turn." Daddy Bruce nodded, and two Roosevelt Street Boys locked the apartment door and stood in front of it. "This club apartment is now the property of the Roosevelt Street Boys."

"Who says?" Andy said. "Rico, did you tell them they could have our club? You're not the leader of the Knights anymore. You're not even a Knight. You can't give away our club."

"No, Andy, I did not. You and Mike did." Rico rubbed his eyes. "Pay attention, you idiot. I sense this will not take long or end well. Try to pay attention."

"Good advice," Daddy Bruce said. "After this meeting, Satan's Knights will no longer exist. They will be no more. All you Knights wearing Knight shirts or jackets, or any-thing else that says Knights on it, take them off and pile them on this table. Also, you and you," Daddy Bruce pointed at two Knights. "Collect any other Knight stuff in this apartment and put it on the table."

"No, no! Now hold up, "Andy said. "I didn't agree to this."

"Andy, who were the brave Knights with you last night?" Daddy Bruce said.

Andy pointed to three Knights seated close to him, who all proudly raised their hands. "Why?"

Rico shook his head and closed his eyes.

"Angelo wanted to be here to do this," Daddy Bruce said. "But I told him I would take care of it."

Daddy Bruce shot Andy in the forehead. Andy and his chair flew backward. There was frozen silence. Daddy Bruce shot the three Knights who had raised their hands. The room burst into frightened screams and pleas.

"Calm yourselves. We have work to do." Daddy Bruce shouted. "Good, that's better. Do you remember your assignments? Everything with 'Knights' on it, put on this table."

Without hesitation, every Knight followed Daddy Bruce's orders. When they were done, they waited in silence.

"Now then, back to our business. This club belongs to the Roosevelt Street Boys," Daddy Bruce said. "Any objections? Hearing none, it is so agreed. Next, Satan's Knights no longer exists. Anyone wearing a Knights' anything, or calling himself a Knight, will be killed. Does anyone object to that? Good, the Knights have been officially disbanded. And finally, it is the duty of all the former Knights in this room to let all the guys who missed this meeting know they're no longer Knights. Do you understand your duty?

Raise your hand if you do not understand, or if you have any questions or objections. No objections? Good."

The Satan's Knights were paralyzed, but one softly asked, "Rico, you got anything to say?"

"Sure, Rico, you wanna say something?" Daddy Bruce said.

"I am taking back leadership of the Knights for a minute," Rico said. "First, I order you all to remain silent about what happened in this club. Rats get killed in traps. Second, I agree that Satan's Knights no longer exist. And third, I agree that we must all tell anyone who missed this meeting that the Knights are over."

"Good," Daddy Bruce said. "Anything else?"

"What about them?" Rico pointed at Andy and the three dead Knights.

"Yeah, good point. Freddy, call Bucky and tell him to bring his truck around. We're gonna make a dump run," Daddy Bruce said to one of the Roosevelt Street Boys. "You ten former Knights get five large, empty metal trash cans with covers. You're gonna load one with the clothing. The other four are for your friends. Then you'll load the truck. The rest of you ex-Knights will clean up this apartment. Okay, let's go."

* * *

After leaving the funeral parlor, Angelo and several Weepers, Angelo's mom, Adam, Rosemarie, and Frank walked over to the Weepers club. Joni was waiting in front.

"I heard about what happened, you know, from Bobby. Anyway, I just wanted to make sure you were okay, Angelo," Joni said. "Is there anything I can do for you? Help you with anything?"

"No, I don't think so, but it's nice that you're here," Angelo said. "We can go grab lunch someplace if you like."

"No, you need to be with your friends and family. I'm fine," Joni said. "I just wanted to let you know if you need me."

"How sweet of you." Angelo's mom smiled. "Come with us, Joni. We'll have a girl's lunch and chat."

Chapter Thirty

"Shut up, Declan"

Heather joined Rico at the East Harlem Diner for breakfast. It was Rico's place for secret meetings or just to have a safe meal away from the neighborhood.

"I suppose no progress on the Nunzio thing," Rico said.

"Progress? Everyone in the neighborhood's been looking over their shoulder for the last month. Ever since your wanker Knights went nuts and almost killed my nephew. I told you we should have killed Mike and Andy. But, no, you trusted them not –"

"Okay, okay, hold it down. I know it's on me. But it's been a month. Everything seems back to normal except that the Knights no longer exist."

"Here's your breakfast." The waitress clattered down two plates of eggs, bacon, potatoes, and toast. "I'll bring you more coffee."

"Thank you," Heather said.

"So, do you have a plan?" Rico asked.

"Today is the first day of autumn, which means tomorrow night at the Cherry – "

"Oh, is that why the schools are closed?" Rico asked.

"No, it's Rosh Hashanah. Good Lord, get a clue. Pay attention."

"Calm down. Go on," Rico said.

"The dance at the Settlement tomorrow night is an annual celebration of autumn. Everyone will be in good spirits and relaxed. Nunzio is always there for these big events. I will get a read on him and maybe an opportunity. The good news is there aren't any Knights to screw up the day. You need to wait for my phone call in your apartment. Got it?"

"Tomorrow night. Got it," Rico said with a nod.

* * *

Nunzio and his lawyer, Declan Ardan, sat in a police interrogation room. A worn wooden table separated them from two detectives.

"Mr. Sabino, I am Detective Goldman and with me is Detective Polini. You have voluntarily agreed to talk with us in the presence of your lawyer, Declan Ardan. Is that correct?"

"My lawyer was the one that agreed for me to talk with you guys voluntarily."

"Do you mind if we record our conversation?"

"You already turned the recorder on, so why ask me now? But, no problem, g'head, record away."

"Earlier this morning, Deputy Mayor Raymond Clarke, was found shot to death in City Hall Park."

"I saw the news," Nunzio said. "Damn shame. Clarke was a good man."

"You knew Mr. Clarke?"

"Yeah, like I said, he was a good guy."

"How did you know him? Socially, professionally, politically..."

"I don't know what you're talkin' about," Nunzio said. "Clarke did me a big favor in delaying the Brooklyn Bridge project back in '57. I owed him for that. And he wasn't full of himself like a lot of politicians. I liked the guy. That's it."

"Do you know who might have wanted to kill him?"

"Now, wait a minute. If you're suggesting that my client had Clarke murdered for political, or any other reason, I am going to object," Declan spoke up.

"I'm not suggesting that at all, Counselor," Detective Goldman said.

"But, since your lawyer raised the question, Mr. Sabino, are you helping your lawyer here win the election?"

"Of course he is. We're friends, and he would benefit from my winning – "

"I'm asking Mr. Sabino, Counselor."

"Absolutely not." Nunzio looked directly into Declan's eyes. "I agreed to help him get the unions behind him if he got on the ticket. But that's it."

"But you would benefit from your friend being the mayor," Detective Polini said.

"First, I benefitted from Mr. Clarke being my friend. Second, Declan is not my friend; he's just my lawyer. And frankly, I don't even want him as a lawyer no more."

"Well, wait, Nunzio," Declan said. "I'm here to protect you from any false charges they may want to bring against you based on this interview."

"You guys have done this before?" Nunzio asked the detectives.

"More than a few times."

"You think my lawyer is doing a good job protecting me from false charges?"

"I think he should be sitting on our side of the table." Detective Goldman smiled. "We're not interested in false charges, Mr. Sabino."

"I didn't think you were," Nunzio said. "Am I free to leave?"

"I do have one thing that you might be able to shed some light on," Detective Goldman said. "A month or so ago, Mr. Clarke met with you at Caffè Fiora on Grand Street. Can you tell us what he wanted?"

"Sure. As I said, I owed Mr. Clarke a favor. He told me he thought he was being followed by some Hell's Kitchen thugs. He wasn't sure, but if he was, he hoped I would be able to tell them to knock it off. As you guys know, I have some weight with thugs."

"Was he being followed?" Detective Polini asked. "Did you tell them to stop?"

"I dropped the ball," Nunzio said. "I knew that Declan was using some Hell's Kitchen Boys for muscle, so I figured I'd ask Declan if - "

"Wait, I have no idea what you're talking about, Nunzio," Declan said. "Who told you that?"

"Your friend, Rico. He said his Knights were running errands for you, but you were using the Hell's Kitchen boys for muscle. Anyway, like I said, I dropped the ball. I reached out to Declan about it, never heard back, and then it just slipped my mind. Sorry about that now."

"That's helpful, Mr. Sabino," Detective Polini said. "Do you know how we can reach this Rico guy?"

"Sure. Give me a card and I'll have him call you," Nunzio said. "Now, am I free to go?"

"Wait. We shouldn't leave yet. Let's restart this in a different way," Declan said.

"Shut up, Declan," Nunzio said. "Detectives, am I free to leave?"

"Yes, you are, Mr. Sabino."

Nunzio walked out without Declan. Pepe was waiting in the car. When Nunzio got in, Pepe asked, "Should we wait for Declan, Boss?"

"No, take me to Fiora's."

* * *

Anna walked to the adult tables at the Cherry Street Settlement. Father Joe greeted her with an autumn smile and a hug as "The Twist" by Chubby Checker, filled the room.

"I thought Frank and Uncle Nunzio would be here by now." Anna said.

"Nunzio is tied up. Something the do with his *stronzo* attorney," Father Joe said. "He needs to get himself a real lawyer."

"I agree," Anna said. "I've never liked Declan."

"Anyway, we're here," Father Cas said. "Where's Angelo's girlfriend? Joni, right?"

"Ah, after all the trouble, Tate's killing, her parents said she could not return to this neighborhood," Anna said. "Angelo can still see her, but the Lower East Side is off limits."

"It's been over a month," Father Cas said. "How sad for Angelo."

"He has had a hard time of it these last few months." Father Joe shook his head.

"Anna, may I talk to you for a moment?" Father Cas asked.

"Of course."

Father Cas took Anna's arm and they walked to the side of the gym.

"Anna, would you have dinner with me sometime?"

"Of course. But I don't need comforting, Father Cas. I'm okay."

"Not to comfort you, although I hope I do that. Just to talk with you and have dinner."

"Talk about what? Angelo?"

"No, no... I am so bad at this."

"Bad at what?" Anna said. "Oh...wait. Are you asking me out on a date?"

"It would be easier if you called me Cas, instead of Father Cas. And yes, I think I am."

"Wow, I, um ..."

"I'm sorry. I shouldn't. I am taking advantage of our friendship, please forgive - "

"No, I would love to, Cas."

"Tomorrow night?"

"Well, let me check my busy schedule." Anna playfully put her index finger to her temple. "It looks like I'm free then." Anna smiled.

"How about I fetch you at seven and we walk over to Forlini's?"

"Sounds good." *Holy crap. What the hell am I doing? With a priest! Ro is going to love this.*

"You just made my evening, Anna. Thank you. I'd ask you to dance, but that might - "

"Yes, that would."

CHAPTER THIRTY-ONE

"You learn best from mistakes if they don't kill you"

Danny was walking toward Lilly's when Johnny pulled up in a '59 Chrysler New Yorker.

"Danny," Johnny said. "Get in, we need to talk."

Danny climbed into the passenger seat. "What's up?"

"The Army ain't gonna do nothin' about your buddy, Elwood," Johnny said. "All about politics at the Pentagon. Deals with the governor and a senator. Same bullshit."

"What about the captain? He said he – "

"Captain Reinart, turns out, is a stand-up guy," Johnny said. "He resigned his commission over the military's refusal to follow through on this. He made a stink up the ladder, but in the end, he walked away from promises of promotions, choice of assignments, the whole nine-yards. Just said bullshit, someone needs to do something for Elwood, and he resigned."

"Okay. Thanks, Johnny" Danny shook his head and started to get out of the car.

"I'm not finished. Is there more you want us to do about this?"

"I got to do what I got to do."

"What's that?"

"I'm going back, find the sheriff, and kill him. I have to."

"Yeah, we thought you'd say that."

"We...who?"

"Me, Ben, and Henry. We got this. You stay here and get ready to be a cop. Yeah, I heard you passed the test. Congratulations, kid."

"Thanks, but not a chance. I love that you guys would do this, but I gotta be part of it," said Danny.

"Okay, but we treat this like a military operation, and Ben is in charge. Not you. Ben."

"Fine with me."

"Done. I'll let you know when we're ready."

* * *

"Mr. Sabino, Declan is standing outside," Pepe said. "He wants to apologize and explain why he did what he did with the cops. Do you want to see him?"

"It's Sunday. Tell him to go to church and confess his sins to a priest. I ain't in the forgiving business."

"Will do, Boss."

When Pepe returned, Natale signaled him for a phone call in her office. And then she brought a small pot of coffee to Nunzio and an empty cup for Pepe.

"Pepe's on the phone with Naples. I'm guessing he'll need some coffee." Natale said. "You need anything else, Papa?"

"I'm good. Thank you."

After ten minutes or so, Pepe returned to Nunzio. He helped himself to one of Nunzio's cigarettes, as Nunzio poured coffee into Pepe's cup.

"Did you get the message about the cops to Rico?" Nunzio asked.

"Done. Rico said he'll do whatever you want."

"Good. Now what's new in Naples?"

"You're not gonna believe this. The waitress was Angie Zara."

"*Impossibile, è morta* – she's dead. Killed in '57 by ... Lanzo ... what did they say? How is this possible?"

"Everyone thought the whole family was killed at their estate in Pozzuoli back in '57. Angie, Fabia, Aldo, the servant, and even Mr. Jewels. All the bodies were there and accounted for. All dead." Pepe said. "But now, another look found the dead girl they thought was Angie was really Adele Ingannare. She worked at Aldo's bank. She and Angie were friends and the same age. Adele was visiting at the time. They now think Angie was hiding somewhere in the house when Lanzo arrived."

"He thought Adele was Angie," Nunzio said. "And never searched the house."

"Right," said Pepe. "They think Angie hid in Italy, takin' odd jobs here and there until she decided it was time for her vendetta."

"So, the waitress we thought was hiding because she saw Lanzo's murder was the assassin herself."

"Yeah. She shot Lanzo at close range with a .32 Baretta. They think she used a silencer, since nobody heard nothin'," Pepe said. "Maybe the bartender helped her or maybe not."

"Do they know where she is now?"

"They think she's still in Italy. Maybe changed her name. But they will find more about her now and get back to us fast."

"Lanzo, my dear friend, you should've searched the house," Nunzio said to the ceiling.

"He made a big mistake, Boss."

"There's a story they tell in Naples about a horse thief who is about to be hanged for his crimes," Nunzio said. "When he was asked if he had any last words, he said, 'This has certainly been a lesson for me'."

"That's funny, Boss."

"What's that Italian saying about learning from mistakes?" asked Nunzio.

"You learn best from your mistakes, but only if they don't kill you."

CHAPTER THIRTY-TWO

"My killer is Angie Zara"

Monday afternoon, Nunzio and Father Joe walked into Lilly's, where Frank, Heather, Johnny, Danny, and Detective Hartz were toasting with glasses of champagne.

"Now this is the best welcoming I've ever received," Father Joe said to much laughter. "And I've been welcomed by the Pope."

"What's the occasion?" asked Nunzio.

"My little brother, Danny, just passed the police test. He starts NYPD training on November first," Frank said. "Hold up. I've got two more glasses here."

"To my brother, Danny. One of New York's finest. Always."

"Cheers!" everyone shouted.

"Come join us. We've got pastries, coffee and all the booze you could dream of," Frank said to Nunzio and Father Joe.

"Love to," said Father Joe as the group gathered around the table.

"I heard you had a run-in with the law," Hartz said to Nunzio. "You good?"

"I think so. You know those detectives on the Clarke case?"

"I do," said Detective Hartz. "They're straight, and between us, you got no worries."

"Thanks, Hartz," Nunzio said. "I also should thank your girlfriend, Frank. What's your name again, dear?"

"Heather."

"Right. You taught me not to underestimate women, and how right you were."

"What happened?" asked Frank.

"It's a long story, but the short of it is a friend of mine was murdered in a Naples trattoria couple of months ago. Everybody was looking for a waitress who saw the killing. But, after Heather mentioned the modern women, I told them the waitress might be Lanzo's killer, and they should find out everything they could about her. Turns out the waitress was Angie Zara."

"Angie Zara? From the neighborhood?" Frank asked.

"I was surprised too," said Father Joe. "She and her mom moved to Italy over ten years ago. I think her mother remarried."

"How old would she be now?" Frank said.

"I'm not sure, maybe 21," said Father Joe.

"You sure about her being Lanzo's killer?" Frank asked.

"Positive."

"How'd she do it?" Danny asked. "Just curious."

"She walked right up to Lanzo. All he saw was his waitress coming. She put a .32 caliber Beretta with a silencer against his head and *ba-boom*," Nunzio said. "Then she just strolled out of the trattoria and vanished."

"Did you say a .32 Beretta with a silencer?" Detective Hartz asked.

"That is correct, my friend. Point blank. *Ba-boom*."

"You, Mr. Sabino, just solved the Mac murder case," said Detective Hartz. He lifted his glass toward Nunzio and said, "My killer is Angie Zara."

"Don't thank me. Thank Heather," Nunzio said.

"Why did Angie kill Domingo too?" asked Johnny. "Her brothers were Knights."

"Good question," Hartz said. "At least a couple of Knights seemed to help her."

"Do you think Rico is her main go-to guy?" Frank asked.

"I don't think so," Nunzio said. "Maybe a few of his Knights might be moonlighting without his permission. He was very upset about his Knights getting knocked off. Rico wound up losing his whole organization."

"But why did she kill Domingo?" Frank asked.

"My guess is she was gettin' rid of witnesses," Nunzio said.

"Do you think Angie is still here in the City?" Johnny asked.

"Good question. If Mac was her only target, she's probably back in Italy, or wherever," Detective Hartz said.

"Mac's not her only target," Nunzio said. "She's still here."

"You?" asked Frank.

"Me," Nunzio said. "Here's the short of it. Back in '57, when this guy Lanzo killed Angie's mother and stepfather, and thought he killed Angie, they had a guest, Timothy Jewels. Jewels worked for me but was one of the guys who planned the hit on me three years ago."

"I remember that, with a couple of Knights." Hartz nodded.

"Right. So a couple of days after Lanzo hit the family, he called me to make sure I wasn't angry with him about killing Jewels. On that call, he told me that before he shot Jewels, Jewels said he worked for me in New York. Lanzo, being Lanzo, said, 'Signore Nunzio Sabino said to say hello, and goodbye. *Ciao e ciao.*'

"Now, assuming Angie was hiding in the house, she must've heard Lanzo talking to Jewels and believed I had something to do with the hit on her family. I'm telling you, she's still in the City." *Only Pepe knows that I asked Lanzo to hit Angie and her family. I want to keep it that way, and anyway, I told them enough.*

"I'd offer you protection, but you don't want that." said Hartz. "Anyone have a clue as to a description?"

"Italian, dark hair, dark eyes, early 20s," Father Joe said. "Probably looks like half the women in this neighborhood."

"My guys in Naples are working with the police to find out more. I'll let you know." Nunzio twirled his glass.

"I have a good contact in Interpol. They have fingerprints, photos, everything. I'll ask them to put together a composite if they can," Johnny said. "They're fast. I'll pass along whatever they send me."

"This is terrific," Hartz said. "Hey, and thanks, Heather."

Heather sat stone still and silent. She smiled weakly when she was thanked, but said nothing. She just stared at an invisible spot between now and then.

CHAPTER THIRTY-THREE

"The wounded can kill you; the dead can't"

At dusk, Danny Terenzio, wearing a dark shirt and clerical collar, drove along Reese Road in Georgia. The stolen '56 Chevy he was driving had smoke billowing out of its hood. He spotted the sheriff's car just ahead. Danny pulled alongside the sheriff's car, honked, smiled, and waved. He cut in front of the sheriff and pulled to the side of the road. The sheriff turned on his red flashers and stopped behind Danny.

"It would appear you're havin' car problems, Father," said the sheriff walking up to Danny's window.

"Good evening, Sheriff Forrest, I appreciate you stopping." Danny smiled.

"Do I know you?"

"You do. Think about it." Danny said.

"Well, first let's take a peek at where all that smoke is coming from."

"It's coming from a small smoke bomb I put under the hood."

"Now why on earth would you do that?"

"Tell me when you see it."

"See what?"

"You'll know when you see it."

"What?" The sheriff looked to each side, up, and then down. "See whaaa – "

"Bingo," said Danny. "That's it."

"Oh, now hold on, son. That's a shotgun." The sheriff took one step back.

"You see it. Good for you, Sheriff Forrest. Now, don't move another inch."

"Why are you pointed that, that – "

"It is a Remington Automaster 878. It contains three 12-gauge bucks."

Danny and the sheriff looked at the headlights of another car that pulled up behind the sheriff's car.

"Wait a minute. You're no minister," said the sheriff. "You're the white soldier with the colored boy we arrested a while ago."

"Yeah, Sergeant Elwood Wallace Patterson. He was my friend. Say his name."

"Sergeant Elwood Wallace Patterson." The sheriff stared at the shotgun. "Now, just give me a minute here."

"You don't have a minute. That's my ride behind us."

"Let me have a last cigarette? It's the Christian thing to do."

Danny fired all three buckshots into Sheriff Forrest, sending most of the sheriff splashing across the darkening road.

Danny set the timer on two explosive devices. He left one in the Chevy. He took his shotgun, the second device, and a small canvas bag with him. On his way to the '59 Chrysler New Yorker behind him, he tossed the second explosive into the sheriff's car.

When Danny got to the Chrysler, Johnny was standing up with his M1C sniper rifle, from a one-knee kneeling position along the driver's side of the car.

"Thanks for the cover, Johnny," Danny said.

"No problem."

Danny and Johnny climbed into the back seat. Ben was driving and Henry was in the shotgun seat. The Chrysler skidded a bit as it took off.

"What the hell am I skidding on?" Ben asked.

"The sheriff." Danny said.

"Oh, shit," Ben said. "If we have a flat, I ain't touching the tires. Just set this car on fire."

Henry was looking at a map. "So, we're headed to an old wooden meeting house on Holcum Road along the Chattahoochee River."

"Danny, I don't know what you and the sheriff were talking about, but no chit-chat at the meeting house, okay?" Ben said.

"Hey, I just made the bastard say Elwood's name."

"Did you know the bastard undid the hold-down strap on his pistol?" Ben asked Danny.

"No, are you sure?"

"Positive," Johnny said. "He also started to bend his knees."

"What?" asked Danny.

"While he was saying Sergeant Patterson's name," Johnny said. "My guess is he was thinking about dropping to the ground and firing a couple of Hail-Mary bullets into your door."

"If I hadn't been fast enough with the trigger, the shotgun would have been clumsy from the driver's window," Danny softly said. "Jesus."

"I had him cold," Johnny said. "One more second and I would have fired."

"Listen, Danny, these guys can't honor your friend," Henry said. "They don't know how dumb they are. They think the reason they ain't rich and famous is because of the Coloreds, Jews, Italians, Catholics, and anyone else who's not them."

"You're right," Danny said.

"Good," said Ben. "No chit-chat at the meeting house. I have two goals for this operation: complete success and bringing everyone in this car home safely."

"Got it," Danny said. "What are we looking at?"

"My guy, Topo. Yeah, that's really his name," Ben said. "Told his Klan he had four ministers who wanted to join. We will be facing about 20 members when we get there. They're all armed, so no one will be surprised that we are walking in with weapons. Deputy Sheriff Lee Arsch is the Klan leader. Johnny will stay outside to watch for any late-comers. Topo will introduce us to Deputy Arsch. He might recognize you, Danny."

"No chit-chat," Danny said. "Just bang."

"Good," Ben said. "Topo is going to walk outside right after introducing us, which might stir up some of these guys. Henry and I have our military Browning automatic rifles with 40-round open boxes. We will clear the room."

Henry lit a Lucky Strike. "Anyone want a smoke?"

"I'll take one," Danny said. "You know that fuckin' sheriff asked me if he could have a final cigarette?"

"What did you say?"

"That's when I shot him."

"I did a mission in Korea with a captain in the French Foreign Legion," Johnny said. "He told me he allowed an enemy spy to have a smoke before he was executed. The spy pulled out the longest cigar he ever saw. His riflemen sat down while the spy smoked and entertained them with stories. Ever since then, the captain carried Camel cigarettes cut in half."

"Why didn't he just tell them no cigarette?"

"The captain was French."

"There's the road to the meeting house," Henry pointed.

* * *

The Chrysler pulled up along the tree line on the dirt road leading to the front of the house. Johnny rolled out of the back seat with his rifle and vanished into the trees. The other three men walked through the front door into a smoke-filled room. A dozen or so men were there. Some were seated with shotguns on their laps, some were standing. Most were smoking. A wooden table in the back had several bottles of whiskey, a plate of jerky, and a pitcher of water on it. A Confederate flag and a Nazi flag hung on the wall behind the table.

"Welcome, preachers." Topo walked up to the three preachers with two men in tow. "Ministers, this is Deputy Arsch and Judge Jolly."

"Nice weapons," Judge Jolly said. "Are those military-grade BARs?"

"Anyone in the bathroom, outhouse, or anywhere else?" Ben asked Topo.

"No, sir, but not everyone is here, yet." Topo walked out of the house.

"Now why in hell would you want to know that?" Deputy Arsch asked. "Where you goin, Topo?"

Danny obliterated the deputy's head, and then Judge Jolly's head, with one shot each of 12-gauge buck at point-blank range. His next shot took out a man raising a handgun. Ben took the leftside of the room and Henry took the right. The house rattled and shook with the *tat-a-tat, tat-a-tat* of the two BARs.

* * *

Outside the meeting house, Johnny looked over at Topo, who sat on the front wooden steps smoking a cigarette as the eruption and clatter of gunfire filled the night. Topo stood up as a 1948 Ford pickup truck come down the dirt road toward the house. Three men were crammed together in the cab, and one large man stood in the back of the truck.

Johnny raised his rifle and squeezed off a perfect headshot. The large man crumpled to the bed of the truck. Johnny's next shot took out the man in the passenger seat. He blocked the right door as he slumped over. The driver opened his door and jumped out. The middle man reached for the steering wheel to control the truck before Johnny's bullet hit him in the head. The pickup rolled into a large ash tree. Johnny saw a flash from the driver's weapon as a dogwood branch to Johnny's left shattered.

The driver raised his rifle again, but a gunshot made him drop his weapon. Topo was standing on the porch with a gun in his hand. *Son-of-a-bitch Topo might have just saved my life.* Johnny was surprised that the driver was halfway down the driveway, stumbling towards Topo and the house. *The stronzo doesn't know it was Topo who shot him.*

Johnny raised his rifle, but before he could fire, Topo shot the driver in the chest with his .38 pistol. The driver sat in the dirt with both hands on his wounds, staring at Topo. Johnny finished checking the dead guys in the truck. Topo shot the driver in his right foot. The driver howled.

Johnny walked up to Topo. "You okay?"

"Yes, sir." Topo shot the driver in his left foot.

"Make him stop shooting me," the driver said to Johnny.

"They never liked me 'cause my mom is Italian. Never let me join," Topo said.

"You know what *topo* means in Italian?" Johnny said.

"Mouse," Topo said. "My mom told me I was always little and quiet."

"You're Italian. You don't wanna join them," Johnny said. "They're pieces of shit."

"You're right."

"Why'd you shoot his feet?"

"He always made fun of my feet. Said I had little-girl feet."

"Help me," said the driver. "Please."

"*Topo, amico mio*, when seeking revenge, we Italians say: 'The wounded can kill you; the dead can't.' One shot to the chest knocks him down. Good. Then one shot to the head completes the revenge and ends the risk to you. Understand?"

"Yes, sir."

"Do you want me to do it?"

"No, no, no, wait!" the driver pleaded and cried.

"No, sir," Topo said to Johnny. He raised his .38 and fired one shot into the driver's forehead.

Danny, Ben, and Henry walked out of the now-quiet meeting house.

"I see we had some late arrivals. Who's this guy?" Ben pointed at the dead driver.

"Topo had my back on this one," Johnny said.

"So, you got your story straight about what happened here, Topo?" Ben asked.

"Yes, sir. Some Alabama boys we been feuding with did this. They were all hooded, but I recognized their trucks," Topo said. "You need to shoot me."

"Who's gonna come get you?"

"My brother. He's about fifteen minutes out. There's a phone inside."

"Okay, Topo, call your brother now," Johnny said. "I'll shoot you after the call. Bring out some towels or sheets, a chair, and the whiskey."

Topo was back out in minutes. "He's coming."

"Put the chair against the house and sit in it," Johnny said. "I see you're right-handed so the first shot will go between your left arm and chest. Just let your arm hang limp. Take a big drink of whiskey. Henry will soak the towels in the whiskey for you to hold on the wound. Stay still."

"Ready." Topo plopped into the chair.

Johnny's bullet was perfect and embedded itself in the chair.

Henry gave Topo a soaked towel to press under his arm.

"Now, I'm gonna give you a hero's scar," Johnny said. "The bullet will take off a small piece of your left ear and burn a scar along your cheek. No one will ever mess with you again, Topo. My nephew has one."

"Did you give it to him?'

"No, he got it from an asshole."

"You know who?"

"Don't know his name," Johnny said. "But I know he's dead."

"Okay, I'm ready," said Topo.

"Take a big drink. And stay real still."

The shot was masterful and the bullet went through a window in the house.

"Put this towel on your face wound," Henry said.

"Topo, you good?" Johnny asked. "Can we leave you here?"

"Yes, sir. Hurts awful. But I like having a hero's scar. I'm good."

"Topo, I owe you," Ben said. "If you ever need us, you know how to reach me."

"Yes, sir."

"Gentlemen, let's go home," Ben said. "Big guns in the trunk, handguns in the car. We'll do three-hour driving shifts with the shotgun seat awake for the driver."

The four men climbed into the Chrysler and headed north.

CHAPTER THIRTY-FOUR

"Guns for Weepers"

Pepe parked Nunzio's black Cadillac in front of the Weepers' storefront. Several Weepers were seated on chairs on the sidewalk.

Pepe rolled down his window and asked, "Is Angelo inside?"

"Yeah, you want me to get him?"

"Not necessary."

Nunzio and a large man carrying a small duffle bag got out of the car and walked into the club.

"Uncle Nunzio," Angelo said. "I just saw you pull up. I was coming out."

"No, you stay," Nunzio said. "I want a minute alone with my nephew. The rest of you guys wait outside."

"What's up?" Angelo asked as the other members quickly filed out.

"Rocco here has a bag with twelve Colt .38 Specials and twelve boxes of ammo. All of the guns are clean, untraceable. There is also one chrome-plated gun, modified so it can't shoot. It has *Tate* engraved on the handle. You should make a wall of honor, Angelo, and hang Tate's gun on it. He is your first, and God willing, your last casualty. No Weeper should ever forget him."

"Geez, Uncle Nunzio, thank you." Angelo wiped tears from his face.

"You decide who gets the guns. I also have a good-size safe comin' to your club today. If the guns are gonna stay here, you should keep them and the ammo in the safe. You will be the only one with the combination unless you decide to share it. You're the leader of the Weepers and these are your decisions."

"Should I get holsters?" asked Angelo. "You know the kind that go inside your pants, or around your – "

"No holsters. These are unregistered guns. You get caught with one, you say you found it. If you're wearing a holster, it ain't gonna play well. And if you use one of these guns, wipe it down and throw it in the river. I'll get you another one, *capisci* ?"

"Yeah, got it."

"Where do you want Rocco to put the bag of guns?"

"In the back near the bathroom."

Then Angelo asked, "Uncle Nunzio, are you comin' to the Halloween dance at the Settlement tonight?"

"I wouldn't miss it, *Gattino*."

* * *

The South Street Boys, generally known as Popeyes, wore Popeye masks. The Weepers wore Lone Ranger masks. Other gangs wore Superman capes, top hats, and Batman paraphernalia, to the Halloween dance at the Cherry Street Settlement. To the surprise and delight of Father Joe and Father Cas, the adults dressed like priests, even the women.

"I Want to be Wanted" by Brenda Lee was playing to a crowded dancefloor, and Angelo was dancing with Liz.

"Is Joni still grounded from you?" Liz said.

"Her father is just worried 'cause of all the trouble with the Knights and the deputy mayor getting killed and all. I can still go out with her, but not here."

"Are you?"

"Her school is having a dance called the November Affair in a couple of weeks and she asked me to take her."

"Cool. Where else do you guys go for dates?"

"Um, honestly, I don't really have enough money to go on a lot of dates."

"What do you mean? All you need is fare."

"Night" by Jackie Wilson began, and Angelo and Liz stayed on the dance floor.

"My father told me if I want a girl to like me, I should take her to a movie or a restaurant she likes. You know, stuff like that. So, she has a good time and thinks it's because of me."

"Your father said that? Wow, Angelo. You don't need to do that. The right girl will just like hanging out with you. Just because of you."

"I don't know."

"I would and what about Audrey?"

"Me and Audrey were like friends and going steady. It was different."

"I always loved that about you two. Being friends and dating. Nice. Stick with neighborhood girls. There's gotta be someone you like."

"I like Marie from my building, but she is too cool for me.

"Tell her that."

"Not a chance. Forget about it."

"I'm serious. Tell her just like you said it to me. Take a shot."

"Maybe," Angelo said. "Let's change the subject."

"Okay, what's up with Father Cas and your mom?"

"He's been really great, especially since my father and Tate died."

"Are you doing okay? I mean about your father."

"He never liked me, ya' know, because of the Zara brothers," Angelo said.

"Sorry, Angelo. Let's just spend the night dancing."

"Alley Oop" by the Hollywood Argyles came on.

"Cool, but not to this," Angelo said.

Angelo and Liz made their way back to the Weepers' corner of the room where two Popeyes were waiting.

"Angelo," one of the Popeyes said. "Are you guys thinking about taking over the projects now that the Knights are gone?"

"No, we're just stickin' with the Cherry Street Park and our storefront club."

"So, no problems with our guys moving in?"

"Not from us," Angelo said. "But you should check with the Roosevelt Street Boys. They took over the old Knights' club at Ten Catherine Slip."

"Yeah. Good advice," the Popeye said. "Will do. Thanks."

Chapter Thirty-Five

"I'm here to kill you"

G iven Rico's warning about Declan planning a hit on Nunzio, Pepe spent the last several nights with Nunzio at the Drake. Nunzio preferred being alone, but he appreciated his old friend's devotion to him. Pepe woke up each morning before Nunzio and had a pot of coffee and some pastries delivered to the suite.

Nunzio would shower, have a quick cup of coffee and a bite with Pepe, and then they would either have breakfast in the lobby or head directly to the Caffè Fiora. Today, Nunzio suggested they have breakfast downstairs. Pepe opened the door, and there stood Declan Ardan.

"I was just about to knock," Declan pushed his way into the suite. Four men with guns, and one man without a gun, followed him inside.

"De, it looks like you finally get to see me," Nunzio said.

"You wouldn't even talk to me," Declan said.

"Talk to me now."

"Too late, Nunzio, my old friend."

"We were never friends, De. So, what is this all about?"

"I'm here to kill you," Declan said.

"Why, De...I didn't think you had it in you." Nunzio smiled.

"Not me personally. These are my guys from Hell's Kitchen, and their leader is this guy, Tommy Sullivan." De grabbed the arm of the unarmed man and pulled him forward. "And you know what, Nunzio? He does what I tell him to do. Me. Not you. Me."

"De, you seem angry. Tell me, did you have my friend Mr. Clarke killed?"

"I told them to kill the deputy mayor and they did."

"That was too bad. He was with us. You would have won. You would've been mayor."

"I still will. I'm taking your advice," Declan said. "You're number two on my list of the four people to kill."

"I told you, De, it's not the killing; it's knowing who the right four people are. And Clarke was not one of them. That was a mistake."

"Sorry about that, Mr. Sabino," Tommy Sullivan said. "Declan said you wanted the deputy mayor killed. I should've known better; I remember he helped you with the Brooklyn Bridge project. I should've called you."

"You should've, but I understand, Tommy," Nunzio said. "I've known Declan all my life and trusted his advice more than I should've."

"I hope you're not pissed at me, Mr. Sabino?"

"We're good, Tommy."

"What's going on?" Declan said. "You guys know each other?"

"We're old friends, De."

"Thanks, Mr. Sabino. Like I said back in '57, I always want you to think of me as a friend. Hey, you still got that gold lighter?"

"I still have the lighter and I do consider you a friend," Nunzio said. "You boys want some coffee and pastries?"

"Thanks, but we better get going," Tommy said. "We'll take care of Declan, unless you want to."

"Whadaya have planned?" Nunzio asked.

"We have a woodchipper facing the river on an enclosed pier in Hell's Kitchen," Tommy said. "I wouldn't eat any seafood for the next week or so."

"I always wondered about that in the movies," Nunzio said. "Can you put a whole guy into a woodchipper?"

"Nah, we tried that once, years ago, when we were first starting out. We put this guy in feet first; the damned chipper jammed. We had to rip the guy out. He was screaming and flopping around on the dock like a fish while we tried to unjam the chipper. No luck. We finally pushed him and the chipper into the river. After that, we bought a chain saw. Now we cut the guy up first. You know, legs and arms off, then cut the body in quarters, and the head separate."

"Wait, please, Nunzio! Don't let them do this!" Declan was shivering and crying. He dropped to the floor into a sitting position, his pants were urine soaked, and he threw up on himself. "Nunzio, p-p-please, let's s-star-start over. We grew up together. Oh, geez, p-please."

"Rich guys never know how to die," Tommy said.

"They never do," agreed Nunzio.

"We could do this quick with a bullet to the head. You give us a hard time down to the car, it's the woodchipper," Tommy said. The men and Declan left Nunzio's suite.

"Let's go have that breakfast, Pepe," Nunzio said.

* * *

Nunzio and Pepe sat at a table in the Drake's dining room and enjoyed Swiss omelets and coffee. The morning paper announced that Maris had beaten Mantle for the American League MVP Award.

"Look at that. Roger Maris won by only three votes and I had Maris against the odds," Nunzio said. "This is a good day, my friend."

"It is, Boss, but for a better reason than you won on your MVP bet."

"You're right. As you said, Tommy came through."

"Tommy promised me."

"You trusted him."

"I did, Boss."

"You're a good friend, Pepe," Nunzio said.

"I owe you my life, Boss."

Chapter Thirty-Six

"This ain't a great street"

Angelo and his mother walked along Orchard Street. His mom had purchased a blue blazer and gray pants for Angelo to wear on his November Affair date with Joni. It was dusk, and they turned left on Hester Street. "He'll Have to Go," "Cathy's Clown," and "Running Bear" created a cacophony of music mixed with shouts and arguments from several windows. Angelo tasted death and the putrid smell of urine as they walked along Hester Street. Smoke was coming from a burning garbage can, and the carcass of an animal too chewed up to recognize was draped over the curb.

"Ma, where ya goin?" Angelo was carrying his new jacket and pants on a paper-covered hanger over his shoulder. "This is Hester, not Canal Street."

"My head's somewhere else."

"You thinkin' about Father Cas?"

"What?" Angelo's mother said. "Why would you think that?"

"Come on, Ma."

"Is it that obvious?"

"Oh, yeah, but it's cool," Angelo said. "This ain't a great street, Ma. We should turn around and head back to Orchard."

"It'll be fine. We'll just turn at Seward Park."

As they approached Ludlow Street, two men stepped out of the shadows to block them.

"Where you goin'?" one thug said. "Grab the kid's suit, Benny."

"You check the kid, I'm gonna check out the doll." Benny pulled out a knife.

"Don't you touch my mother," Angelo roared.

"What are you gonna do, punk?" the thug gave Angelo a quick punch on the tip of his nose, which knocked him against several trash cans. The thug grabbed the hanger with Angelo's jacket and pants.

Angelo shook his head clear and saw his mother pushed against a wall with Benny's hand on her throat and his other hand under her clothes.

"Leave her alone!" Angelo shouted. "I swear I will kill you assholes."

"Shut that kid up, Eddie." Benny said.

Eddie grabbed Angelo by his lapels and lifted him to his feet. He pushed Angelo hard against a lamppost.

A loud slap echoed along the narrow street. Angelo twisted towards his mother. Blood sprayed from his mother's face. He reached for Merlin, his knife. It wasn't there. He had left it home because he was going to try on clothes. And then he remembered the gun. He reached into his right coat pocket, grabbed his .38 Colt, and in one motion, jammed the gun under Eddie's chin and fired one shot. It was louder than Angelo thought it would be. His face and neck were suddenly wet. Angelo instinctively ran his tongue over his lips. The taste of Eddie's blood was salty, a bit sweet, and bitter. Benny froze as Eddie fell straight backwards, dead.

"What the hell was that?" someone shouted from a window.

"Sounded like a gunshot," a voice came from another window.

Benny took off running down Ludlow Street.

"I see you, Benny Vega," a woman shouted. "You got a gun now?"

Benny was quickly returned by two cops with guns drawn.

"That's Benny Vega," another window voice said. "He's bad news, Officer. Lock him up."

"Give me that gun, kid," one of the cops said to Angelo.

"It was his." Angelo pointed at Eddie, and handed the gun to the cop. "And that other guy has a knife."

"That wasn't my knife and I didn't know Eddie had a gun, and we was –"

"Shut up," the cop said to Benny. Then to Angelo and his mother, he said, "Are you two okay?"

"We're alive." Angelo's mother was staring at her son. "Thanks to my boy."

"I'm gonna walk this skell over to headquarters. They have a holding cell in the detective's room, and I'll get a meat wagon over here for the dead guy," one cop said. "You sure you don't need an ambulance?"

"No, we just wanna go home," said Anna.

"Are you from the neighborhood?" the cop asked.

"We are, officer. My brother, Frank Terenzio, used to be a cop."

"Your brother is Frankie? He's got a liquor store now, right?"

"He does. Lilly's on Catherine," Angelo's mother said.

"Okay, listen, give my partner your contact information and a statement. I'll send a radio car over here to take you home. Give my best to your brother. He was a great cop."

"I will. Thank you."

CHAPTER THIRTY-SEVEN

"He's gonna die tonight"

On their way home, Angelo's mom asked the police officer driving the radio car to drop them off at Lilly's. She needed to tell Frank what had happened. A black Cadillac was parked outside the liquor store. Angelo and his mom waved to Pepe, who was behind the wheel.

Frank poured four shots of bourbon. He and Nunzio listened with anger and concern. And when they finished, they all hugged in recognition of life so fragile in this neighborhood. Angelo and his mom walked out of Lilly's, and Nunzio followed.

"Angelo, I think you should come home," his mother said.

"Can I hang out at the club for a little while. I'll be home soon, I promise."

"Okay. Give me your clothes, and...I don't know. Just be careful."

"I will." Angelo kissed his mother and watched her walk away.

"Come sit in the car with me, *Gattino.*"

"Sure, Uncle Nunzio." They climbed into the backseat.

"That was smart tellin' the cop it was the dead man's gun. Good for you."

"Thanks."

"You killed a man tonight. How do you feel?"

"I feel good about it," Angelo said. "I know, I'm supposed to feel bad, or sad, or something. But I don't. I'm glad I killed him. I wish I would've killed the other guy, too. He had his hands all over my mom and slapped her really hard."

"Yeah, well, I got this," Uncle Nunzio said. "You probably saved your mother's life. I'm proud of you, kid."

"We're reading about Machiavelli in school," Angelo said. "He said that it's better to be feared than loved. Do you believe that?"

"He said it's *safer* to be feared than loved," said Nunzio. "And, no, I don't believe that. To be feared tastes like sulfur and steam; to be loved tastes like Sunday dinner with family. If I can't have both, I choose love."

"But if those guys had feared me, they wouldn't have attacked me and my mom."

"I would take a bullet for Father Joe," Nunzio said. "Not because I fear him but because I love him."

"It is the same reason I would take a bullet for you, Boss," Pepe said.

"Your mother is safe tonight because you love her, not because you fear her," Nunzio said.

"The Weepers are gonna wanna know all about what happened. I'm not sure what to tell them."

"Sleep on it," Nunzio said, "And listen, your mom is putting on a brave front for you, but she is still rattled about what happened. So, go home and be with her tonight. Your guys can wait 'til tomorrow."

"You're right. I will."

"You want a ride?"

"Sure, thanks, Uncle Nunzio."

* * *

After dropping Angelo at home, Nunzio told Pepe what had happened to Angelo and Anna while the Cadillac parked in front of the Caffè Fiora. Once inside, Pepe made several phone calls and then joined Nunzio at his table.

"Boss, Benny Vega is in a holding cell at police head-quarters."

"Benny assaulted my goddaughter. He dies tonight."

"I got the Sicario brothers over there. Let me take care of this."

"If you can make it look like a suicide, all the better. But not necessary, my friend."

* * *

Pepe and the Sicario brothers walked into the Madra Rue Saloon across the street from police headquarters and sat at a table for four. The waitress walked over and handed them menus.

"Good to see you, Pepe," she said.

"You too, Meg."

"Mr. Sabino called and said whatever you want is on him," Meg said. "I'm guessing champagne?"

"You have champagne?" Pepe asked.

"No, we have brisket. It's the special."

"Is it fatty?" Pepe asked. "I don't like it fatty."

"Some people do," Meg said. "Here's the secret: if you want it fatty you say wet brisket; if you want it lean, you say dry brisket. What'll it be, boys?"

"Three dry briskets, and three bottles of Ballantine," Pepe said.

"Neal will meet you in front of the men's room when you're ready," Meg said.

As the waitress walked away, three men walked in.

"Take any table boys. I'll be right with ya," Meg said to the new arrivals.

Two of the men sat at a table some distance from Pepe, and the third kept walking over to Pepe. The man handed Pepe a folded newspaper. "Take a look at this, my Italian friend. An Irish Catholic just became President of the United States."

"The country's in trouble now, Detective," Pepe said.

"Burgers all around?"

"We'll have whatever Pepe's havin', Meg."

"Not if it's on the arm," Meg said.

"Mr. Sabino will cover their table too, Meg," Pepe said.

"Okay with me. You guys want Ballantines with your brisket?"

"Sounds good." The detective joined his friends at their table.

"Who's Neal?" Tommaso asked Pepe.

"You'll meet Neal near the men's room," Pepe said. "So, here's the deal: Benny Vega is in a holding cell at police headquarters. Benny assaulted Mr. Sabino's goddaughter. He's gonna die tonight. There are three detectives on duty tonight in the room with the holding cell. They all just came in for dinner. There's a tunnel from this bar to police headquarters."

"A tunnel?" Tommaso said.

"Yeah. It was built around 1910, and it's still there. During Prohibition, the lower level of this bar was a speakeasy. It gave our friends in blue an easy way to enjoy a drink, and it still does."

"Oh! *è fantastico!*" Lorenzo said.

Pepe took a key from the folded newspaper, "This key is for Benny's cell. You two go through the tunnel and hit Benny Vega. If you can make it look like a suicide, good, but not necessary. Then come back through the tunnel to the bar and give me the key. I will put it in this envelope and return it to the detective."

Pepe removed an overstuffed envelope from his inside pocket and placed it on the table. "Any problems with the plan? Anything?"

"The other two detectives," Tommaso said. "They gotta be suspicious."

"They know," Pepe said. "They'll get a cut of the cash in the envelope."

"Where's the tunnel?" Tommaso asked.

"Neal will show you."

"How do we find the holding cell where they got Benny?" Tommaso asked.

"I have a map showing the best way in and out." Pepe handed the map to Tommaso. "What else?"

"When do we go?" Lorenzo asked.

"Right now."

Twenty minutes after the Sicario brothers left, they returned. Their brisket was still warm, and their beers were cold.

"Problems?" Pepe asked as they sat down.

"Benny hung himself in his cell," Lorenzo said. "No problems."

"Good." Pepe put the key in the envelope, the envelope back in the folded newspaper, and walked it over to the detectives.

CHAPTER THIRTY-EIGHT

"Can I call you Uncle Nunzio"

Johnny walked into Lilly's Liquor store and was greeted by Frank and Jokes.

"Let's have a drink," Johnny said.

Frank poured whiskey for Johnny, Jokes, and himself.

"That bad a day?" Jokes asked.

"It will be," Johnny said.

"What's up, Johnny?" asked Frank.

When they were seated, Johnny handed Frank a folder.

"What's this?" Frank asked.

"Where's Heather?" Johnny said.

"Good question. She was supposed to meet me here 20 minutes ago," Frank said. "What's this folder, and why are you asking about Heather?"

"Fuck, Frank, just open it."

Frank opened the folder, looked through it briefly and held up a photo. "This is a picture of Heather."

"It's a picture of Angie Zara. I'm so sorry, Frank."

Frank looked at the photo and then back at Johnny. "This can't be right. There has to be some mistake. Let's go over and talk to her. Now," Frank said. "I have a key for her apartment, and we can look around if she's not there. You got the store, Jokes?"

"I got it. G'head."

Frank and Johnny rushed out of Lilly's. When they got to Heather's apartment, they found it empty. No Heather, no clothes, nothing. Heather was gone.

"Is her phone still working?" Johnny said.

Frank picked it up and there was a dial tone. "Yeah."

"Call Nunzio, Frank. He's one of her targets."

Frank dialed the Caffè Fiora. "Natale, tell Nunzio that if Heather shows up there, she's there to kill him." Frank was still. He stared at the emptiness before him. He hung up the phone and headed to the door.

"What's goin' on Frankie?"

"She's there now."

*　*　*

Natale dropped the phone.

Heather was overwhelmed. The questions were getting too close to her. She had to rush to kill Nunzio but would forget about Anna's family. Then get out of the country fast. She knew this was a risk that had to be taken if she wanted any chance to kill Nunzio. Heather walked toward Nunzio's table.

Nunzio stood up, opened his arms and smiled. "Heather, good to see you."

Heather smiled, "Can I call you Uncle Nunzio?"

Natale was dashing across the room.

Heather pulled her Beretta out of her coat pocket and pointed it at Nunzio. "For my family."

Natale jumped on a table and flew towards Nunzio.

Nunzio was knocked back by Natale's body slamming against his.

Heather fired three quick shots. Two hit Natale's back, one hit Nunzio's shoulder. Heather fired three more shots at Nunzio's men, who rushed towards her. Arturo, the waiter, threw a chair at Heather, knocking her against another table and causing her to drop her gun.

The shots Pepe had fired missed Heather as she fell to the floor. Heather got up. She scrambled for the door. Rico was behind the wheel of her car, waiting. Heather jumped into the shotgun seat as her Chevy screeched down Grand Street.

* * *

Inside the Caffè, Pepe, the cook, and Arturo rushed to Nunzio. He ordered them to take care of Natale first. Natale moaned, face down on the floor. The cook stayed with Nunzio. He removed Nunzio's shirt and started to stanch the bleeding with a napkin.

Pepe carefully cut the back of Natale's blouse open. Blood was everywhere. With the help of Arturo, Pepe managed to slow Natale's bleeding. He covered her wounds with clean cloths, then placed a couple of folded towels under her head and covered her with a tablecloth.

Pepe then turned his attention to Nunzio. The cook had wrapped a cloth around Nunzio's shoulder.

"Natale?" Nunzio asked.

"I don't know, Boss. An ambulance is on its way."

"Did Heather get away?"

"We got three cars chasing her," Pepe said. "Boss, Rico was her getaway driver."

"Rico? Son of a bitch. Rico."

"Papa," Natale said, and then was silent.

* * *

One member of the ambulance team leaned over Nunzio, bandaging his left arm, and placing it in a sling. Two other team members worked on Natale. They stopped and stood up. One of them gently put a clean white cloth over her face and shook his head.

"The bullet passed right through you, Mr. Sabino," said the ambulance driver. "I gave you something for the pain, which will make you sleepy. We suggest you come to the hospital or, at least, see your doctor. But you should be fine. Just take it –"

"Natale?" Nunzio asked.

"I'm sorry, Mr. Sabino. One of the bullets pierced her heart. She's gone, sir."

Nunzio went vacant. Tears streamed down his face.

***

Nunzio was lying on a couch in the lower level of the caffè. The pain medication had taken effect and he was drifting in and out of consciousness.

Nunzio slurred as he asked for Pepe.

"I'm right with you, Boss."

"Did they get her?"

"She boarded the TWA flight to London before we could grab her."

"Get on the phone with the Camorra. Tell them to –"

"Already done, Boss. They will be waiting for her at the London Airport."

"Pepe, she killed my Natale...."

CHAPTER THIRTY-NINE
"Somehow, she vanished"

A dozen British police officers were at London Airport waiting for the TWA flight from New York. Several members of the Camorra also were at the gate waiting for the plane. Officers surrounded the plane on the tarmac after it landed and radioed the pilot to open the door. Five officers boarded the plane before anyone got off. They waited in the front of the plane as the passengers gathered their things. The officers checked every passenger as they exited the plane. Identifications were required. Facial features examined. Heather could be disguised. The police searched everywhere and everything. Heather could not be found.

One of the Camorra filmed each passenger as they got off the plane and entered the terminal. He needed to examine the film closely as soon as he could.

The police promised to stay at the London Airport for another 24 hours. The Camorra would also stay just in case something turned up. One of the Camorra bosses called the Caffè Fiora.

* * *

"Don't make me tell Mr. Sabino you lost her," Pepe said into the phone. "He's resting with pain medication, but when he wakes up, I must give him some hope. Something."

Nunzio slept through the night on a couch in the lower level of Caffè Fiora. In his dreams, he was an eight-foot, 500-pound muscular lion with a red mane. A light rain obscured Natale waving to him in the distance. He started to walk toward her. She waved both hands and gestured for him to stay. He stopped. The air carried the sent of rubbing alcohol and the salty, saccharine smell of death. He was surrounded by snares, pits, and traps with steel teeth. He sniffed the ground but was unable to locate the hazards.

A small fox approached him and crawled between his front legs. The fox was Angelo darting across Catherine Street, risking his life to save Nunzio from certain death three years ago. Now the fox was Pepe, who zigzagged through time and the labyrinth of traps, leading Nunzio to safety. Now Natale was shouting and running to him. Wolves appeared out of the mist behind her. Nunzio rushed toward her. The wolves were upon her. Nunzio's roar rattled the earth and frightened the wolves away, but they dragged Natale with them. She screamed, "Papa!" He rushed into the fog. They were gone.

He woke up late morning, drenched in anguish and wrath. He glared at himself in the bathroom mirror. He looked old. Nunzio squeezed his eyes shut and saw the dead horse against the curb on Pike Street. He opened his eyes, shook his head, and washed himself carefully, avoiding his wounds. Then Nunzio came up to the dining room and sat at his table. Pepe brought him a glass of water and signaled a waiter to bring Nunzio coffee and biscotti.

"My Natale's gone, isn't she?"

"She is, Boss."

"Any word on Heather?" Nunzio asked.

"They examined the film they shot at the airport, over and over," Pepe said. "They questioned everyone who might have seen Heather on the plane. They did see her. She was on the plane when it took off. She could not have parachuted out of it. Somehow, she vanished. The one thing I'm sure of is someone helped her."

Vincent brought a pot of coffee and biscotti to Nunzio and Pepe.

"I think it's time for me and the Sicario brothers to have a talk with Rico," Pepe said. "I know you like him, but he was Heather's getaway driver. I think he knows a lot."

"I'm through with him, Pepe. Find him. Get everything you can outta him, any way you need to. And then, end him."

"Will do, Boss."

"How's Frankie doin'? He's gotta be hurtin.' She broke the heart of his whole family."

"She did," Pepe said. "Frank and Anna stopped by while you were sleepin.' They said to call when you woke up. They're broken up about Natale. You want me to give Frank a call?"

"Yeah, make sure he's okay."

"Will do, Boss."

* * *

Frank, Anna, Pomp, and Father Joe were in Lilly's when the phone rang.

"Pepe, thanks for calling," Frank said. "Anna, Pomp, and Father Joe are here with me. How's Nunzio doing? ...

Ah, good. Tell him how sorry we are, and that we love him ... I know ... I know ... Natale is in our prayers .... Father Joe and Pomp just walked out the door. They're on their way over. Anna and I will come by later." Frank hung up.

"How are you doin' Frankie?" Anna asked. "You know none of this is your fault, right?"

"It's a little bit my fault. I'm this great ex-cop and I missed every damn clue she gave me. You picked up on how Heather knew Rico wasn't in Mussels and Mugs that night. I blew it off. Johnny picked up on the crap about her dead 101st Airborne husband. I blew it off. I blew it all off."

"You were in love, Frankie. And she is one of the best con men I've ever seen. We all wanted to like her. She had all of us fooled. Know what I think? I think maybe she really loved you."

"Yeah. What a sap I was."

"You're no sap."

"Geez, Sis. Here I am feeling sad about her screwing me over, and she shot Nunzio and murdered Natale. I need to knock it off and grow up."

"Nunzio has greater reason for his pain, but that doesn't reduce yours, Frankie, or mine."

"Do you believe that saying? What is it? What doesn't kill you makes you stronger?"

"No. I never liked that," Anna said. "I think that which doesn't kill you makes you a bit more wary, a little more fragile, and a touch harder."

"You're right," Frank said, looking defeated.

"Where do you think she is?"

"No clue. But there are a lot of angry guys lookin' for her."

CHAPTER FORTY

"I know it's never good to meet them"

It was a brisk night in Brewster, New York. The Sunshine Diner on Oak Street was closed. Pepe looked through the locked glass doors. One workman sat in a booth drinking coffee. Rico was wiping down the counter. Pepe banged on the door. Rico squinted toward Pepe then came around the counter and opened the door.

Pepe and the Sicario brothers walked in. Pepe locked the door. A large sign leaned sideways against the counter. The sign read, "Rico's Diner." The middle-aged working man started to get up. Pepe held up his hand and told the man to sit and stay. The man sat back down.

"You're changing the name of the diner?" Pepe asked.

"Yeah, my guy there is gonna hang the new sign tonight. I think my customers will be surprised tomorrow."

"Oh, they will be surprised," Pepe said.

"Pepe, I know if you're here, this must be important," Rico said.

"It's a matter of life and death," Pepe said.

"Is Nunzio, I mean, Mr. Sabino, okay?"

"Cut the shit. We know you drove Heather to the airport," Pepe said. "Do you know the Sicario brothers?"

"Only by reputation. And I know it's never good to meet them."

"Well, this is Tommaso and his brother, Lorenzo. Now you've met them. Soon you will know them."

"Please, let's just have a cup of coffee and talk. Please."

"We're gonna talk," Pepe said. "First, take all the money out of your pockets and the cash register and give it to your guy sitting over there."

Rico did as he was told.

"Now make some coffee. We're gonna talk and you're gonna tell us everything you know about Heather Potter. Everything."

"Sure, right, okay. But I don't know much."

Pepe hung his head for a moment, then looked into Rico's eyes. "I'm gonna let this be your one free pass." Pepe's face was inches from Rico's. "But, from now on every time I don't believe you, one of my associates here will remove a piece of you. It is also up to you if your wife lives or dies tonight. Do you understand?"

"Please, she's pregnant. Please."

"Do you understand?"

"I understand."

"Good. Make the coffee while you tell us about Heather."

Rico stepped behind the counter to the coffee machine with Lorenzo Sicario by his side. When the coffee was ready, Rico carried the pot and cups to the booth where Pepe and Tommaso were waiting for them. Rico poured the coffee and started talking.

"A few months ago, a man followed me into the East Harlem Diner. I like being alone there, ya know, having a quiet dinner away from the neighborhood. Anyway, he sat in my booth and said he represented Heather Potter, who you now know is Angie Zara." Rico said. "He told me she was coming here to kill Nunzio, Mac, and Anna's family. He offered me $10,000 in cash to pick her up at the airport and be her only contact. He gave me another ten grand to get her an apartment, a not-so-fancy car, and anything else she might need. He told me that if she made it back to London, I would get a $25,000 bonus. He set up a wire account for me at the London-American Bank on Canal Street. He said she would only be here a week or so. But if it was longer, I would get $2,000 every week until she left."

"Where'd she get all the money?" Pepe said.

"She has a very rich old man who paid for everything."

"Why put his wife in danger? He could've hired torpedoes right here for that kind of money?" Tommaso asked.

"Heather insisted. She wanted to do it herself. She didn't even want bodyguards. She just wanted me."

"Why you?" Pepe asked.

"Her two brothers—the ones who Mac killed—started Satan's Knights with my brother, back in the day. She wanted it to be payback from the Knights and her."

"Why did she want to kill Anna's family?" Pepe said.

"Heather said she wanted Anna to feel the pain she did when Mr. Sabino had her family killed."

"But she didn't kill the family," Pepe said. "And she stayed longer than a couple of weeks."

"Heather fell in love with Frank. She even wondered about marrying him."

"What about her rich husband?"

"Yeah, she said she would have to go home and kill him first, and then come back."

"What's her husband's name?"

"Phillip."

"Phillip what?"

"Honest, she never told me. She would just say, 'Phillip wants me to come home.' Oh, yeah, he has a boat. Heather said he was having his 50th birthday party on the yacht, and he wanted her to be there with him."

"Where's the boat?"

"No idea."

"Where do you think she is?"

"London. She flew to London."

"We know that."

"She likes having a separate contact. But only one. That's why she was killing my Knights because they knew who she was. So my guess is she had a contact waiting.... Wait, hold on. When I took her to the airport, I dropped her off. I parked and went to her gate to see if she needed help with anything. When I got there, she was talking, more like whispering, to one of the pilots. Or maybe he was the navigator, I don't know. There were three guys and four girls in TWA uniforms. She was talking to one of the guys."

"Could you hear them? Were they joking? Flirting?"

"I couldn't hear but they looked all business-like," Rico said. "Then your guys showed up, walking to the gate. Heather spotted them. She said something to the guy she was talking to and he hurried her out to the plane with the rest of the crew following slowly behind them. They boarded the plane before any passengers did. I cut out before I was spotted."

"Anything else you can remember?" Pepe said.

"That's it, I swear to God. That's all of it."

"I believe you." said Pepe.

"Is my wife safe?"

"Yeah."

"Will it be quick?"

Pepe nodded. "Go behind the counter and stand next to your cash register."

Rico cried as he walked to his death. He thought about Hector and Ernesto. He had blown it. He had stayed too long. All the plates he was spinning came crashing down. He stood very still.

Tommaso walked up to him on the other side of the counter. "Close your eyes tight and count out loud to five."

"One, two, thr –"

Tommaso's bullet hit Rico square in the forehead, knocking him straight back against a stack of dishes that shattered and flew in all directions. The seated workman screamed.

Pepe walked over to the workman. "Give me your wallet."

"Here, please don't kill me," the man said trembling as he fumbled in his pocket.

"Shhh, listen to me." Pepe looked through the man's wallet and then returned it to him. "We now know who you are and where you live."

Pepe leaned toward the frightened man, one hand resting on the table, the other on the seatback near the man's head. "Here is your story: two colored guys robbed the place and killed Rico. You were hiding under the table, so they didn't see you. That's why you still have your wallet. The money from the dead guy and the cash register is in your pocket. You call the police 20 minutes after we leave and tell them that. And you're richer and safe. You tell them anything else and we will find you. Do you understand?"

"Yes, I understand. Twenty minutes."

"Good."

CHAPTER FORTY-ONE

"Where the hell is Heather"

Detective Hartz, Frank, Jokes, and Johnny were having lunch around the table at Lilly's. They were talking about all that had happened in the last few months, and wondering where Heather was when Nunzio and Father Joe walked in.

"Nunzio, you got rid of the sling," Frank said.

"It was more trouble than help," Nunzio said.

"Speaking about help, help yourselves to heroes on the counter, and soda, coffee, beer, and anything else you might like. Come join us."

"Good idea," Father Joe said. "So, what's the topic?"

"All that has gone on these last few months," Frank said. "Where's Pepe?"

"Back at the Caffè. Me and Joe decided to walk over."

"Where the hell is Heather anyway?" Johnny asked.

"Given what Pepe found out, I figure she disguised herself as a stewardess," Frank said. "Cut and colored her hair in the bathroom, put on a uniform, flirted with the cops, and walked away."

"I don't know. You'd have four stewardesses getting on the plane and five getting off?" Hartz said.

"Or she swapped with a stewardess," Frank said. "So, four on and four off."

"I'd love to see the film that was taken," Hartz said.

The phone rang and Frank answered it.

"Nunzio, it's Pepe."

"What's up?" Nunzio said into the phone. A pause. "Okay, thanks for the call."

"Everything okay?" Frank asked.

"Everything's good," Nunzio said. "You mean what you said about watching the film, Hartz?"

"I did."

"Pepe said the film just arrived, airmail express, whatever that is. I have a projector in the lower club level. Who can come?"

"Jokes, can you watch the store?"

"Like always, I got it, Frankie," Jokes said. "The rest of you guys should go."

"Let's say 4:00 pm." Nunzio said.

* * *

At 4 o'clock on the dot, they all gathered in the club level of the Caffè Fiora. There were drinks, including a couple of bottles of Chivas Regal, and a spread of food. A large screen was set up in front of a long table, so everyone seated would be facing it. One of Nunzio's guys owned the projector and would operate it.

The film began after everyone got a plate of food, drinks, and sat down. The whole film lasted an hour and a half.

"Let's watch it again," Hartz said.

The film played a second time.

"Nothing jumps out to me," Father Joe said. "It looks like the same crew members got on and got off."

"I agree," Pepe said. "Even the pilots, the ones Rico told me about. Nothing suspicious."

"Something's wrong," Hartz said. "It's like I can walk into a diner and sense something seems off. Can I see it again? Not the whole thing, just the part when the crew gets off the plane."

"Sure."

Hartz leaned across the table, staring hard as the scene replayed. "Okay...okay...wait...wait... Go back...a little more...stop there. Okay, go forward ... good ... okay ... bingo. It's the copilot."

"What?" Johnny said.

"Whadaya see, Hartz?" Frank asked.

"Show us," Nunzio said.

"Okay, go back to the crew getting off the plane," Hartz said. "There are three guys and four women. They each have a shoulder bag and are pulling a small suitcase on a wheel cart."

"Got it," Johnny said.

"Now we lose them for a couple of seconds when the truck passes in front of the camera, okay?"

"You think the truck did that on purpose?" Nunzio said.

"No, no, it didn't even know anyone was filming. It just drove past," Hartz said. "But go back to just before the truck blocks the camera. Okay, notice that small flatbed vehicle parked close to the crew. It has nothing on its bed."

"Got it," Johnny said.

"In the distance is a private plane. See it?"

"Yeah," Pepe said.

"Right now, the copilot has a shoulder bag and is pulling a small suitcase, right? See it?"

"Yeah, got it," Johnny said.

"Okay, so the truck passes and we can see the crew walking into the terminal. They all have their shoulder bags and suitcases, except the copilot. He just has his shoulder bag. Go back a couple of frames, before they get to the terminal. See the flatbed? Moving toward the private plane? Now it has a small suitcase and wheeled cart turned upside down on it."

"How do you know he's the copilot?" Father Joe asked.

"The older guy with the same wings has more sleeve stripes, so I figure he's the pilot. The other guy has different wings so I'm guessing navigator, which leaves the copilot."

"Cool," Pepe said.

"So, the copilot put his suitcase on the flatbed," Johnny said. "The flatbed takes the suitcase to a private plane. It's like a drug deal. How do we tie this to Heather?"

"The copilot's suitcase looks just like the other crew members' because they are new and supplied by TWA, with the logo prominent," Hartz said. "Except, his suitcase has a couple of holes in it."

"So does mine," Father Joe said. "So, what's in the suitcase? Is there money or drugs or what?"

"Hold on," Frank said. "Heather told me her stepfather beat her and her mother with a belt when he was drunk. Heather would scrunch up and hide under their sink."

"And what was in the copilot's small suitcase, Frank?" Hartz said.

"Not what, who," Frank said. "Heather was in the suitcase. That's why the holes."

"Bingo," Hartz said.

A stunned silence hung over the room.

"So now we need to find out who, and where, this copilot is," Nunzio said slapping his hand on the table as he stood up.

"That's what my security firm does," Johnny said. "I got this."

"Brilliant detective work, Hartz," Frank said. "Best I've ever seen."

"Does that mean we can open the Chivas Regal now?" Hartz smiled.

CHAPTER FORTY-TWO

"The next time I see her, I'll kill her"

The Thanksgiving dance at the Cherry Street Settlement found Father Cas and Anna dancing together to "My Heart has a Mind of its Own" by Connie Francis. Father Joe could only smile. Nunzio, Hartz, Frank, Pomp, and Danny were hanging out at the adult table and talking about Danny's first month as an NYPD cop. Most of the teens in attendance were dancing, joking, and enjoying the huge Thanksgiving spread provided by Nunzio. Angelo danced with Liz, and they stayed on the dance floor when "Only the Lonely" by Roy Orbison came on.

"How was the November Affair with Joni?" Liz asked.

"It was fine."

"Did you tell her about you shooting that guy?"

"Not a chance. Her father hardly lets her see me now."

"You need a neighborhood girl, Angelo. Did you talk to Marie?"

"I told you, she is way outta my league."

"And I told you to give it a shot."

"And I'm dancing with the prettiest girl in the neighborhood. So why are we talkin' about other girls?"

"I got nothin' to say to that except you have good taste. Hey, your Uncle Johnny just walked in. Talk about cool, he's really cool."

"Yeah, he is."

* * *

Johnny walked over to the adult table and asked that the guys who watched the airport film step out. Once they were outside, Johnny handed each guy a folder.

"In those folders is the following information," Johnny said. "The copilot is Blake Dickenson. He lives in London, and you'll see that his address and biography are in there. He did this for money. He has done other jobs for Heather's husband. Her husband's name is Phillip Borovkov, a Russian and part of the Russian aristocracy. He should not be underestimated. He lives on his two-hundred -foot yacht with a twelve-man crew and bodyguards. He has an ex-wife and two adult children living in Spain. I don't know where his yacht is right now."

"Just before coming over here tonight, I got a call from Heather," Frank said. Everyone looked up from their folders and zeroed in on Frank.

"What did she say?" asked Johnny.

"She said she loved me and maybe we could be together."

"What did you say?" Nunzio asked.

"I said the next time I see her, I'd kill her. But here's the thing. In the background, I could hear some men talking in— What's that language?—Afrikaans, I think."

"South Africa," Johnny said. "I can take care of this."

"No. She killed my Natale," Nunzio said. "This is for me. Her husband is Russian, you said?"

"Yeah, Russian," Johnny said.

* * *

The next morning over breakfast with Pepe at the Drake, Nunzio went through the folder more closely.

"Pepe, set up a meeting for me with Boris Anoushka at his club in Brighton Beach as soon as you can," Nunzio said.

"Will do, Boss," Pepe said. "But me and the Sicario brothers need to be with you."

"Good idea, Pepe."

* * *

Pepe pulled up in front of the Café Alexander on Neptune Avenue in Brighton Beach and rolled down his window. Two large men walked to the Cadillac and looked inside.

"Mr. Sabino, welcome to the Café Alexander," one of them said. "I'm Vlad, but most people call me Bill, and this is Sergei. I'll take you and your men to Mr. Anoushka's private dining room. Sergei will take charge of your car if you allow."

The grand interior of Alexander's was stunning. White walls with red drapes trimmed in gold surrounded the room. White tablecloths, beautiful flower arrangements, and red linen napkins covered the tables in the main dining room.

Boris Anoushka's private dining room was also his office. It was a large room with hints of the main dining room, but with more wood and less gold. A serpentine mahogany executive desk rested in the center of a huge bay window. On one side of the room was a long dining table. The rest of the room was filled with comfortable stuffed leather chairs. At each chair was a side table with a plate, and two glasses. One glass had water, the other was empty.

Upon a mahogany serving table were crepes with red caviar, shrimp cocktails, burrata with oranges, Greek salad, puff pastry with cheese and meat, filet mignon kababs, and a bowl of fruit. There was also coffee, tea, Coca-Cola, cranberry juice, and assorted pastries.

Boris stood in the middle of the room with his arms apart and a smile on his face. Attractive women stood to either side of him.

"My dear friend, Mr. Sabino, welcome," Boris said.

"My dear friend, Mr. Anoushka, thank you," Nunzio said.

"Unless you prefer to sit at the table, I thought we could sit around this room, eat, drink, and talk like brothers."

"Excellent," Nunzio said.

"This is Krista. She will bring you food. And this is Alexandra. She will bring you vodka, or whatever you wish to drink," Boris said. "Everyone, please be seated. Bill, you stay."

Krista and Alexandra circulated with plates of food and Russian Standard Vodka as the men got comfortable in the chairs.

"You know, Nunzio, you never need your guys for protection when you come to see me," Boris said.

"They're not for my protection," Nunzio said. "They are the light in my closet."

"Nice, in Russian we would say, *svet v moyem shkafu* – same thing," Boris said. "Pepe sent a folder over with the information about Phillip Borovkov, so I could be better prepared for this lovely meeting. I am so sorry about your daughter, Natale, my friend."

"Thank you."

"It is a difficult situation, you understand. We have different countries, different governments, different politics."

"I do not agree, my friend. We – you and I – are bigger than our countries. Our governments want power, money, control. They are all just corrupt business models. Capitalism, Communism, whatever. They have the power to pass laws that make what they do legal. They can do whatever they want," Nunzio said. "No, I don't agree. If I needed something, I would come to you before I would go to my senator. With you, I can make a mutually beneficial deal and know you will honor it. With my senator, I must give him money to get what I want and he might not honor our deal. No, my friend, we are stronger and more honorable than our countries."

Boris was quiet for a moment and then nodded. "Okay, the man you are interested in, Phillip Borovkov, is very rich and connected to the Russian aristocracy. He is married to Heather Potter, he calls her *Lapochka*. He owns a yacht named *Oodovolstvie*. It means pleasure. He is presently off the coast of South Africa. He will be having a big party on his boat in two weeks. It's his 50th birthday."

"What's the hard part?" Nunzio said.

"The hit would not be hard. I can do that. No problem," Boris said. "The blow-back would be the hard part."

"Tell me."

"There are four countries with people who could get angry: Russia, China, South Africa, and Italy. I can take care of those in Russia and South Africa with my contacts. I assume you can quiet the Camorra in Italy and the Mafia in Sicily. Borovkov has connections in both organizations."

"Not a problem," Nunzio said. "Tell me about China."

"China could be a problem. Borovkov is an arrogant asshole, but the Chinese government loves him. I'll have trouble with the Russians if I can't say the Chinese will look the other way."

"Okay, I'll deliver the Chinese," Nunzio said. "What else?"

"If you can do that, it's a go from my end."

Nunzio nodded. "Now, what can I do for you?"

"As you know, I control one-fourth of Brighton Beach. The Italians control the rest, and they control Manhattan Beach, Coney Island, everything else. I pay the Italians 15 percent of my end," Boris said. "I want all of Brighton Beach, from Corbin Place to Ocean Parkway, from the ocean to Shore Parkway. All of it. That will still leave the Italians all the rest — Manhattan, Coney, the rest."

"That's a lot."

"I will pay them 15 percent of the whole thing."

"You will pay them 25 percent of the whole thing," said Nunzio.

"Twenty percent."

"Done."

"Good," Boris said. "Let me know when you have the Chinese and I'll finish it."

CHAPTER FORTY-THREE

"Black Tiger Tea"

The next afternoon, Nunzio and Pepe walked along Mott Street to the Hào chī Diner. They sat side by side in a red faux-leather booth for six.

"Gentlemen welcome. Do you need menus?" a waiter asked.

"No, I would like to have black tiger tea with Mr. Lĭngdǎo Sēnlín," Nunzio said.

"I will have a cup of black tea and two almond cookies," Pepe said.

The waiter vanished and a young man returned with a pot of black tea, two cups, and six almond cookies.

"I am Rĕn Sēnlín, Mr. Sēnlín's grandson. He is resting and will not be able to join you. Please enjoy your tea and cookies."

"Is your grandfather ill?" asked Nunzio.

"No. He is simply resting. Whatever you want to say to him, you can say to me, and I will pass it along."

"Do you know who I am?"

"You are Nunzio Sabino and your friend's name, I believe, is Pepe."

"Did you tell your grandfather that I wanted to talk with him?"

"No. I will not trouble him. You may talk to me."

"This is a most important matter. Please tell your grandfather I wish to have black tiger tea with him. Not with his grandson. With him."

"This is not Little Italy, Mr. Sabino. You have no power here. My family has the power in Chinatown. If you don't want to talk with me, then talk to each other. Enjoy your tea and cookies. They are on the house." The young man bowed slightly and walked away.

"May I kill him, Boss?"

"Let's go, Pepe."

Nunzio and Pepe slid out of the booth, left the diner, and walked back to the Caffè Fiora in silence. Once inside, Pepe poured two glasses of Chivas and sat down with Nunzio.

"How much do we close down and when?" Pepe asked.

"This is a win for us, Pepe."

"A win?"

"His grandfather will want to do me a favor because of the way we were treated by his grandson."

"But we must retaliate in some way, so the grandfather knows of the insult."

"Oh, we will, my friend. Close it all down," Nunzio said. "No deliveries, no garbage pickup, get a street repair on Mott Street in front of the Hào chī Diner with a lot of jackhammer noise. Close the street, no tourist buses, no parking. Nothing moves in Chinatown. Nowhere in Chinatown, starting now."

"I'm on it, Boss."

* * *

Mr. Sēnlín spent the next three days appeasing store owners, workers, and families, promising to get to the bottom of the shutdown. Chinatown was hurting. Finally, a waiter told him about the Nunzio incident with his grandson. Mr. Sēnlín was relieved to discover the source of the problem, but devastated to learn his grandson was the cause.

Mr. Sēnlín walked up Mott Street to Grand Street. His grandson walked behind him carrying a silver ceremonial tray. On it was a carved ceramic pot of hot black tea, four carved cups, as well as a plate of their finest appetizers and almond cookies. When they entered the Caffè Fiora, they stood silently at the door until Pepe saw them and escorted them to Nunzio's table.

The grandson stood at the table holding the silver tray. His grandfather placed the food and the teacups on the table and filled the teacups. The grandson placed the tray on its side against the wall and stood next to his grandfather in front of Nunzio.

Nunzio stood up. Mr. Sēnlín and his grandson bowed.

"Mr. Sabino. My sorrow for your daughter, and for your mistreatment by my family.

"Please sit. Pepe will join us."

"You came to me for black tiger tea," Mr. Sēnlín said. "As I explained to my feckless grandson, black tiger tea requests a life-or-death favor. I am here to apologize and to grant your favor if it is within my power."

"I accept your apology, but I don't know what I can offer in return."

"Your forgiveness for my family's insult is all I need in return. What may I have the honor of doing for you?"

"The person who killed my daughter is married to Phillip Borovkov, a wealthy Russian, whom I understand, is a friend of the Chinese government. I want to take my vengeance, but I don't want to anger the Chinese government."

"I know who this man is. He is not a friend; he is not even liked. But he does do business with many Chinese government officials and businessmen. I assure you they will not take notice. You are free to do as you please."

"Thank you," Nunzio said. "What can I do for you? Please, let me do something."

"If you would be so kind as to let me expand from Bayard Street up to Canal Street, I would be a hero in Chinatown."

"But not cross Canal. That will still be Italian. And you'll continue to pay 20 percent of it all."

"Agreed."

"Done," Nunzio said.

Mr. Sēnlín thanked Nunzio, and with his grandson walking behind him carrying the loaded tray, they headed back to Chinatown.

"Boss, what's black tiger tea?"

"There is a belief that if you drink tea made from the ground bones of a black tiger, you will gain super-strength or immortality."

"Why a black tiger?"

"There are no black tigers. They are like dragons. Me and Lǐngdǎo Sēnlín use black tiger tea as a life-and-death favor code."

"*Buono*, cool."

"Pepe, call Boris and tell him to go. Then end the strike in Chinatown."

"Will do, Boss."

"I gotta let the Camorra, Mafia, and our guys here and in Coney Island know about our deal."

"I already told them it would be coming. I'll make sure they all support you on this."

"Thank you, Pepe."

CHAPTER FORTY-FOUR

"You're under arrest for assault and battery, I think"

anny Terenzio, after little more than a month, already loved being a cop. The NYPD added a street experience experiment to their training. After a month, and qualifying with their firearms, the recruits would go out on the street for two weeks and then return for another month of training and evaluations.

Danny was working four to midnight for his two weeks. He spent his first couple of days in Central Park, then the South Bronx, and now on Manhattan's West Side. He loved it all. He walked with pride and a friendly demeanor, greeting neighborhood residents and sometimes receiving a nice response.

As Danny approached the end of the block, he saw a small crowd gathered in a circle, looking inward and shouting. His street sense told him there was a fight. He pushed his way through the outer perimeter to find a police sergeant kneeling over a middle-aged man on his back. His first instinct was to assist the sergeant.

"Sergeant, I'm Officer Terenzio. Can I help you?"

"Yeah, send this crowd home," the sergeant said.

"Okay everybody, break it up," Danny said. "Go home. We have this under control."

"Please, Officer, it's my father on the ground," a twenty -something girl said, "Please help him."

Danny turned to the sergeant and reached down. "Let me help you up, Sarge."

The sergeant punched the man on the ground. "You gonna pay me now?"

"I don't got the money. My bodega is not doing well, I swear. On Friday, I will borrow enough to pay you. I promise, I pay Friday." The man on the ground covered his bruised face with his hands.

"What the fuck?" Danny asked. "Sarge, what's goin' on here?"

"This guy's on the pad, but he's always late." The sergeant punched the man again. "Well, no more. Now he pays on time, like everyone else.

The man's face was bloody, his daughter was crying, and the crowd was angry and scared.

The daughter screamed and pleaded to leave her father alone.

"Sarge, don't hit him anymore," Danny said. "Get off him and let him up."

The sergeant looked at Danny. "You fuckin' rookie. You do what I tell you. Move the crowd away from me. Use your nightstick if you have to."

"Let him up, Sarge!"

The sergeant pulled his arm back for another punch, but Danny grabbed it. The sergeant pulled free and punched the man in his head.

With a singular motion, Danny firmly grabbed the sergeant's arm, lifting and twisting him sideways into the street. Danny pulled the sergeant's arms behind him and cuffed him. "You're under arrest for assault and battery, I think," Danny said. "On your feet."

"What the hell do you think you're doing, rookie? I will have your badge before you finish your fuckin' training."

"Does your father need an ambulance?" Danny asked the man's daughter, who was kneeling over her father.

"He said he will be fine," his daughter said, "and he doesn't want to press charges."

"No such thing as civilians pressing charges. That's only in the movies," Danny said. "I witnessed the assault and I'm making the arrest. Period."

"What's your name, Officer?" the girl asked.

"Danny Terenzio."

"Thank you, Danny."

As Danny walked away holding the cuffed sergeant by the arm, the crowd shouted *"Viva la Policía!"*

CHAPTER FORTY-FIVE

"You're all dead"

After walking a couple of blocks, Danny saw a radio car in front of A-Plus Car Rentals. "Maybe, we can bum a ride to the stationhouse, Sarge."

"You stupid fuck. Let me go now, and I'll forget all about this shit," the sergeant said.

"Officer," Danny said to the cop standing in the doorway of A-Plus Car Rentals. "Any chance we can get a ride to the stationhouse?"

"Sure thing. I'm almost finished here. What the.... Is the sergeant arrested?"

"He is."

"Ha! A rookie arrested a sergeant. Now I've seen it all. What did he do?"

"Kenney, don't encourage him. He's a rookie who doesn't know his ass from – "

"Assault and battery. I'm pretty new, so I think that's right," Danny said.

"What's your name, kid?" Kenney said.

"Danny Terenzio. What's goin' down here?"

"Well, see this fella?" Kenney pointed to the man in the suit standing inside the store. "He rented a car from A-Plus, and it looks like he returned it ten minutes late. Bruno won't give him back his driver's license unless he pays him another $50 in cash, which the suit doesn't have."

The three cops joined the man in the suit inside. They walked over to Bruno, who was standing in front of a small desk.

"Look, I'll make it easy for you. I'm a lawyer," the suit said to the cops. "Give me the guy's full name and I'll sue him and the company."

"What's your last name, Bruno?" Kenney said. "And where's Mr. Tiranno?"

"*Vaffanculo*, I ain't tellin' you nothin," Bruno said. "Mr. Tiranno is on an important call. Anyway, you can't come in here without a warrant."

"We don't need a warrant to walk into a place of business," Kenney said. "What's your whole name and where is this suit's license?"

"*Fanculo*," Bruno said.

"If I knew what you said, I'd probably be pissed off," Kenney said. "But I don't –"

"I know what he said," Danny said. "He called us fucking pigs."

Danny shoved his way past Bruno and grabbed the lawyer's license and rental contract that were on the desk. Bruno caught Danny's wrist with his large hand. Danny placed his other hand on top of Bruno's hand and twisted his arm in an Aikido move, sending painful rockets through Bruno's arm, shoulder, and neck. Bruno bent over in pain. Danny reached into Bruno's pocket with his left hand while still controlling Bruno with his right. He removed Bruno's wallet. Bruno tried to pull away. Danny undulated Bruno's arm and released him. Bruno yelped and collapsed in agony.

"I'm gonna kill you, cop," Bruno said. "I ain't just blowin'– "

Another man in a suit walked into the main business area from the backroom. "What's goin' on in here?" The man helped Bruno to his feet.

"Mr. Tiranno, these crazy cops just busted in here. That cop has my wallet, and the customer's driver's license and rental contract. He just took them and almost broke my arm."

"Ain't I paying you cops enough?" Tiranno asked, agitated.

"You ain't payin' me, pal," Kenney said. "And you ain't payin' Danny here, either."

"That's because you're too stupid to know what's good for you, Kenney. Yeah, I know who you are," Tiranno said. "But your sergeant here gets his share plus yours, asshole. Now, you *stronzo*, give me Bruno's wallet and the customer's contract and license, and get the fuck outta my store. And do it now! All youse guys. Now!"

Tiranno tried to pull the wallet out of Danny's hand. Danny shoved him over a chair and onto the floor. Bruno rushed toward Danny, who struck him in the throat, causing Bruno to gasp and drop to his knees. Tiranno got up and reached inside his jacket. Danny thought he might be going for a gun, drew his own revolver, and shoved it hard into Tiranno's forehead.

"I've killed men, *stronzo*. And it didn't bother me a bit. Not one fuckin' bit," Danny said. "So, if you got the balls to pull it, do it. Please. Fucking do it."

Tiranno put his hands in the air. "You're dead cop. I'm a made guy. Connected. You know what that means? It means you are fuckin' dead. No one in this precinct is gonna try to help you. Dead."

"Come on at me, you piece of shit," Danny said.

"Not just you. Your family, and you two cops with him." Tiranno said scrambling to his feet. "All youse guys."

"Now, hold on, Tiranno," the sergeant said. "You can't be threatening a –"

"Did you just threaten my family? And my fellow officers?" Danny asked.

"You're all dead," Tiranno said.

"There are three rules to threatening someone." Danny picked up the phone on the desk and dialed. "Do you know what they are?"

"That's my business phone," Tiranno said. "You can't use it."

"Hello, this is Danny. Is Pepe there?"

"Pepe? I know someone named Pepe," Tiranno said.

"Hello, Pepe, it's Danny...yeah...I'm lovin' bein' a cop, yeah...Is my uncle doin' okay? Good. So, there is this guy... Tiranno. He runs, right, A-Plus Rental, right. Anyway, he said he's going to kill me, my partner Kenney, and my whole family. Yeah, he said that. To me. He is right here standing next to me. I will put him on."

Danny handed the phone to Tiranno.

"It's for you."

"Hello, Pepe?" Tiranno said slowly into the phone. "Yes, I can hold for Mr. Sabino...Mr. Sabino, sir, I had no idea...no, sir... *Ho capito, signore* ...I am so sorry for what I said, sir...I swear, I had no idea...no sir...never...no sir... forgive me...thank you."

Tiranno hung up the phone, with a blanched face. He looked at Danny and bowed.

"We okay?" Danny said to Tiranno.

"Yes, sir, whatever you want. Keep the contract and license. No charge for the rental car. Whatever you want, Officer. My apologies."

"So, you're not going to kill my friends and family?" Danny smirked.

"No, please forgive my *commento stupido, no, mai.*"

After they left A-Plus, Kenney asked, "What are the three rules to threatening someone?"

"Know who they are; know who they know; and be prepared to die."

"Cool, but you're probably better off just killing them," Kenney said.

"Yeah, that's my view."

"You still want to arrest this sergeant? They're just gonna have a laugh, and then the detectives will cut him loose."

"One cop might think it was the right thing to do," Danny said. "That would make it worth the laughs and the what-not."

"Let's do it," Kenney said.

After turning over the sergeant to the detectives, Danny got back in the radio-car with Kenney.

"Where's your partner?" Danny said.

"I lost him six-months ago. I don't know who your rabbi is but thank him for me."

"And you haven't filled the seat yet?"

"Not yet, the guy I'm riding with today made a collar and is doing the paperwork right now. I want to show you something."

"What?"

Kenney pulled up in front of Martin & Sons. "See all these double-parked trucks? Go in there and say, 'Merry Christmas' to whoever is at the counter."

"Really?"

"Just do it."

Danny did it and returned. "They gave me this envelope."

"What's in it?"

Danny opened it and looked inside. "Money."

"How's it make you feel?"

"Not good," Danny said. "Look, Kenney, if you want this, I don't give a shit. But I don't."

"Good," Kenney said. "Go give it back."

Danny did and returned. "They were upset. They said they need to double park. I said 'Don't worry about it; we just don't want your money.'"

"Good. I wanted you to see how easy it is to get a little cash," Kenney said. "I don't give a shit if other cops take it. Politicians take bribes everyday to pass laws that the guy bribing them wants. They passed a law saying they can take it; they call it a 'contribution.' But if a cop takes a buck, it's a bribe. When politicians pass a law saying they can't take a bribe, then I'll give a shit about cops takin' money. For now, I don't want to be part of it. It makes me feel slimy. You know?"

"Yeah, I feel the same way. I don't want anyone owning me or what I do."

"Listen, if you wind up in this precinct, you can have a seat with me if you want one."

"I'd like that."

"I'll keep the seat open until we find out where you land," Kenney said. "You're gonna make a hell of a good cop, Danny."

CHAPTER FORTY-SIX

"Pine for past love and die"

Father Joe and Father Cas sat in a middle pew at Saint Joseph's church on Catherine Street.

"Cas, over these past three years I have come to know you and to love you," Father Joe said. "You are a good and compassionate young man."

"Thank you, Joe, I feel the same. But why are we –"

"I also love Anna as if she were my daughter. She has not had an easy life and deserves better."

"Joe, my affection...love...for Anna will never cause me to act upon it in any way contrary to my commitment to the church. I can assure you that –"

"My point, Cas, is that you two should be together. I can tell you're in love with each other. I think you should get married. I don't care if no one knows or if everyone knows. And you may leave the priesthood or stay while you're married. That's up to you. I will support you and remain your friend and mentor either way. God could not have made a more perfect couple than you and Anna. I have always believed in God's will over the church's doctrine. I ask you to give it some thought."

"I don't know if she feels the same way about me."

"From my observations, and probably those of everyone who knows you two, you guys are in love. So, how might you find out for yourself?"

"I've been waiting for her to say something first."

"You see her as Anna, she sees you as Cas and as a priest," Father Joe said. "The distance from you to her is shorter than the distance from her to you. You need to ask the question."

Father Cas smiled. "I will."

* * *

Heather Potter stood at the rail of Phillip's yacht, the *Oodovolstvie*, gazing at the western cape of South Africa. She saw white beaches and lush vineyards around Stellenbosch and Paarl, and the craggy cliffs at the Cape of Good Hope. The beauty of South Africa's shore was breathtaking as the sun was setting. But she was thinking about Frank, their long talks, making love, his kindness.

"Lapochka, what are you doing here?" Phillip was suddenly next to her. "Actually, I don't care. Get inside and join my birthday party."

"Mr. Borovkov," one of Phillip's men approached Phillip and spoke Afrikaans to him.

"What did he say?" Heather asked.

"Rico is dead and we should cut our bank connection," Phillip said. "We should cut anything that ties us to him. Now get inside and act like you're having a great time. It's my birthday. You know what they say here: pine for past love and die."

"Lovely, I'll be right in."

The last time she had spoken to Frank, she called him from shore, just to tell him she loved him. He said he would kill her but she knew he didn't mean it. He loved her. And after she killed Phillip - which must look like an accident — she would be a wealthy woman and she would marry Frank. They would have children and live in Paris or Athens...anywhere they wanted. And they would be gloriously happy.

* * *

On shore, Aidan Ambroos, a Dutch mercenary, and leader of a seven-man team, watched the 200-foot yacht through night-vision binoculars. He confirmed the name, *Oodovolstvie*. He shifted the binoculars to the nearby dock. He watched the three men guarding the Royal Rover runabout that took guests to and from the yacht. Two of the men stayed on shore and the third drove the runabout.

It was quiet, and all three men sat in the runabout smoking and drinking and talking a little too loudly. They didn't hear the mercenary team approach. *Thub, thub, thub*, and the three men were quickly replaced by three mercenaries in the runabout, while the other mercenaries dragged the dead bodies into the brush. The mercenary dressed as the pilot drove the runabout slowly toward the yacht. Two others wore tuxedoes and posed as passengers in the boat.

Four others in frogman suits and wearing knapsacks hung onto the side of the runabout with only their heads above water. The four frogmen went underwater when they got close to the yacht. The runabout stopped and signaled to the two men on the yacht who were there to check guests and help them board.

One of the tuxedoes hung over the side of the runabout pretending to throw-up, much to the delight of the two men on the yacht. After ten minutes, a tapping on the underdeck of the runabout signaled that frogmen were back. The pilot waved to the men on the yacht to indicate that he was taking the two guests back to shore.

"*Perfek*," Aidan said out loud to himself. He watched his frogmen change clothes and take up guardian positions in the brush on the shore. His three other men continued to pose as the runabout crew, in case anyone from the yacht was watching.

Aidan lowered the night-vision binoculars. It would be a mistake to wear them. He felt the anticipation of a child waiting for Christmas. He watched. The ocean around the yacht turned inky black and deep purple. Or maybe indigo. Aidan did not believe the color indigo existed, but there it was. Then he saw streaks of pink in the silent ocean. And then the flash ... bright yellows and blues with a blinding white center as the sound reached him. The sound of a thousand angry lions, the shout of a furious God. The enormous yacht was lifted five feet above the ocean and bent in half.

Aidan covered his ears at the sounds of human screaming, and the screeching and ripping of metal and wood. Blast after blast sent shock waves toward shore and shot 30 feet into the air particles of glass, cloth, wood, steel, and mangled bodies, all on fire. Large waves were now hitting the shore, and it was time for Aidan to get his small army out of there. They had completed a difficult mission without losing a man. This was a great success, and they would be paid handsomely.

They celebrated in Cape Town, where Aidan called Boris Anoushka to deliver the news.

"Mr. Anoushka, it is done."

"Good. Payment will be released to you in one-hour. Bravo, Aidan."

* * *

After hanging up with Aidan, Boris called the Caffè Fiora.

"Pepe, it's done."

"Thank you." Pepe said.

Pepe walked over to Nunzio with two glasses and Chivas Regal.

"What's this?" Nunzio asked.

"That was Boris on the phone. It's done."

CHAPTER FORTY-SEVEN

*"Be a fox to recognize traps
and a lion to frighten wolves"*

N unzio and Pepe sat at Nunzio's table sharing dinner
and talking about life and middle-age dreams.

"Pepe, you have been my protector, confidante,
and best friend for more than 30 years."

"You have been the same for me, Boss."

"This next year will be our biggest challenge, my
friend."

"What's up?"

"In the past few months, I have survived two assassination attempts. I have been wounded in my heart by the loss
of my dear Natale and in my shoulder by a bullet."

"But you've won. So, what's coming, Boss?"

"We have a few guys who would like to see me break
up my empire so they can have a small one of their own.
And a lot of our guys expect me to take it easy for a little
while and celebrate our victories."

"You think some of our own guys might come at you if
they think you're relaxed or in the dumps. Who?"

"Franco Diffidente, our Brooklyn capo, is unhappy
about my deal with the Russians. But he ain't ambitious or
foolish enough to come at me. But Giacomo Slealmente,
our capo in the Bronx, is smart, ambitious, and might be

able to recruit Franco and his crew to join him in a move against me."

"Boss, I can take care of Giacomo tomorrow."

"No, my friend, I ain't sayin' Giacomo is gonna come at me. I'm sayin' if someone in our organization is thinking that way, it could be him. And then, the Chinese and the Russians now know I gave up territory for a personal favor. That was my weakness, Pepe. They might be willing to join an effort against me or offer me help for more territory and money. Poachers know the lion is most vulnerable after a big kill and meal...they think the lion is sleeping."

"We would never let that happen."

"I also made a couple of other mistakes, Pepe. You warned me about Rico and Father Joe warned me about Declan. I did not take them seriously enough. I had too much ego. And I trusted Rico and Declan more than I should have."

"We have soldiers in the Bronx and Brooklyn loyal to you, Boss. I'll tell them to watch for anything that looks like a move against you. I know them, and like you said to Boris, they'll be our light in the closet."

"Good. Tap a couple here in our backyard, too."

"Will do."

"Let's talk to Tommy Sullivan about getting his support, and ears on this."

"You have done more than anyone building an empire. But Boss, even the lion looks for shade when it gets too hot. No one would think any less of you if you stepped back for a moment. I would make sure all stays strong and running smooth for you."

Nunzio was surprised by Pepe's suggestion, "Step back?"

"Maybe it's time to just enjoy what you have."

"That's not my way, Pepe. You know that I love this neighborhood and the people in it too much to leave it to greedy and lying politicians. I also admit I love the power, the respect, and even the hot water. I have an empire here that reaches beyond our city. It all keeps me awake and vigilant."

"You're right. Anyway you're too young to retire, Boss. So, what should we watch out for?"

Nunzio was going to say *"Beware of the smart, ambitious capos or soldati in our own organization that, out of some fake concern for me, think it might be a good time for me to retire … you know … for my health."* But instead, he said, "Anybody who wants to get close, who hasn't been close before. Anything that smells like rotten fish."

"Are you worried?"

"No. This is the good part, Pepe. Of all the reasons I love this *vita nostra* – this life of ours – it's living my way. It is destroying those who think they can take what is mine. It is the attack by fools who underestimate me. The killing of my enemies. The hot water is what gets me up in the morning."

"What's your way for what's coming, Boss?"

"The lion can't tell if there's a trap, and the fox can't defend himself against wolves. So, we will be a fox to recognize traps and a lion to frighten wolves."

"Maybe if we pretend that you are sitting back, recovering, the traitors will come out of the shadows quicker," Pepe said. "But we must be ready with our own traps. And when they show themselves, do not wait for an attack but slaughter them immediately with such force that no one will ever think of coming at you again."

Nunzio was still uneasy by Pepe's 'stepping back' comment. *After 30 years is it possible that he would betray me? Not a chance, not Pepe. Be alert...no more mistakes.* But he simply said, "Good idea, my friend. Now let's have a drink to celebrate our victory and victories to come."

"To your way, Boss." Pepe held up his glass.

THE END

ACKNOWLEDGMENTS

Thank you to my wife, Attorney and Law School Clinical Professor Emerita, Judith Olingy, and our son Gerard "Josh" Chiarkas, who were my relentless and terrific line editors.

Thank you, Attorney Marilyn Kliman, my brilliant initial content, story, and line editor, and dear friend.

Thank you, Mark Schmitz, my wonderful friend, and extraordinary artist, https://www.zebradog.com/ for your beautiful and engaging cover art and design.

Thank you to my friend, editor, and extraordinary poet, Sandra "Sas" Kuehn, for her encouraging and helpful comments on early drafts and her poem.

Thank you to my daughter, Erica Chiarkas, and my son, Gerard "Josh" Chiarkas, who brought *Nunzio's Way* to life through their captivating audio book performance. Gerard "Josh" Chiarkas also narrated the audio book for *Weepers*.

Thank you to my publisher, and friend, Kira Henschel of HenschelHAUS Publishing, without whose guidance, knowledge, and wisdom, you would not have read *Nunzio's Way*. https://henschelhausbooks.com/

Thank you to my publicist, marketing guru, and friend, Valerie Biel, President of Lost Lake Press https://lostlakepress.com/ for helping *Nunzio's Way* reach more places than I could have imagined.
Thank you to my brother John and my Uncle Mario for their suggestions, advice, and encouragement.

Thank you to Christine DeSmet, https://christinedesmet.com/ for her valuable critiques and encouragement.

I am also grateful for the support and encouragement of my brothers (Ralphie, Bill, Doug, James, Jeff, John, Mark, Mitch, Pat, Steve, Tom, William, Tim, and Catul) in the JDS Society of Madison, Wisconsin.

I am grateful for the support of my brothers and sisters in the, Wisconsin Writers Association https://www.wiwrite.org/; the Blackbird Writers https://blackbirdwriters.com/; the Public Safety Writers Association https://policewriter.com/; and the Madison West Writers Group https://www.meetup.com/madisonwestwriters/.

Thanks to Tom Kenney, my NYPD partner, for teaching me more about the law in action, good judgment, and common sense than all my formal education.

And I thank God for granting me more second chances than I deserve.

ABOUT THE AUTHOR

Nick Chiarkas grew up in the Al Smith housing projects in the Two Bridges neighborhood on Manhattan's Lower East Side. When he was in fourth grade, his mother was told by the principal of PS-1 that, "Nick was unlikely to ever complete high school, so you must steer him toward a simple and secure vocation."

Instead, Nick became a writer, with a few stops along the way: a U.S. Army paratrooper, a New York City police officer, the Deputy Chief Counsel for the President's Commission on Organized Crime, and the Director of the Wisconsin State Public Defender Agency. On the way, he picked up a doctorate from Columbia University, a law degree from Temple University, and was a Pickett Fellow at Harvard.

How many mothers are told their children are hopeless? How many kids with potential simply surrender to despair?

That's why Nick wrote *Weepers* and *Nunzio's Way*—for them.

The author would be delighted to hear from you.
Please visit his website: www.nickchiarkas.com.

Please enjoy the thrilling preview of
Weepers (Book 1 of the Weepers series)

Available from your local independent
bookstore, Amazon.com and from the
publisher,
www.HenschelHAUSbooks.com

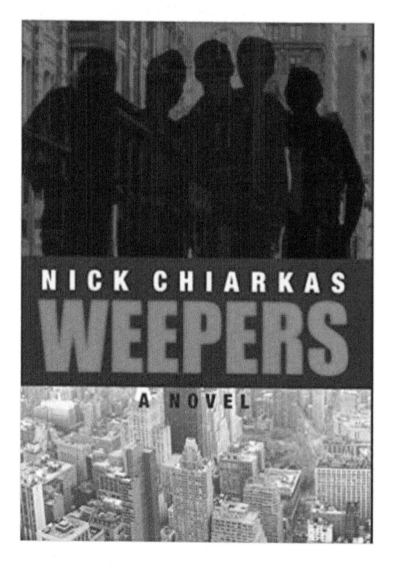

1951

CHAPTER ONE

"If it moves toward you, you're food."

"**A**ngelo, don't get too far ahead."

"I won't, Papa."

Angelo had never been happier. It was the night before Christmas, he was with his father, and it was snowing. Not a chilling, icy snow, but a powder of flakes—perfect forms floating to the streets of New York.

The few maple and ash trees that stood watch along the cement playground on Cherry Street were dressed in white, with crystal-gloved fingers reaching down to the silent sidewalk. Those brittle bushes that had managed to survive another summer pouncing of playful children now nestled comfortably under a downy white cover.

Angelo heeded his father's warning and shortened the distance between them. Even at seven years old, he knew these streets were unsafe. This was, after all, the Two Bridges section of Manhattan's Lower East Side.

"Doesn't it look just like that glass ball that snows when you shake it on Nonna's table?"

"Yeah, but a little colder." His father followed behind at a steady pace, pulling a two-wheeled metal shopping cart filled with brightly wrapped Christmas gifts.

"Yeah, it sure does, but a little colder." Angelo giggled and turned to grab for a particularly large flake that seesawed down like a feather from a pillow fight. The ash on his father's cigarette brightened momentarily.

Like a dragon, his father streamed smoke from his nostrils and the corner of his mouth. Mixed with the vapor from his breath, it left a brief trail before disappearing behind him.

"Wouldn't it be funny if Nonna looked at her snow globe and saw us walking?" Angelo asked in an effort to continue the connection with his father. "What would she say?"

"Jesus, kid, I don't know." Angelo's father took a quick drag on his cigarette and flicked it into the snow. "Try to catch a snowflake on your tongue."

"Okay." Angelo danced in circles with his opened mouth to the sky.

"Don't cross Catherine Street without me."

"Okay, Papa."

"How's that eye doing?"

Angelo instinctively touched the left side of his face with a wet mitten. "It's okay. It don't hardly hurt no more."

"Good." His father's voice was suddenly stern. "But, like I said, it was your own fault."

Angelo didn't respond. He was absorbed by the memory of sterile pads on his eyes, the aroma of tomato soup and alcohol in the hospital, and his mother's weeping.

"Hey, you hear me?"

"Yes, Papa." Angelo again felt the snowflakes on his upturned face. "My fault. I know, Papa. My fault."

"You better believe it's your fault."

Angelo's father was not a big man. Mostly he seemed calm, though Angelo had witnessed just how rapidly things could change with little provocation. He'd learned to read the cues quickly and respond accordingly. He was pretty sure he didn't need to respond at that moment, but threw back another "I know, I'm sorry, Papa," just in case.

Angelo walked alongside the burgundy brick walls of Knickerbocker Village. Beyond the narrow park to his left that separated Cherry and Water Streets, he could see the Journal-American newspaper building. The Journal's loading platform on Water Street, usually lively with shouting men and the comings and goings of trucks, was quiet. Instead, three Christmas trees stood on the platform, each beautifully decorated with colored lights and an illuminated gold star on top. "How come nobody stole the trees, Papa?"

"They belong to Uncle Nunzio."

Angelo nodded.

After a slight pause, his father spoke. "Angelo."

"Yeah?"

"That stuff I said...it wasn't your fault, kid. None of it was your fault. You're a good kid, Angelo. Beats me...it just beats me." His father shook his head in private puzzlement.

Angelo stopped walking and turned around.

His father winked. Angelo smiled and resumed his dance in the snow. Beyond a veil of falling snow, Angelo could see black-jacketed, shadowy figures moving within the projects. Two standing there. Four more moving together, a white mist kicked up at their feet.

"Papa, see those guys?"

"Don't worry about it. They're just punks."

"I wish I was a lion. Pompa said they're the king of the jungle."

"He would know."

Angelo's attention alternated from the black-jacket shadow-punks to the Christmas lights dancing in the projects' windows. "Will Uncle Johnny be home before the new baby comes?"

"Probably."

"I bet he ain't scared of the projects. I bet he ain't scared of nothin'…just like you, Papa. Just like a lion."

At the corner of Cherry and Catherine, Angelo stopped, waiting for his father to catch up. He looked back up Cherry Street and was stunned. Less than twenty feet away, the cart stood alone in the snow. Angelo stared in disbelief. He ran to the spot where his father should have been. He grabbed the handle of the cart, looking down at the abandoned presents.

He knew his father had been right there pulling the cart. He squeezed his eyes shut tight, opened them, and still his father would not appear. He turned in circles, scanning the quiet street for some sign of where his father had gone. His foot slipped. He fell. He got up. Nothing. No one. Not a sound.

"Papa," he shouted into the silent night. "Papa!"

No response. Not even an echo. The solid brick walls of Knickerbocker offered no clues. No cars moved and no footsteps could be heard. Nothing. Just the cart standing there filled with Christmas. He was alone.

"Papa, please!"

Angelo fell to his knees in the snow and cried into already soggy mittens. In a breath between sobs, he heard something. The hairs stood up on the back of his neck and goose bumps flooded his small body.

"*Aspetta, aspetta,*" someone whispered. Just that. Hushed, deep, and nothing more.

Startled, Angelo jumped to his feet. Eyes wide, his head whipped around. There was no one. Terror tightened its grip as he looked across the street at the projects. Like hyenas spotting a lost lion cub, the black-jacketed punks were moving cautiously toward Catherine Street. Toward him.

Angelo looked at his own building, 20 Catherine Slip, on the edge of the projects, about a block away. He locked his grip on the shopping cart in a failed attempt to pull the cart with him. It was too heavy and the punks were coming.

The boy already knew the first rule of the jungle: *If it moves away from you, it's food; if it moves toward you, you're food.* He took a deep breath and released the handle. The cart toppled onto its side as he ran as fast as he could toward home.

Angelo cut diagonally across the snow-covered street without looking toward the black-jacketed punks, for fear it would slow him down just enough for them to get him. He kept focused on his building. The cold air and snow were clouding his eyes and burning his lungs, but 20 Catherine Slip was getting closer. He tripped on the edge of the sidewalk in front of his building and fell face down, sliding in the snow. Even while skidding, he was getting up, finding his footing and running. The entrance was now in front of him and he flew through the door and into the lobby.

Slipping in a puddle of melted snow, Angelo slammed into the wall of mailboxes to the left of the door. Amidst the muted cacophony of Christmas music from several first-floor apartments and the scent of pine and pie, he noticed for the first time the sound of his own crying. Fearing that his sobs might attract predators, he tried to control himself, planning the safest route to his fifth-floor apartment.

Not the elevators. They were unreliable and he could be trapped. He cautiously entered the stairwell. Grabbing the banister, he dashed up the first flight of stairs. A sharp pain from the cold air burned through his lungs and heart. *Only to the fifth floor*, he thought. His ankles felt like weights as he continued up, pulling himself along with the banister as fast as he could.

His breathing was shrill and strained rounding the third floor landing. The acrid smell of urine replaced the stale stairway air as he stopped abruptly at the fourth-floor landing. He didn't recognize the man who lay on the floor with his head and shoulder propped against the wall. Any other time, Angelo would have run down a floor to the elevator or back stairway. But tonight he had no time for detours and he was running out of steam. He had to keep going.

Angelo moved cautiously, stepping over the thin, extended arm. The young man did not move. White crusts covered the stranger's lips below unblinking eyes. Angelo's eyes remained locked on the ghostly figure as he turned toward the next flight of stairs.

Angelo grabbed the banister and snapped his head toward the fifth-floor landing and safety. Once there, he slammed open the firewall door and shot down the hallway to his apartment. He threw himself against the locked door and pounded.

"Mama, Mama, hurry, Mama!"

After a moment that felt like a lifetime, his mother opened the door and reached down to him. Angelo collapsed into the harbor of her arms.

"Angelo, my baby, what is it?" She kneeled and embraced him in the doorway. She looked at her son, and then past him. "Where's your father?"

Angelo, unable to speak, cried and gasped for air. His mother lifted him over the threshold and inside the warm apartment as he tried to control his sobbing.

"Frank!" she shouted, but her brother was already behind her.

"What's goin' on?" Uncle Frank asked.

"Calm down, my baby, tell us what happened." Her tone comforted Angelo. For the first time since he'd turned to look back up Cherry Street, Angelo felt safe. The warmth and smells of home rolled over his body like a tonic.

Anna Pastamadeo's black hair accented her warm and worried gray eyes.

"Mama, we have to find Papa."

"What do you mean 'find Papa'?"

"He disappeared on Cherry Street. Just gone. We have to go find him."

Uncle Frank grabbed his leather jacket off the closet doorknob. "Cherry Street...you see anybody, anything I need to know?"

"A voice...I don't know." Angelo choked down a lump of fear. "P-Please find my—"

"Anna, lock the door and call Pop. I'll be right back."

Angelo heard the stairwell door open and close as his uncle went into the night.

His mother locked their apartment door. "Okay, Angelo, okay." With some effort, she lifted him up, wet clothes and all, and carried him to the living-room couch. The room was lit only by the Christmas tree in the corner near the window. She held Angelo in her lap, swallowing him in the sanctuary of her embrace.

There, in between sobs and shivers, he told her what had happened. Angelo knew she had to swallow hard and hold on. He knew she remained calm for him.

He told his mother all of it—the Christmas trees at the *Journal-American*, catching snowflakes on his tongue, his father saying he was a good kid, hearing someone say *aspetta*, the gifts tumbling into the snow—all of it.

"Your father said you were a good kid? He said that?"

"He really said that...to me."

"Huh... and after he was gone you heard *aspetta*?"

"Yeah. The cart fell over. I couldn't pull it. And then I ran home. I just left."

"Don't worry about it, Sweetheart. I'm glad you left it there and came right home."

"No. Mama, I left Papa. I should've looked for him. I got scared and left him."

"You did right, Angelo."

"I got scared of the punks with the black jackets and I ran."

"Punks with black jackets? Knights." His mother nodded. "Did they hurt your papa?"

"No. They were in the projects. I just got scared of them and all. And I ran home instead of looking for Papa. I should've been with him. Walking with him."

"Angelo, you did just what you were supposed to do. Uncle Frank will find out what happened." She gently unfolded Angelo from her lap. "Come to the kitchen. I'll call Pompa."

Angelo nodded. Pompa, his grandfather, would make things right.

* * *

Angelo took a hot bath, put on his pajamas, and was halfway through a slice of bread when Uncle Frank returned with the shopping cart and damp presents.

"Did you find Papa?" Angelo choked back despair.

"Not yet, kid. Angelo, I found these cookies in a napkin on the presents."

"They're from Mrs. Monahan."

"Angelo." Uncle Frank kneeled on one knee. "Tell me exactly where your father was the last time you saw him."

"Right where the cart was."

"Did you notice any cars coming down the street?"

"No."

"Don't answer so fast, Angelo. Close your eyes. Try to picture it, kid."

Angelo closed his eyes. "No, no cars. No people. Nothing." He opened his eyes.

"Okay, when you turned around and Mac—when your father was gone, do you remember any empty parking spots?"

Angelo closed his eyes tighter this time and pictured the cart standing there on its own. He remembered looking around for his father, but nothing about the cars parked along the street, except they looked like rolling, snow-covered hills.

"I don't remember any empty spots. I'm sorry."

"Don't be sorry, that helps. Do you remember anything else that seemed different when you turned around and your father was gone?"

"No, I was scared, kinda still am a little."

"Ah, hey, kiddo. Don't you worry about nothing. Your Uncle Frank's here and I ain't quitting 'til I find him. And, Angelo, I'm not going to let anything hurt you."

"Angelo," his mother said softly, "it's time for bed now."

"But, I wanna help find Papa," he protested as he turned from his uncle to his mother.

His mother's and uncle's eyes met for a moment.

"If you wanna help get a good night's sleep. Tomorrow, think about what you saw. You know, with your eyes shut, and trying to picture what you might have seen."

"Okay, Uncle Frank."

"Now I need to talk to your mother. You go to bed, and don't worry about nothing."

Uncle Frank's stubble was scratchy and he smelled like cigarettes and Old Spice. But his hug made Angelo feel safe again.

Instead of turning into his bedroom down the hall, his mother led Angelo to her bedroom.

"You sleep in here with me tonight, Angel."

"Okay, Mama." Angelo climbed into the large bed and under the thick comforter, a hand-me-down wedding present from his mother's parents. He rolled over onto his back as his mother brought the cover up to his chin.

"Angelo, are you sure you heard someone say *aspetta*?"

"I think so, Mama."

"You know it's Italian. It means—"

"Wait."

"That's right, Sweetheart. It means wait. And that's what you heard?"

"That's what it sounded like."

"Okay, Angel. No more tonight."

"Mama," Angelo said as his mother turned out the light, "I'm sorry."

She stopped short in the doorway. Backlit by the hall light, Angelo could see her frown. "Angelo." She walked back to the bed. "You have nothing to be sorry for. Nothing."

Bending over him in the dark, she placed a hand on either side of his face—carefully avoiding the fading bruise near his left eye—and kissed him on his head. A stray tear moistened his forehead.

"Wait here." She needlessly adjusted his cover. "I'll get something for you to drink."

"What?"

"Something Pompa used to make for Uncle Frank and me when we couldn't sleep."

"And for Uncle Danny, too?"

"Danny, too." She smiled. "You say your prayers and I'll be right back."

"Okay."

In minutes, his mother returned. She placed a glass on the nightstand and then helped Angelo sit up. Holding the glass to his mouth, she said, "Here, drink this."

"What is it?"

"Warm milk, some honey, and a touch of brandy. It will help you sleep, Sweetheart; now drink it down."

Angelo took a sip and made a face. His mother held it back up to his lips until he was finished, then placed the empty glass back on the nightstand as he nestled in beneath the covers. Gathering her skirt in front, she lay down next to him and began to hum a familiar tune while gently stroking his head.

He stirred when he felt her get up. She touched her lips to both his eyelids and his forehead. "God grant you peaceful dreams, my baby."

After she left, Angelo listened to the muffled voices through the closed door. When Pompa arrived, he heard his mother's voice augmented by her fear.

He could hear enough to know she was telling Pompa the story he had told her. He heard her say, "*Aspetta, aspetta!* Angelo heard it."

"Shhh, Anna. You'll wake the boy," Pompa said. "Frankie, what do you make of the gifts still being there?"

He heard Uncle Frank say, "That bothers me, too, especially since Angelo said some Knights saw him." Uncle Frank continued in little more than a whisper. "I figure the Knights saw something that scared them enough to keep them away."

Angelo tried to stay awake, but exhaustion and the brandy took hold of him and, through silent sobs and clinging fears, guided him into dreamless sleep on that chilly Christmas Eve.